Gene Clark
April – 54.

The Red Doe

BY DRAYTON MAYRANT

The Red Doe

By

DRAYTON MAYRANT

PEOPLES BOOK CLUB
CHICAGO

The Red Doe

1

LEX MOURNE SAT ON THE WOODPILE BEHIND THE LOW LOG
farmhouse to rest from the full cord he had split and to
try his new hunting horn.

It was old Dun's left horn, but he had no sentiment
about that. When the cow went dry he and his father had
butchered her. They had given presents of meat to the
Gaylords and the Hawkins', according to custom between
close friends of the section. They had also put to use every
scrap of horn, hide and hoof. The moccasins Lex was
wearing now and the leggings he wore in winter were
made of leather cured by him and then cut and stitched
by Shoemaker Brevard over on the Wateree.

The horn he had scraped and polished was a lovely
thing. Streaks of brown-to-amber ran the length of its
curve. Lex had cut and fitted to it a mouthpiece of bone,
and he was carving on it a running hound. He had not yet
made up his mind what the hound was trailing. It could
be raccoon, possum, fox or lynx; for in season he hunted
all four.

He pressed the smooth mouthpiece to his lips, and the
sound poured sweet as water. Its pitch was higher than
most cattle horns, and it had a range of several notes. Lips
puckered and lungs deflating, he held them as long as he
could. Back to him over the steep red hills and the deep
green of their gullies came echoes of the trial of old Dun's
left horn. . . .

Those were years when other bugles were blowing along

the Atlantic seaboard from Boston to Savannah. Even on remote farms in the High Hills of Santee farmers paused at their plows to hear the echo of that calling.

War had not yet reached far inland. British attack was centered on the rebellious seaports, and some rice plantations along the coast had suffered. So it was from those sections that the majority of the militiamen had come. There were many patriots in the Back Country; but there were many farmers who still called it a rich man's war. Others smoked in silence and listened to the echoes. . . .

Lex Mourne knew of the Minute Men at a town far north which bore his name. He knew that a Virginia farmer called George Washington was in command of the Continental forces. He had heard that farmers in that civilian army often went absent without leave at planting time or harvest. He could not see the wrong of it, for a man must reap to live. Yet he kept recalling what his schoolmaster in the log schoolhouse had said about the right of a man—even a poor man and a farmer—to have a say in the government to which he paid his taxes.

He was thinking about it that night as he walked the path through the gullies which led to Hawkins' water mill. He had grown up with Edisto Hawkins and Jeems Gaylord, and they were still his closest friends. Since childhood the three had been accustomed to meet in the loft above the floor of the mill. Now that school days were past and they were men and did a man's work, they still went every Saturday night to the old meeting place. And there they talked of the events whose echoes drifted inland—events which men were discussing all through the American colonies, and fighting about wherever invasion had reached them.

At a little palmetto log fort on an island in Charles Town harbor, the planter Francis Marion was serving under General Moultrie with the rank of militia captain.

This was the closest that war had yet come to the High Hills of Santee. But the Huguenot Francis Marion was no stranger to the hill country, and to Lex Mourne's father he was an old friend. "He's a small slim man," said Farmer Mourne. "I'd make two of him on the steelyards. But there ain't a gray fox in Santee Swamp that knows the country better. He's hunted the varmints all his life and he's easy in a saddle like I'm easy sitting here by this fire of white-oak logs."

Lex thought of this horseman, now dismounted for artillery work on the coast. Horses were his passion, and as he walked through the night he pictured a running cavalry fight across the woods and hills he knew. Would invasion ever penetrate the seaboard defenses and over-run these red clay ravines and slopes? He and his father talked about the chances every night, when they lighted the bayberry candles for the short aftersupper time before they went to bed. The question would remain in his mind while he undressed in his room close under the low eaves. It would trouble him until he threw open his window and glimpsed the Great Square of Pegasus high in the west. Then thoughts of the stars would take his mind from the world and war. His schoolmaster had taught rudimentary astronomy, and it had been Lex's favorite study. The constellations having anything to do with horses were the ones which interested him most.

Tonight as he climbed the steep path to the crest of the hill, the stars ahead seemed to grow clearer and brighter. He stopped to look north where Auriga the Charioteer was driving. Faint and low in the southeast the Archer rode with drawn bow. It came to Lex Mourne that these same stars were shining on New England, on the camps of Staten Island and the South Atlantic coast.

He figured in his mind the difference in time which would cause them to shine at a different hour upon Eng-

land. There was latitude also, he knew, to be considered.
Was the Archer too far south for Englishmen to see? He
knew that they were a nation of horsemen. Like him, they
would probably find equestrian constellations most pleas-
ing. He had often dreamed of seeing and riding the horses
raised on English estates. But he knew that was a vain
hope. His country was at war with England.

He could not know that these same high stars had a
year before looked down upon events in England which
would influence his life.

For there on a country estate two hostlers had held
lanterns high above the sides of a box stall deep in straw.
"A filly it is," one of them had said, "and the spit of the
old mare, Squire."

Squire Fay had looked, and his younger son had looked
with him. The red mare stretched exhausted, but the foal
was on its feet. Although its coat was dark and still wet,
the tint of henna shone through the bay. With legs fan-
tastically long for a short woolly body, it tottered on toy-
like hooves. As the mare stretched her neck and moved
her head to lick this precious offspring, it switched its
small bush of a tail gaily and defiantly.

Twelve-year-old Edmund Fay, watching beside his
father, was just as enthusiastic about the foal as its dam
was. He longed with all his heart to own it. But he knew
that the foal would go to his brother Evelyn.

Evelyn Fay was now riding the mare's older colt with
his troop, and that colt was now a four-year stallion. Edmund had heard his father read many letters from this
older brother: letters filled with complaints—complaints
that he needed money and a second horse. Like his father,
Edmund took pride in the fact that Evelyn was gazetted;
but, although only twelve, he loved horses enough to realize that Evelyn was a horse killer. Perched on the side of
the stall, he looked at the baby filly with his heart in his

eyes and with a great hurt in his heart. He shared his family's pride in the fact that his grandfather had developed the Red Doe strain at the family estate, Fay Green Riding. It was a sturdy, courageous strain and belonged to the Fays alone. Little Edmund loved a Red Doe as he loved the old house in which he lived. But Evelyn would get the old home, and the foal, too, just as soon as she was old enough to be ridden. Why was a four-year stallion not mount enough to carry Evelyn through this colonial war?

He saw that the mare was licking her foal and the filly was tottering nearer. With its broad forehead between the protruding eyes it butted feebly against its mother's ribs, lowering its pointed muzzle and by instinct and scent finding the teats swollen with milk.

Above that stable twelve months before, the Winged Horse had fled and the Charioteer whipped onward, and, too far south for England to see, the Archer pursued the Scorpion.

And standing then by the Red Doe's stall, Squire Fay had heard the trumpets as he too thought of Leftenant Evelyn Fay. He had heard the same trumpets that Lexington Mourne was now hearing upon one of the Santee hills half a world away.

2

THERE WERE NOT TO BE FOUND IN ALL THE WORLD TWO countrysides more different than the formal lawns and parks and white-fenced paddocks of the land where the Red Doe filly was foaled and the land where the young farmer was walking that summer night. As Lex looked away from the celestial steeds that rode the skies, he saw a terrain of jungle and wood which might have appeared impenetrable to anyone who did not know it as he did. It was to be the downfall of more than one magnificently drilled British regiment. Their drums and scarlet coats and compact formation would make a ridiculously easy target for men who knew the northern woods or the southern swamps of America.

But Lex was no longer thinking of war. Pegasus and Sagittarius and Auriga had turned his thoughts to earthly steeds. On his father's farm there were only two horses. They were powerful draft animals, and Farmer Mourne and his son saw that the beasts got their rest and food as surely as they themselves did. That was why Lex was now walking the three miles to Hawkins' mill, instead of riding bareback on Blaze or Congaree.

Neither horse was a pleasure to ride, for their backs were as broad as benches and they set their large feathered feet down with jarring force. Every time Lex mounted one of them he thought of the thoroughbreds at the Lane plantation on Santee River. At school he had become friendly with Toff Lane and had more than once visited in his home. When he had first arrived, Lex had felt out of place, but the Lane family soon put him at ease. Mr. Lane was merrier and less formal than Farmer Mourne. Pretty Mrs. Lane was easygoing and scatterbrained; husband and children and servants followed in her wake retrieving all the things that she misplaced or dropped. With the adaptability of youth, Lex had found himself at home amid luxury. By the second day it had seemed to him no longer strange to stroll with Toff to the stable yard and find a well-groomed saddle horse ready for him. Although not accustomed to such service, he was horseman enough to appreciate the Negro groom who stood on the off side with one hand on the bit ring and the other holding the stirrup of the flat Somerset saddle. As he recalled those visits he could see in his mind's eye Toff's twin sisters, Margaret and Sophia, who were only a little younger than he: Peggy with her loose dark curls around an exquisite oval face, and Fire's tumbled mass of flaming hair. . . .

Those visits had been joy to Lex; and Toff had visited him in return, finding a new kind of excitement in the bear hunts in Wateree Swamp and the club meetings in the old mill.

In fact Toff was the only outsider ever allowed at those meetings—and he was allowed only because he had earned a place the hard way. At school he had been man enough to accept and to carry gracefully a derisive nickname given him because of his fine clothes and his wealth. He bore it good-naturedly and did not resent teasing; but any boy who indulged in spite or insult discovered that in a fight there was nothing soft about Toff Lane.

Jeems Gaylord, the blacksmith's son, was the only man who had beaten Toff. The fight had not been at school, for neither Jeems nor Edisto had ever gone to school. It had been when Toff first visited Lex. They had gone by the gully path to the meeting in the mill, and there the young

men had begun to talk of the Battle of Lexington. Toff
had said: "I wish I'd been there. I'd like to fight the
limeys."

"Trouble is," Jeems Gaylord sneered, "your crowd won't
do the fighting. You rich, rice-planting toffs will sit at
home or ride horseback while poor men fight your war."

There had been no stopping it then. All Lex and Edisto
could do was draw a rough circle on the floor and stand
by with meal sacks for towels and buckets of cold water
from the mill pond. Jeems had been knocked down almost
at once by a blow whose science was unknown to him.
But in two seconds he was up and on his feet and—Lex
could see—more dangerous than before. He had never had
a boxing lesson, but he was a born fighter and was now
learning from every move that his opponent made. It had
gone on for nine rounds, with both boys bleeding and
Toff weakening. After Jeems broke Toff's nose he had
been careful not to strike there again. But he had not
slackened his savage attack, and—since Toff still refused
to say "enough"—had closed both of Toff's eyes and finally
put him out with all his strength in a blow on the chin.
Then, bloody and staggering and with two broken fingers
on the hand that forged horseshoes, he had helped Lex
and Edisto bring his opponent to—and had apologized
for his sneer as soon as Toff was conscious.

After that Toff Lane had been an honored guest at the
club.

Remembering all this, Lex Mourne descended the next
to last hill on his path, and found himself crossing the
deepest and darkest ravine on the way. Now and then a
roosting bird flew up from a branch that his shoulder
brushed, but it was too dark for him to see its flight. The
small animals of the night fell silent as they heard his step;
but suddenly from ahead came a heavy rustling and a low
growl. Lex knew it was one of the black bears so numerous

in the Wateree Swamp. When they reared they were as tall as a man, and they were bad-tempered if molested when feeding. This one, Lex told himself, must have found berries or a nest of grubs.

He had no false pride about avoiding an encounter. He knew that darkness would give the beast an advantage. But the gully was so thickly grown that he wished to keep to the path; and with the stout hickory cudgel he carried, he felt himself a match for any swamp bear. So he gave a threatening shout and increased his gait, thrashing about him with the hickory stick.

At once there was a squall, and something the size of a half-grown shoat rushed against and between his legs, almost upsetting him. As Lex clutched to keep from falling he dropped the stick. And as he stooped to grope for it, he realized that he had come upon a she-bear with cubs.

The cub which he had inadvertently struck and which had in panic collided with him was now squealing with terror as it rushed through the bushes behind him. Its mother, infuriated, was rushing to the rescue. As Lex's hand found his cudgel and he straightened up, the old she-bear was upon him with a roar and a swipe of her paw.

The blow was meant for his face, but he ducked his head as he tried to swing away from her. Her claws thrust like knives into his left shoulder, shredding his heavy homespun shirt and raking flesh and muscle down to his left elbow.

Sick with the pain and the impact, the young farmer knew that her next move would be to seize him with both forelegs, hug him close and sink her teeth in his neck. There was not enough room to strike with the stick, but with his unwounded hand he raised it between them as a guard. It was at once torn from his grasp, and he heard it crack between the bear's fangs. He fell back a step and pulled his hunting knife from its sheath at his belt. If the beast gave him time to turn he could outrun her on the path; but he knew that if she once seized him his only chance would be to stab her in belly or throat while her grip left his right hand free.

The cubs decided the matter. From somewhere back of their mother they now set up a racket of redoubled squeals and squalls. The black bear slashed out once again, in the air between herself and Lex. With the same movement she swung her heavy body around and away, dropped to all fours, and went crashing through the bushes to her young.

3

LEX MOURNE LEANED AGAINST THE TRUNK OF A GUM TREE
and listened to the bear and her cubs smashing their way
through the underbrush. He felt his whole body trembling
with excitement and relief. Only the circumstances of
darkness and of being thrown off guard by the charging
cub had put him at the mercy of the bear. But he did not
fool himself that he had not been at her mercy. He knew
that if she had seized him his chances against her would
have been less than equal because of his mangled arm.

Every second now increased the burn of the pain. Blood
was running freely from the long, deep gashes. He felt it
on the back of his hand and dripping from his fingers. He
realized that he must get help, but he waited to catch his
breath and to be sure that the aroused bear was out of
hearing and would not return. He knew he had brushed
shoulders with death, and yet he felt ridiculous. The black
bears were not man-eaters, and even without firearms a
grown man was supposed to be capable of coping with
one.

Hawkins' mill was now less than a half mile ahead,
while he had put his father's farm nearly three miles
behind him. The thing to do, he realized, was to get on to
the mill, where Edisto and Jeems would be waiting for
him. As he moved, his foot struck the cudgel where the
bear had dropped it, and he reached down to pick it up.

He walked more slowly than he had before, using the
raised stick as a guard to protect his left shoulder. Even

11

the light contact of a twig made him wince as it brushed the torn flesh and tendons; he could feel that the bleeding was copious, and he knew that he must move on before he became faint. He cleared the gully and climbed the next hill—then stopped on its summit to rest from the unusual weakness shaking his lean six-foot frame.

He was not gazing at stars now but looking for the light in the mill. Down in the valley beside the pond he saw the doorway outlined in a dull yellow glow.

Grateful for descent instead of ascent, he managed to cover that last hundred yards. As he staggered into the lantern light, Jeems and Edisto leapt to their feet. Before they asked any questions they helped him to a pile of sacks, removed his shirt and examined the mangled arm and shoulder. Edisto brought a bucket of water, and they washed the slashes clean in spite of his groans and protests.

Only then did Edisto ask: "Was it a bear or a bay lynx?"

Before Lex could reply Jeems said: "Bear. Look at the size of those claw marks."

To Lex he added: "Were you fool enough to go after one in the dark with only a stick?"

Lex told them what had occurred. "It wouldn't happen more than once in a man's lifetime."

"It wouldn't," Jeems said drily, "because either his lifetime would end or he'd learn sense enough not to let it happen again."

Edisto was more sympathetic. "When my father was my age he rode under a tree where a wildcat had built her nest in a low fork. She thought he was after her kittens, and she dropped on him. Pa said he and the cat rode for a quarter mile together, with the cat biting and gouging both him and the horse and the horse bucking with every jump."

Lex grunted as the cold spring water stung his wounds.

"I'd rather fight one on foot than take it to ride with me. How'd he ever get it off him?"

"He didn't get it off him; he got off it. At the end of a quarter mile he fell off the horse, and he's been saying ever since that he ought to've had sense to fall off sooner."

While he talked, Edisto was tearing a clean meal sack into strips for bandaging. He began to wind these tightly around Lex's arm and shoulder. Jeems was for more drastic measures.

"Bear claws carry poison. Thing to do is heat an iron red-hot and burn those cuts out right now."

Lex disagreed violently. "You're worse than the bear. Just tie them up and stop the bleeding. They're washed clean with good spring water."

"One of the Couturier boys over at Eutaw Springs died from a bear clawing him last year. Marks weren't any deeper than yours, but he got the lockjaw."

The alternative was horrible, but Lex still resisted and Edisto re-enforced him.

"I heard Doc Wallace say that when a slash bleeds enough it cleans itself."

"Mine have bled aplenty," said Lex. "Get along and tie them up, then fetch our cider keg."

The cider was always furnished from the Mourne apple orchard, and a keg of it was kept in a hollow tree near the mill. For Hawkins was no jolly miller. He was stern and lantern-jawed, and he preached total abstinence. The juice of his apples was drunk fresh by himself and his family. He allowed none put by for fermentation. It was Lex's chore to see that the club keg was kept full from the generous supply of hard cider that he and his father made each year. Now he gulped it gratefully from a long-handled hollow gourd. Its sparkle ran through his body, and its infinitesimal alcoholic content at once soothed and strengthened him.

Jeems had brought a hard cheese, such as only his mother could make, and Edisto was unwrapping from a towel a long loaf of still-warm bread. Food was better than physic for a man of Lex's youth and strength. He ate heartily and held out his dipper for more cider.

"I talked last week with a fellow was at the Siege of Savannah. He don't think much of the Britishers or the Frenchies."

"How'd he get home," asked Jeems, "if they had him in the army?"

"He had to get home to plant his crop. His wife's up by Williamsburg on a farm with three small children. You think any man's going to fight while his family starves and his land grows up in grass?"

"Savannah ain't our country," said Jeems; "but I told Pa he better start training Gavin to do something more than just pump the bellows. General Moultrie licked the British in Charles Town harbor, but I hear tell they're coming here—and if they do I'm going to enlist."

"Pa says," contributed Edisto, "that the British are going to win. He says the men who've accepted parole are the ones with sense."

Lex and Jeems knew that Miller Hawkins always took the grimmer view. The three sat through half of the summer night; each one thinking his thoughts, and each one thinking differently, while they argued. Although Jeems was now the one most anxious to fight, he had been voicing the opinion of the countryside when he told Toff a year before that it was a rich man's war. Now its echoes were nearer and louder.

Lex said: "War or no war, I got work to do Monday. Can you get the ox, Ed, and give me a ride back home? I'll rest up tomorrow, then I'll have to plow with one arm. Grass grows fast as fire in the early summertime."

4

SUMMER WENT ON ITS SLOW, HOT WAY IN THE HIGH HILLS of Santee. Daybreak came at four thirty at its earliest period; at longest the southern twilights lasted until after eight. On those warm, still nights, relieved only by the coolness of evaporation from trees and grass, the stars seemed closer and they took on a yellow luminescence. All through June the whippoorwills still called their amorous sorrow. Lex Mourne's sight was keen enough to find them in the darkness, squatted on a line with some tree limb instead of roosting crosswise as other birds did. The chuckwell's widow was the one that lilted four notes instead of three.

But although they haunted the barnyard and came close to his window, the night birds' crying could not keep him awake. He knew that he had to be up and start the day's tasks with the day's first light. His father was not a slave owner. All that was done on farm and in house was done by him or his son. The older man first milked and fed the cow and penned her calf with her, then let out the poultry —which had to be housed at night because of foxes and wildcats—in time for them to get a meal of worms and insects the night had brought out. Lex threw corn on the cob to the hogs, saw that all water troughs were refilled, fed and curried the two horses. Then he returned to the farmhouse and with his father prepared and ate a breakfast of hot biscuits or spoon bread, with boiled bacon and apples either fresh or dried. Only in Toff Lane's home had he tasted coffee and tea. For the day's three meals he had his choice of sweet milk, buttermilk, and cider hard or soft.

At other, no more prosperous farms there was more variety, because those farms did not lack a wife and mother as this one did. Mistress Gaylord was known as the best cook in the neighborhood. She crystallized fruit, slicing and coating it with sugar and placing it on a board in the hot sun. When a small boy, Lex had watched her do it. With Jeems, he had sat by it to brush away flies and wasps, and had run to help carry it indoors when a sudden rain came up. Both she and Mistress Hawkins made jams of the berries and wild haws and fruits. Both were generous in sending by Jeems and Edisto china pots of these sweets to the womanless farm. Lex's knowledge of cooking extended to stewing fruit, which he sweetened with wild honey if it was tart. But conserves and confections were far beyond either his or his father's culinary skill.

He remembered his mother vaguely. She had been soft and deep-bosomed, with masses of light brown hair. Although her face was not clear to him, he could still feel the touch of her arms around him and hear her rich, low voice in an old English ballad:

> *"Lord Thomas, he was a bold forester,*
> *And a chaser of the king's deer . . ."*

The Mourne farmhouse had been brighter then, as if lighted with more candles. His father recalled it each evening when he went lonely to bed.

> *"Fair Eleanor, she was a brave woman;*
> *Lord Thomas, he lovèd her dear."*

Malvina Mourne had made a Junoesque figure as she rocked her first baby to sleep, or as she went singing about

her household tasks. She had been shaped to follow her
man into the wilderness, and to bear him strong sons to
till the land he took up. She was triumphantly happy and
completely without fear when she knew that she would
have a second child. Lex's birth had been easy and swift,
and Lex had been normal and straight and strong. He had
yelled when hungry and kicked when wet and fallen asleep
while she sang:

> *"She dress'd herself in gallant attire,*
> *Her tiremen all in green,*
> *And every borough that she rode thorough*
> *They took her to be some queen."*

But in the fifth month of this pregnancy she had sick-
ened with a fever which came upon her every second day,
causing her to alternate between cold chills and burning.
She had lost the baby and she had died, leaving her husband with a four-year-old son. When that son remembered
her now he always heard her voice:

> *"They buried Lord Thomas beneath an oak tree,*
> *Fair Ellen beneath the church spire;*
> *And out of her bosom there grew a red rose,*
> *And out of her lover's a briar."*

It was one of the few songs Lex knew, and he whistled
it this morning as he hooked the trace chains on Congaree.
The first corn had been broken and the fodder bound, and
the first cartloads of it would go today into the barn. As he
forked it—sweet and pale brown and dusty—up and over
the hay rack, his left arm still gave him a twinge of pain.
But that encounter with the black bear had taken place
two weeks ago, and he had healed cleanly and quickly in
that time.

Midsummer was beginning today. The sun, although only two hours up, was hot on the slope of the cornfield. When Lex had got the fodder in, he would plow under the stubble and roots. Then, as soon as the first good rain had mixed it with the red earth, he would sow a second crop from selected ears of the first. Miller Hawkins believed that a short, stout man should drop seed corn. He never let Edisto sow it—to Edisto's gratification—but did it himself with the help of his fat younger son. He warned Farmer Mourne every year that when the corn was dropped by Lex he risked having the stalks grow thin and gangling and tall like Lex. But Farmer Mourne only laughed at him, and Lex still dropped the seed corn.

The sun now burned in a steel-blue sky and Lex's shirt was drenched with sweat. Congaree's bay coat was wet wherever leather or chain touched him. He stood between furrows with his big head drooping until his muzzle nearly touched his front pasterns, too listless even to snatch a mouthful to right or left. In the melon patch above, Lex saw his father weeding. The muskmelons were over and the pumpkins coloring. Soon the gourds, long of stem and fantastic of shape, would be ready for cutting and drying. They were used not only for drinking utensils; Lex hollowed and hung them on trees for the martins to nest in. Martins were welcome in any barnyard because they attacked on sight and chased the chicken hawks.

The road to the barn led uphill and past the melon patch. As he drove his next load in, Lex shouted: "Look where you're walking, Pa! Remember what happened to Ranger."

Ranger had been his tawny hound who tracked possum and coon for him on winter nights. Last spring the old dog had been bitten by a copperhead moccasin which was sunning itself in the melon vines. Lex found and killed the snake, but the hound died. Edisto's dog had a litter of pups under the mill floor now, and Edisto had already told Lex to take his pick of them. But they were still too young to be taken from their mother. Also Lex knew that when he brought his puppy home, he would have to guard it for months from the ferocious yellow cat that held sway in and around the barn. The cat, although unloved, was respected and valued as a destroyer of rats and even of small snakes. But it would resent—and could destroy— a young puppy which it would consider an interloper.

Farmer Mourne did not take advice from his son.

"I killed moccasins before you were born. Sun's overhead. When you get that load in, call me and we'll eat."

They ate roasting ears of corn, with a couple of squashes split and baked. Lex brought a big jug of cool milk in from the springhouse. It was pleasant indoors, for a small breeze found the hilltop, and the tall white oaks and sycamores shaded the low roof from the sun.

When Lex went back to work, he harnessed Blaze to the cart and left Congaree switching his tail in the shadow of the barn. Except for the change of horses, afternoon was to him exactly the same as morning, only the sun was hotter and the red dust rose from baked earth that needed rain. At sundown, when he put in his last load and fed and watered the stock for the night, he heard a rain crow calling from the next hill across the ravine. It was still crying in mournful repetition when he wiped the last of his blueberry jam from his plate with a hunk of bread.

"Think rain could come before tomorrow, Pa?"

"Not a chance, son. Sunset was too red."

"I got a full half-day's work to do in the lower field. I'd sure hate to see that fodder get wet."

"You've spread fodder to dry before this."

"I know—and I haven't yet failed to find some of it sour, too."

The rain crow continued calling while they sat and

talked for the aftersupper hour. A free Negro named Adlai Johnston who owned and farmed his small place nearby had stopped to bring them a sweet-potato pie made by his wife and to borrow a share for his hand plow.

"Adlai brought news too," Mr. Mourne told his son. "He watched a band of Tories in green uniform ride by his farm this morning on their way to join the British."

Lex said hotly: "Tories are worse than real Britishers. Jeems says any man who lives here but fights for the king is a traitor to South Carolina."

"Young Gaylord's head is as hot as his forge. But, all the same, I can't stomach Tories."

"It makes me feel like joining up now. If I just had a horse to ride—"

"Well, you won't get Blaze or Congaree—and you won't join up neither. So long as the war leaves us alone, we'll leave it alone. Get on to bed now, son. Another day's work is waiting for us."

5

IN LATE SUMMER THE SYCAMORE LEAVES LOOKED LIKE PLATES of green gold which had been hammered so thin you could see sunlight through them. One by one they floated down, making pale mats around their boles which still soared leprous-white and scarred by long rags of scaling bark.

Lex had always loved to see their trunks like ghosts in the moonlight. Standing on the piazza with his father one evening, he said: "Pa, I wonder why the sycamores shed bark all year round."

Yadkin Mourne had been raised on both sacred history and legendry. He was grandson of an itinerant Calvinist preacher who had traveled the Great Road from the north to Mecklenburg County in North Carolina. Of that preacher's many sons, only Yadkin's father had followed the Catawba Path farther south. But in this even more remote land he had taught his own sons all he had learned— taught by the method his father taught, with the aid of prayer and a hickory limb. Now his son Yadkin looked scornfully at his own son.

"What did I get by sending you to that school on the Winyah? Schoolmaster filled your head with crazy star pictures in the sky and with even crazier talk about taxation. But he sent you back home ignorant of why a sycamore peels its bark."

Lex's craving for knowledge made him humble to gain it.

"I don't recall Master Ward telling us much about trees.

21

He learned us why you can make candles of some berries and not others; and he told us that orange-colored vine that blooms in the woods ain't poison at all."

"Oh, he did! Did he? Well, *I* tell you it's *cow itch*. Don't I know when I've seen my own cow come in with her nose and her belly broke out?"

"Might be she got hold of something else that was real poison," dared Lex.

"Might be nothing! Why would it have got the name of *cow itch* if it ain't?"

Unable to answer that, Lex asked: "Why does a sycamore shed all year, Pa?"

"The Bible tells it," said Farmer Mourne, "and you're old enough to've known it before. It was when the Lord Jesus Christ was passing through Jericho, and such a crowd waited to see Him that only tall folks could see."

He paused to glance at his long-limbed son. "You and me would of had a chance. But there was a little fellow by name of Zacchaeus. Saint Luke said he was a publican. Do you know what that means?"

"Yes," said Lex. "It means he kept an ordinary, like the one old man Jones built on the Catawba Path."

Yadkin nodded, pleased at proof that the schoolmaster had taught something. "That's why I always tell Hawkins that he's plumb wrong refusing to set foot in an ordinary and not drinking the cider God gave him to drink."

Lex was in agreement with that, but he prodded: "Why?"

"Why? Ain't I just told you that the Lord Jesus picked out this man Zacchaeus to stay with that night? Don't it stand to reason if Jesus thought it wrong for a man to keep an ordinary, He'd not have gone to sleep in that man's house?"

"Sure He wouldn't," agreed Lex. "But what about the sycamore's bark?"

"You ask me what about sycamore bark when I just explained to you? You got a head much thicker than that same sycamore wood. I told you—didn't I?—that this Zacchaeus was a little man. He wasn't as tall as Hawkins and was hardly half as broad."

"Yes, Pa, but you didn't say—"

"Didn't say? I'm saying it now. This Zacchaeus couldn't see in the crowd, so what he did was to climb up in a sycamore tree by the road. The Lord looked up there and saw him and hollered to him: 'Zacchaeus, hurry up 'n come down! I'm going to stay in your house.'"

As Lex still gazed at his father, Yadkin raised his voice. "Ain't you got it yet in your wooden head? Soon as Zacchaeus heard that, he was so glad he just let go and slid down that sycamore bole. He slid so fast he tore all its bark to ribbons; and ever since then a sycamore sheds its bark straggly twelve months a year."

Lex remembered that legend of the sycamore tree whenever he looked from his window on moonlit nights. Colors of the autumn were now brightening the hills. He had put in the second corn crop. The gourds and pumpkins were cut; the last fodder was in the barn loft. All day long the cicadas still sang, but the nights were getting chilly. The wild persimmons would not sweeten until frost had touched them, but Lex knew that possums and coons did not wait for frost. He had brought home from Hawkins' Mill the hound pup Edisto gave him. It was black-and-tawny, with paws of a size that promised a big dog. After one encounter with the yellow cat, it stayed away from the barn. Lex named it Vidette because of stories he was hearing about sentries set at camps in the Low Country.

One day he and Vidette walked the edge of the Wateree Swamp in search of a lost boar hog. He was teaching the dog to hold one trail, and he hoped it had struck the scent of the boar as it sniffed uncertainly and yelped excitedly.

Suddenly it raised its head, gave full tongue and started to run.

Lex followed silently for a half mile, leaping from tussock to tussock and splashing through pools as the trailing hound pup led him deeper into the swamp. He knew that a fox would run higher ground, and he told himself that a coon or possum or wildcat would by now have taken to a tree. When Vidette, without warning, led him up on an Indian mound, he stopped short in surprise at what he saw.

Two men, dirty and bearded, stood over a smoky fire. Both held long backwoodsmen's rifles, and both looked furtive and mean-faced. Although Lex had stopped short, the pup ran on, and the nearer man kicked it savagely.

The brown and green of Wateree Swamp went red before Lex Mourne's eyes. His dog shrieked, rolling on the ground. He clenched his hands as he strode forward.

"I don't know where on earth you came from; but I know I'm going to kick you back to wherever it is!"

"Stand where you air," said a whining voice. "One step more, youngun, I'll shoot."

Lex stood—for the second man had his gun against his shoulder. He felt Vidette crawl over his feet, and he felt himself shaking with terrible rage. His one desire was to lay hands on the stranger who had kicked his dog. He had never before seen such men or heard such voices. The hill country he knew was peopled by farmers and artisans— clean, sturdy folk, mostly of Scotch-Irish descent. These men were skulking and ragged, and their expression was vicious. The long barrel of the rifle did not waver, and the nasal voice was speaking again.

"We-uns comes from the mountains, and we don't aim to take no sass from you-uns in the lowlands. Turn your back an' git goin' now—lessen you craves a dose of lead."

6

THE STRANGERS IN THE SWAMP WERE A MATTER OF SPECULA-
tion to the families of Mourne and Gaylord and Hawkins.
The sparsely settled section was still troubled at times by
depredations of the outlaws called "Schofilites." Yadkin
Mourne suspected that his tall young son had met two of
these; but, because he knew the boy was hot-tempered,
he tried to minimize the incident.

"After all, Lex blamed the man and threatened to kick
him. Even a Schofilite won't stand for that."

"He kicked my pup." Lex's voice went harsh, and the
blood rose in his high-cheekboned face up to the line of his
thick hay-colored hair. He looked down at the sleeping
puppy sprawled across his feet.

"Might be he thought he'd get dog-bit. That pup's as
big as a small hound now."

They were sitting around the blacksmith's forge, and the
blacksmith disagreed. "Any man with eyes can see it's just
a puppy. Any man kicks a puppy needs killing."

"Well, don't you strive to make my boy hot-headeder
than he is. He and your boy already went after the
strangers."

"They did. And I'm glad, Yadkin Mourne, that my boy
went with yours."

He turned to Lex and Jeems. "You say you couldn't find
trace of them?"

"We found a trace, all right," Jeems Gaylord told his
father. "The ash of their fire was still on the mound where

25

Lex saw them. But it had rained that night and the water was high in the swamp, and Bell Mouth lost the scent."

"And you think if that old hound can't find them they can't be in the swamp."

"Well, Pa, no dog can trail through water."

"Let be!" begged Farmer Mourne. "What good can come of trailing them? You ain't sure they're Schofilites, and ain't no law prevents a mountain man camping in the High Hills."

The trail seemed there to come to an end, as it had done in Wateree Swamp. During that fall and winter they heard no more of the strangers, and spring brought pleasant excitement to the quiet neighborhood. Edisto's sister Luraline Hawkins was promised to a young German from the Saluda, and the wedding was set for early summer. It meant a full day and night of games, contests, enormous meals, and all the horseplay of a charivari. Lex Mourne looked forward to attending it and hoped to get Sal Gaylord as his partner.

She was a plump black-haired lass with a merry eye and a ready laugh, and Lex was not the only lad caught by her easy favors. Jeems told him: "She's older than you are. Sal won't own to it, but she's past seventeen."

"Well, I'm 'most seventeen; and Sal just comes as high as my shoulder."

Jeems picked up a bent horseshoe and threw it a hundred feet, to land near a bantam rooster that was taking its dust bath in a hollow. With a squawk of indignation the diminutive fowl flew up in a cloud of pulverized earth.

"I bought him four years ago when I first started raising bantams. He ain't grown any since then. He's little—but he's old."

But even the knowledge of Sal's advanced age did not keep Lex from seeking her out. He had started going to see her in very early spring, when the honeysuckle was in bud. The path he now walked to the Gaylord place was a tangle of its green vines and scented blossoms. Lex thought to himself that if moonlight was to be smelled instead of seen, it would have this honey-smooth and yet poignant sweetness. He had always liked to think about stars and trees and flowers. Sal did not; and yet association with Sal was this summer making him more conscious of any beauty. Through the darkness the bay buds shone white in the dark laurel of their leaves. They took his thoughts back to the avenue of magnolias which lined the back road to the Lane house. Although Sal Gaylord was waiting for him, he began dreaming of Peggy Lane. She was the loveliest girl he had ever seen, and whenever he saw her he thought of a yellow rosebud. Sal resembled a sunflower: hearty and gay and bright, turning as the sunflower does to follow whatever attracted her. Little Fire, Peggy's twin, would be neither a rose nor a sunflower. At her home was a house under glass with rare flowers whose names Lex did not even know. But although they belonged to her, none of them suited Fire, he thought. She was wild as a bird, and she often bridled a horse for herself and rode bareback in the woods and fields, forgetting the dinner hour and frightening the plantation. When Lex had been there he had once gone with Toff on a two-hour search. They had finally found her lying on her stomach by a creek and watching a flock of white heron at fishing. Toff had started to scold her.

"Can't you behave like a lady, as Peggy does? It's not fair to the stable men for you to run off this way. They get blamed."

She had rolled over and sat up, mud on the skirt of her homespun house dress and rebellion in her long, smoke-gray eyes.

"You had no right to scold Sam or the others, Toff. They

were busy harnessing the coach for mother when I took father's hunter. Father's not riding today."

She had slipped the bridle, and the thoroughbred had been grazing near her. Now he threw up his head and moved nervously.

"You took him and you turned him loose. He'll run off and leave you miles from the house, one of these days."

As he spoke the thoroughbred backed and reared and wheeled and started off in a run.

Fire's eyes were darkened by tears, but they were tears of anger.

"You made him do it, by riding up with two horses and yelling at me like this. I won't ride back behind you! Lex, will you take me up?"

Lex had started to dismount, but she had screamed at him: "Stay up! Just give me your right hand and stick out your left foot!"

He had done so, and she had gone up as lightly as a bird, clasping the right hand held out to her and using his left foot as a step. But he still disapproved of her. He had no use for women who rode astraddle like men. He had seen and admired Peggy in her big sidesaddle with her long skirts sweeping as she rode. The women of the High Hills, although they had no saddles, sat sideways on horses or mules or oxen. Sal, he thought to himself, would never ride astraddle.

He was now near the Gaylord place, and he recalled that Sal waited for him. Her small front porch was overgrown with vines of the white moonflower, and the bench on which she sat was carefully placed in deep shadow. She pressed her short plump body against his lean frame and turned toward him her lips, as a sunflower turns to the sun.

7

TO LEX, IN HIS ROMANTIC MOOD, THE FLOWERING OF THAT summer seemed an appropriate frame for Sal Gaylord's bright picture. She had made herself a new yellow dress, in which she looked more sunflowerlike than ever. Her smooth, red-cheeked face, too large for her body, was still undeniably pretty. She frizzed her hair with a hot iron, Lex learned from Jeems, making her head appear even larger. In comparison, Lex found himself recalling that Peggy Lane had begun to bunch her hair up on her head in curls, while Fire either wore hers in braids or let it fly loose.

But the memory did not decrease his admiration for Sal. He liked the way she smelled of clean starch and baking bread as she giggled on the bench, now pressing against him, now pouting and pulling away in order to make him follow. She had agreed to go with him to the wedding, but had taken care to tell him of other offers she had.

"Serenius Brown from across the swamp asked to partner me to the Hawkins'."

Serenius was the son of Preacher Brown, and Lex was both impressed and gratified.

"I'm proud you favored me. I'll come by for you in the cart soon as it's full day."

Many young couples would go afoot, and like most stout women Sal loved to ride. "I'll bring a quilt for us to sit on and to cover our—"

She stopped and giggled shrilly. Lex flushed, but in his

mind he applauded her modesty because she had stopped short of mentioning legs. . . .

A few days later Lex and Sal were driving across the dewy, flower-freckled fields, his knee touching hers under the patchwork quilt. Down in the gullies it was cool, but the sun was warm on the hill slopes.

"Luraline picked a good day for her wedding."

"She picked a good man too," said Sal. "He somehow reminds me of you, Lex."

Lex was pleased with the compliment. "I reckon he's stouter than I am. But—didn't *he* do the picking?"

"If you think that now," Sal told him, "you'll learn better before you get much older."

Lex had no reply to that. He was still thinking it over when they met Mary McEden walking with Hugh Baker and took the other couple into the cart with them. Slim little Mary's voice was regretful.

"Hugh says Miller Hawkins won't allow any square dancing."

"Or any hard cider," Hugh added—with even deeper regret.

Lex laughed. "I don't figure to help Mary get the dancing she loves. But most every man that's going will carry a jug. You just feel under that straw you're sitting on."

Mary felt—and brought to light a young roasting pig with an apple securely jammed between its ghoulishly grinning teeth.

"No, that ain't what I mean. Pa sent that to help out with the dinner. He's coming over later, riding Blaze. He and I killed that pig late last night and hung it in the springhouse for me to take in the cart."

"I got the jug," said Hugh. "I wish I'd thought to bring one myself."

"You needn't trouble. I got enough. We grow more apples than we can use."

All during that festive day Lex's cart was a rallying place for his friends. The girls did not drink hard cider. Any one of the fathers there would have taken his belt to a daughter who touched it. But the dour miller noticed with silent resentment that his men guests were strolling between games to gather in groups around certain vehicles or saddle packs on the ground. The cool, sharp apple juice caused no drunkenness. It merely made them more appreciative of the good food he had provided, which was supplemented by bread and pies and meat brought by the guests.

To one side burned the barbecue pits, which had been lighted the night before. In front of the farmhouse a space of hard sand had been cleared and swept for the frolics. Mary McEden's small foot was tapping it as she longed to be swung in a reel by her partner. But Sal was hovering over the big wooden table upon which were set out the prizes for the contests. Custom would force Lex to give her anything he won; but as she checked the list of games she doubted that Lex would win anything. She knew he could outride all the other men; but neither Blaze nor Congaree were built for racing, and on the other hand Lex was not built for wrestling.

First events of the day were the foot races. They were not arranged according to distance, but for fat men and thin men, old men and young ones.

Yadkin Mourne, aged forty-one, led the older men by half a field, and Lex shouted louder than anybody else.

But Lex did not distinguish himself in the young men's race. His long legs were capable of covering distance when they got in stride, but the eighth of a mile was too short for his easy, swing-from-the-hip horseman's gait. Sal was plainly disgruntled.

"Seems like you could of done better. You're taller than Jeems, and yet he came out ahead of you."

Jeems, however, had not won. It was in wrestling and other feats of strength that he excelled. His sister's eyes were fixed enviously on the Rose of Sharon patchwork quilt that Link McDougall was handing to Patience Reese amid laughter and remarks that were broadly suggestive.

Lex did not even compete in the wrestling. He knew that a tall thin man had no chance at all. But he perceived that Sal was sulking. Her brother and the partners of her girl friends had been winning, while her partner of the day had not. Realizing all this Lex was disturbed, for he had no horse for the horse races. So he took refuge in the shade of a gum tree, drinking cool cider with Jeems Gaylord and Hugh Baker and the preacher's son Serenius Brown from across Wateree. Serenius was chunkily built and already getting bald, but he had ridden to Luraline's wedding on a leggy four-year-old that his father used on his circuit. Now he was gulping down swallow after swallow of the fermented apple juice which was forbidden in his home and thereby made more alluring.

"You couldn't sit that colt in a run," Jeems Gaylord was telling him. "But you could use a keg hid out in your woodhouse, and Lex could win this race."

"Two kegs," said Serenius Brown, and held up two thick fingers.

Lex won the race on the preacher's bay colt. Sal pushed boldly through the crowd to meet him as he dismounted, and she caught his arm and walked with him to the table of trophies. The prize was a dress length of indigo-dyed homespun and flax-and-wool, known as linsey-woolsey.

"It's for you," he said hoarsely to Sal, not even touching it; and she snatched it and held it against her to the accompaniment of whistles and personal questions.

"Going to make a wedding dress of it, Sal?" inquired Edisto.

She laughed loudly. "That's for me to know and you to find out."

Lex, his ears red with embarrassment, stood and endured in silence the shouts and catcalls evoked by that display of wit. But his eye was caught by a figure on the edge of the crowd: Parson Brown's son standing on tiptoe and holding up a broad hand with two stubby fingers outstretched.

8

THE CREAM OF THE ENTERTAINMENT HAD BEEN SAVED FOR afternoon. Dinner occupied more than two hours. It was served by the women and eaten sitting on benches, on chairs brought from the house, or upon the ground. Lex ate with Sal and Mary and Hugh. He ate pork and beef and boiled fowl and roast corn and potatoes and beans and apple pie.

Afterward there was a short rest, while the older women went in the house and the younger ones gathered to laugh and talk in bunches. Then Miller Hawkins came around the corner of the piazza, carrying a big gray gander in his arms.

"Help me hang him up on the pole, boys," he ordered.

Lex stepped back as the others went willingly forward. The gander was swung by the legs, head down, from a crude yard on the pole. He flapped his wings in protest and curved his long neck and hissed, and the weight of his body began to make the thongs cut into his flesh.

Serenius Brown was already astride the brown colt which he had let Lex have for the race in exchange for two kegs of cider. He was too clumsy for jockeying, but this was work suited to him.

The rules stipulated only that contestants must ride at a gallop and that the first one who succeeded in pulling the gander's head from its body received the gander as prize. Serenius galloped as slowly as he could make the colt go. His thick, strong right hand seized the dodging,

34

darting neck in a grip which appeared to pull it out to twice its length. The thongs held, and the downy thighs were dislocated by the jerk. The gander honked in agony, beating its wings vainly, and the crowd howled applause. But Serenius' sweaty fingers slipped from the orange beak, leaving the maimed bird fluttering as the next man rode down on it.

Lex walked off toward the spring at the foot of the hill. Behind him sounded the yelling which told that another contestant was doing his best to tear a living creature apart. The path on each side was cool with fern, and the bubbling water was lighter than any cider. As he drank from his cupped hands Lex tried to forget the gander. It was a popular game all through that section as well as up in Mecklenburg and farther north. A gander for boiling or roasting was a prize worth trying for.

Yet he did not go back. He sat for hours by the green spring, watching the black or gray squirrels who scolded him from the trees. With dusk a raccoon family came seeking water in single file. Lex lay motionless, watching them, his gray leather leggings as still as two lichen-grown sticks. The two old coons were in the lead and were followed by six young ones. One by one they drank from the pool, raising their ringed masks and licking their whiskers daintily. Then, still unfrightened, they turned and racked out of sight to begin the night's hunt for food.

It was not long after that he heard Sal coming down the path. She was calling: "Lex! Lex! Edisto said you'd be down at the spring!"

He rose and met her.

"Why'd you leave me, Lex? When the goose pulling was finished I looked all 'round for you."

"It took you long enough to miss me and start to look."

"I was watching the goose pulling—just like everybody else."

"Not like me. I never did favor that kind of sport."

"Jeems and Edisto said that's why you went off. But you don't need to be so squeamish. Preacher Brown's own son rode in it, and he got the gander second try."

"He can keep it. He's not man enough to ride a race or to rassle a man."

"He didn't keep it. He gave it to me. Might be you just jealous, Lex."

"Might be," said Lexington Mourne.

Slow rage was rising in him, and it was increased by the fact that he knew he was jealous. Sal caught at his hand, but he jerked it away. He wanted to be left alone in the cool twilight of the hills. Yet he could not relinquish Sal. With her flushed cheeks and her scattered hair she was even more desirable. He knew in his heart that no other girl would have refused the gander. But the man who won it had offered it to Sal.

She came closer, head on one side and her full mouth pouting. "You don't have to act this way, Lex. I could get me another boy, but—but I like you best. . . ."

He caught her in both arms and put his mouth down on the waiting mouth. It was still greedy and clinging to his when he lifted his head again.

Dark was closing around the spring as they walked slowly, hand in hand, up the path to the farmhouse. Some of the guests were already tuning up for the "shivaree," and as they approached they heard the harsh notes of homemade fiddles and beaten pans. The house was unlighted, but lanterns were hung in the yard. Supper was in progress, with Luraline and her bridegroom sitting side by side on a bench and trying to eat. The girl was plainly terrified and the young man apprehensive. Nobody was drunk, but the mood of the crowd had changed. Lex could feel it through Sal's hot hand, like a charge of electricity. Laughter was too loud and too high, and coarse jokes were being shouted. Nobody was drunk; but the same effect of the forbidden liquor had been achieved by cruelty to an animal and by anticipation of putting the bride to bed.

Edisto strolled up to Lex. He said: "Luraline's scary. I'd help 'em get away if I could."

"Now, don't you go spoiling the fun," Sal ordered him sharply. "Whoever heard of a wedding without a shivaree?"

For an hour more they all milled around, watching the bride and groom in the way a hound watches a raccoon it has treed. When Lex saw Luraline reach for her husband's hand and draw him into the shadows, he hoped they might escape. But just behind him Serenius gave voice to a bellow and charged forward. Lex stuck out a long leg, and Serenius tripped and rolled heavily. But he was up again, and the crowd in pursuit with him.

The girl ran for the farmhouse, the young man for the woods. Sal abandoned Lex and joined the screaming women who followed Luraline. Lex and Jeems and Edisto stood in the deserted yard, among overturned benches and the remains of the food.

In less than fifteen minutes Johannes Heidt was dragged back into the lantern light by his whooping captors. They had tousled and pommeled the young German, and his long blond hair was hanging over his eyes. They carried him on through the farmhouse doors, giving him loud advice and roaring loudly at their own wit. At Luraline's bedroom door a short delay was occasioned by the fact that the women inside were trying to hold it shut.

As the door was forced open, Lex, in the rear of the crowd of men, caught a glimpse of a big square bed with Luraline cowering in it. Then, as Johannes was thrust in, her shrieking women attendants broke in a rush that knocked the men aside as they forced their way out.

9

THE CHARIVARI LASTED UNTIL EXACTLY MIDNIGHT. HAVING
put the young couple to bed, their guests continued for
hours to mock-serenade them. Making all the noise they
possibly could, they marched around and around the Hawkins house. Many, like Lex, had hunting horns. Others
drew raucous notes on homemade fiddles. Most beat as
hard as they could on pots and pans and wooden buckets.
For hours there was bedlam on the miller's premises.

It was a chance heaven-sent for the young courting
couples. Two by two they dropped away into the shadows
beyond the farmyard. Lex was not unwilling when Sal's
hand tightened its grip and she drew him toward the more
solid darkness of shadow cast by a black walnut tree.
Under it their isolation was accentuated by the noise and
the moving lanterns a hundred yards away. Sal sank bone-
lessly down upon a root and pulled him to a seat beside
her.

They occupied the border line between two different
countries. In front of them raged the uproar of horns,
sawed strings, improvised drums and human shouts. Behind them fields—star-pale and half-harvested—sloped, and
small voices of the night sang low but steadily. Lex's
country-bred ears could recognize the different insects
taking part in that chorus, as a musician can recognize the
different parts in a symphony. He sat still with Sal's hand
in his, leaning back against the walnut trunk and feeling
the night breeze cool on his hot body.

She squeezed his fingers. "Seems like you're dumb-struck, Lex."

"I was listening to the night singers out there in the field."

"Why you want to listen to bugs? I been hearing them every night since I was born. I—"

"Hush, Sal! That's a dog fox barking across the gully. You ever seen one bay the moon—with his brush drooping —and his muzzle raised so high his throat was bent in a bow?"

"I got no wish to see one. The varmint might be mad. Only use I have for one is when it's skinned for a side-the-bed rug."

"I'll get you one before Christmas," he promised. "I'll get you the biggest red fox that runs in the High Hills."

"Will you, Lex? The floor's cold to my feet when I get up winter mornings."

Her voice broke in a giggle. "Wonder if Luraline got a foxskin in there by her bed."

In spite of the night wind Lex felt his face growing hot again. To think of Luraline's bedroom seemed to him just as bad as to invade it. He tried to change the subject without reproving Sal.

"I never met Johannes until he came courting Luraline. Might be he runs foxes up in the Saluda."

Sal's voice sharpened. "I heard say he already raised a house for her—a big house with piazzas and carving on the banister rails. Serenius' pa rides up there on his circuit. He tells as how those German boys work hard and marry early, 'stead of running foxes and coons like the boys 'round here."

Her easy giggle bubbled, taking the sharpness from her words. "Serenius says his sister Lizzie is all set to catch her a Saluda boy."

It drew the answer she was working for. "Don't you go catching any Saluda boy, Sal."

She leaned against him, whispering: "What you mean, Lex? You mean you wouldn't want to see that?"

He put an arm around her and pulled her even closer. The noise of the charivari had ceased, but neither noticed that. She was soft and young and the only girl he had kissed.

"I mean it's a sight I couldn't stand to see."

He was still kissing her when Jeems' shout startled them both. "Lex," he was yelling. "Lex! Where 'bouts you and Sal?"

With one movement Lex withdrew his arm and leapt to his feet. "Here!" he shouted. "We're right here! What you want, Jeems?"

As Sal's brother approached she did not rise but demanded angrily of him: "Why you ain't in the shivaree? What you want with Lex?"

"It's Sunday morning and the shivaree's stopped. Everybody's going home, and Pa's done gone and took my horse. What I want is a ride home in Lex's cart."

"Sure," said Lex. Although he was tingling with Sal's kisses, a small cool breeze of relief blew suddenly through his heart.

Sal's voice went higher. "How you know Pa took your horse? Why you can't ride home in the cart with Ma and the younguns?"

"Pa left word for me with Miller Hawkins. He and Lex's pa went off more than an hour ago on the horses, and Ma and the younguns went along in the cart."

Sal tried to speak again, but Lex raised his voice above hers. "Must be some reason, Jeems, to cause 'em to go like that."

"That's what I reckon," said Jeems; "and I reckon to find out from Ma."

The trip from Hawkins' to Gaylords' seemed long to Lex
and Jeems, but it was too fast for Sal and Congaree. The
last two, for different reasons, had looked forward to
taking it in a slow walk. Lex kept the horse in a trot, leaning to smack him with the rope lines whenever he slackened gait. Sal sulked, and the two young men speculated
in worried silence. When they reached the Gaylord gate,
Sal jumped down and ran through it without a good night.
As she pushed open the cottage door her mother appeared
with a candle in hand.

"That you, son?" she called. "I'm glad you come."

"What's the trouble, Ma?" asked Jeems as he walked
swiftly toward her.

Lex followed him up the walk, while Congaree began
to eat the wild rose vines on the fence.

"There's trouble at the Johnston place. Two hours ago
the oldest Johnston boy brought a message to Lex's pa,
and your pa went over there with him."

Jeems demanded: "Why didn't he call me? Me and Lex
would have gone along with them."

"That's just what they didn't want. They say you boys
are too brash."

"Brash or not," said Jeems, "we're going. I'll get my
rifle, Lex."

"Your pa loaned it to Mr. Mourne—and he took his.
Jeems, I'm scared!"

They left her standing in the door, as other pioneer
women had stood, while they ran for the cart and Lex
lashed his horse to a gallop.

10

THE JOHNSTON HOUSE WAS QUIET AND DARK WHEN CONGAREE, breathing hard, pulled the cart through its lane gate. But two horses whinnied at him from the grove of scrub oak to one side, and two figures came down the steps from the piazza.

Jeems was over the big left wheel before it had ceased turning.

"What's the matter, Pa? Why did you go off without telling me?"

"Because I wanted to keep you clear of trouble," his father replied. "Mourne and I have settled it all. Why did you come after us?"

"Ma's scared half to death. Seems like you could have told us."

"I got a message," said Farmer Mourne. "Adlai Johnston sent his boy. Seems like two men he'd never seen before came to his house after dark and made threats against him."

Johnston had moved up behind them. Yadkin Mourne turned to him. "You tell them about it, and tell them what the men looked like."

Johnston's voice was softer than those of the white men. It slurred its consonants, and its vowels were liquid and sad.

"All I knows is when I come up from feedin' my stock tonight, I finds two strange w'ite mens sittin' here on the piazza."

Jeems asked quickly: "Where were your wife and children?"

"They been hidin' back in the house, I finds out atterwards, Mr. Jeems."

Lex demanded excitedly: "What did the men look like?"

"They looks diffunt from anybody 'round here. They built tall and stringy, and they looks like wile mens wid hair all over they face. I ain't never seen sich mens befo', and I don't know who they is."

"I know," Lex told him. "They came out of the swamp. Those are the same men who kicked my puppy and threatened to shoot me."

Yadkin Mourne said slowly: "It sounds like it, son."

"They musta come outa the swamp," Johnston agreed, "'cause they gone back somewhere. But befo' they went, they tole me if I don't do like they says they burn my house down wid my wife and chillun inside it."

Lex and Jeems spoke together. "What did they tell you to do?"

"They tole me I gotta turn my house and all my lan' over to them. They say, where they comes from, they don't 'low no black mens to live."

Blacksmith Gaylord spoke. "I lived a year in the Blue Ridge. Those people didn't allow a Negro in the mountains. If one came, they'd run him back to the lowlands. This fits with what Lex told us just as close as a good shoe fits a horse's foot."

"This ain't the mountains," said Lex. His voice was hoarse with anger. "This is the High Hills of Santee, and it's *our* country—not theirs!"

"It's our country," said Jeems, "and we won't have any mountain men doing their meanness here!"

"Hold your temper," said Farmer Mourne. "We ain't letting 'em do it. I told you Gaylord and I had it fixed before you two got here."

"How'd you fix it? You know well enough, whatever those men told you, they're lying and coming back."

"They didn't tell us anything. They went off before we came. I didn't want you boys in this, and neither did Gaylord; but since you got here you might as well know it all." He turned to Johnston. "Tell 'em the rest of it, Adlai."

"I tole 'em I'se a Free Negro, an' I got the rights of a w'ite man here. I tole 'em my father belonged to the Hugers down in the Low Country. He save Mr. Huger's boy from drownin', an' Mr. Huger give him an' my ma all two they freedom. He give 'em some money too, and they buy this lan' an' live here in a log cabin. After they die I works the place. You all knows I works hard, an' I manage to buil' me a nice house."

Lex said: "I know. You built it—and you'll keep it."

Jeems asked: "What did the mountain men say to that?"

"They say, so far's they concern, no black mens is free. They say it ain't fitten for w'ite mens to camp in the swamp w'ile a black man got a good house on the hill."

"So far as I'm concerned," swore Lex, "they won't camp in the swamp long. When the people around here know what's happened to you, we'll have a big enough pack of dogs and a big enough crowd of men to hunt them out of this country and send them back to the mountains."

"The sheriff will attend to that," said his father. "You hold your tongue if you want the rest of the story."

They wanted the rest of the story, although they were fully determined to hunt out the mountaineers without benefit of law. They were hot with youth and rage, but Johnston's voice was still soft. It held neither resentment nor anger, only a tragic resignation.

"I seen it warn't no good to talk wid 'em. All two of 'em had long guns. They order me go git my wife and chillun. They say, 'We kin scare 'em, if we can't scare you.'"

"Did they hurt any of them?" asked Jeems.

"No, Mr. Jeems. They jist rant and rave, same like they done at me. They holler so loud the littlest chillun start cryin'. I only bring ten head of 'em out. I figure those mens can't know I got 'leven. So when I goes back in the kitchen w'ere they all hid, I tells my oldest boy to slip out the back way and run fas' as he kin to Mr. Mourne's place. I knowed Mr. Mourne would do all he could for me."

Yadkin Mourne turned to his son. "The child found our house empty, so he came on to Hawkins'."

"He's just twelve years old," said Lex, "and he must have run three miles."

"It don't hurt him none to run," said Adlai Johnston. "He fine Mr. Mourne at Mr. Hawkins' place, and Mr. Mourne brung him on home on the horse behine him. Them mens was still here, tellin' me what they goin' to do, when I hears the horses comin' in a gallop. They jump up soon as they hears that, and they tell me, 'You say one word 'bout this an' you'll git a bullet from behine a tree someday.'"

"Of course they're Schofilites," said Lex. "Some of them are left around here. Hanging's too good for them! We need the Regulators—"

His father broke in. "The sheriff can do his own hanging. When you or the Regulators run a man with dogs and put the lynch law on him, you're doing just the same thing those men are trying to do to Johnston."

"What are you going to do then?" Jeems demanded furiously. "You going to let Schofilites stay in the swamp and come out whenever they choose and shoot Adlai and burn his house?"

"Shut your head," the blacksmith said, "and don't give Mr. Mourne any sass. He and I got this matter fixed without interference from you young cubs."

He moved toward the two horses tied to the scrub oak

trees, throwing over his shoulder: "You come along with me, Jeems! You got a long ride to work off your hotness. I'm sending you straight on for Sheriff Cebron now."

"Take your gun," advised Yadkin Mourne. "Varmints like that might ambush you."

"They might—but in that case the rifle wouldn't help me. You and Lex may need the guns if they try to come back here tonight."

"I reckon you're right," said Yadkin Mourne. "Jeems is welcome to ride my horse. He's a mite faster than yours, although he ain't any racer. Lex and I'll take turns on guard until Jeems brings back the sheriff."

Then he and Lex and Adlai Johnston stood in the farmyard's darkness and heard the heavy hoofbeats receding.

11

TWO DAYS LATER JEEMS RETURNED WITH THE SHERIFF, WHO at once deputized both Jeems and Lex to help him. But although the three men quartered the swamp with hounds, they found no trace of the Schofilites.

"By this time," said Yadkin Mourne, "they'll be up in the Piedmont and headed for the mountains."

"That's what you said last time, Pa, after they kicked Vidette and threw a rifle on me."

"Shucks, boy! *You* threatened *them* and were more to blame then than they were. This time they threatened to burn a house and kill an innocent woman and children, as well as a man. They know the law'll be after them."

Summer passed into autumn with no sign of the fugitives. But Lex and Jeems still spoke of them and kept an eye out for them on possum and coon hunts during the following winter. The High Hills had given no sanctuary to the raiders named after their corrupt patron Schovell; but they were known to have friends in the stone hills beyond. Lex wondered whether they were sheltering there. But just after he and his father had finished the spring planting, he got a letter from Toff that made him forget all else.

Lex, I'd expected by now to be in Charleston with my militia troop. But smallpox has broken out there, and we've orders to wait awhile....

47

"—Listen, Pa! He wants me to go over there. Think you could spare me for a couple of weeks?"

Can't you come over for a few weeks? It may be our last time together for nobody knows how long.

"I'd be right glad to be rid of you. You can take Blaze if you want him."

"No. Quickest way will be to get Jeems to ride the Camden-Georgetown road with me. When we get north of the Lane place I'll strike through the swamp afoot, and he'll bring the horses back."

"How'll you cross the river?"

"I'll write Toff a letter now, saying I'll get to the river before sunset one week from this Sunday afternoon. He'll bring a dugout across for me. If 'tweren't for my bundle of clothes I'd swim."

Long before that day broke Lex and Jeems were riding southeast. Shortly after noon they had reached the place on the high road which was directly north of the Lane plantation. Santee Swamp lay on their right. Jeems climbed down from Blaze and stood looking at it.

"This ain't your country. Sure you can find your way?"

"Sure," said Lex. "It's dead south of here, and besides I got my compass."

"How many miles you reckon it is from here to the river?"

"Hardly more than two on a beeline. But I'll have to do some winding around because the water's high."

"Give me hill country any time. You always got your landmarks there. That's why I'd rather run red foxes than hunt the swamp varmints."

"You got landmarks in the swamp if you just look out for them. Soon as I get a little way in I'll find a trace

I know. Last year Toff and I used to paddle across and hunt coon on moonlight nights, clear from the riverbank to this road."

"Better not get yourself lost," warned Jeems as he threw a leg across Blaze. "I don't crave Serenius Brown for a brother-in-law."

"You keep him off till I get back. And, Jeems, you've no need to lead Congaree. He'll follow after Blaze if you just slip his bridle."

He stood to watch Jeems out of sight, then turned and struck south into the swamp.

Within a hundred paces its twilight closed around him. Tall trees reared their naked brown boles in a desperate reach for sunlight, and the limbs and leaves crowning their tops made a thatched roof which filtered its light. As far as Lex could see the bladed wampee was thick and green. Its heart-shaped leaves brushed the old leggings he had worn for wading, and in places they grew as high as his knees. Gray moss hung from the cypresses, shot with a yellow-green pallor. The henna cypress needles, smaller and more delicate than needles of the pine, had during the winter fallen everywhere. They heaped themselves between the gnarled roots, and they floated in rusty rafts upon the sherry-colored expanses of water.

Lex had found a canal bank and was trying to follow it. But, unlike a man-made canal, the watercourse twisted and widened, broadening into a long lagoon that ran east and west. From it came the bellowing of hundreds of bullfrogs. He followed for a quarter mile east, then waded where it narrowed. By now he was wet almost to the waist, and he thought he had gone about half the way. He recalled just such a lagoon when he and Toff had been hunting one night. The dogs were chasing an old raccoon which had eluded them before, and it had taken to water there and thrown them off its scent again.

On the other side he looked back at the spot and assured himself he was right. He checked with his compass and glanced upward through the trees, figuring by the angle of the citron light that he had a little more than two hours before sundown.

Shortly afterward he came upon the faint trace of a path. The swamp growth was bending so low across it that he took it at first for an alligator run. But as he pushed through he found it cleared to the height of his shoulder, and down in its loam he spied the print of a cloven foot. He stooped and examined it carefully. The wild hogs known as "razorbacks" had cloven hoofs just the size of a deer's foot, but he knew that a hog's toes stamped themselves more heavily. Being a deer path, it was apt to lead out to the river; for the deer's chosen habitat was timberland and broom field. They were not swamp dwellers, but they skirted the swamps and came into them occasionally when seeking to hide.

The deer path was easy walking, although narrow and overgrown. It had been laid out by primitive road builders who, instead of cutting curves and leveling obstacles, merely followed the high ground patiently for the longer way. This ridge above the water was taking Lex too far east, but he decided to stay with it since the water looked deep on the right. In less than an hour he realized that he was reaching the edge of the swamp. The cypresses were making way for tupelo and water oak, and he began to see holly, magnolia and bay pine. Suddenly, between their trunks, he glimpsed the Santee's tawny tide, rolling its soiled foam and flotsam from the High Hills down to the sea.

The deer path had led him too far east, as he figured it would do. He stood for a moment on the marsh edge, looking upriver for landmarks. He recalled the alley of pyramidal cedars which led from South Bank, the Lane house, down to the river. They were tall and their pointed tops easy to distinguish, but they must be too far upstream for him to sight. He told himself that he could be no more than a mile downstream, and he turned west to follow the shore in that direction.

His moccasins squelched in the fresh-water marsh, and his leggings felt slimy and cold. He knew he had cured the hide too well for it to shrink, but wet leather was never comfortable. He thought with satisfaction of the real boots in his bundle, and he shifted the straps which held it across his shoulders. Before Peggy Lane saw him he would be dressed in his store clothes. Toff's servant would bring an oval tin bathtub into the room and would pour both hot and cold water into it. But Lex could not bring himself to tie his hair back with a ribbon like Toff's. If Jeems or Edisto heard of that they would make his life a torment. Anyway it was too short, although it came down over his neck and ears. He had brought a jar of bear grease along, and he would rub some in it to make it stay brushed in place. By the time Peggy saw him, he—

A shout from the river interrupted him there. He stopped and looked and saw a paddle being waved through a gap in the willows. Toff's voice came to him: "Here we are! We've been rowing upstream and drifting back down all afternoon."

Lex's heart gave a great jump under his doeskin hunting shirt. Toff had said *we*. Could Peggy have come with him?

He waded as fast as he could through the marsh to a place where he could see Toff holding the dugout against the shore. And as he ran, stumbling and sinking in the mud, a girl stood up in the boat and waved a blue bonnet at him.

12

AS LEX SAW THE BLUE BONNET RISE ABOVE THE LOW WILLOWS
along the bank he heard Toff's voice again, this time in a
howl of anguish.

"Sit down! You'll upset the boat! Haven't you got any
sense! Ow-w-w—"

The exclamation ended in a loud splash, followed by a
second one less noisy. Reaching the bank, Lex saw the
dugout turned on its side with Toff trying to hold it from
being swept away. Just beyond it a girl was struggling in
deeper water. He jerked the pack straps off his shoulders
and plunged in.

"You hold the boat while I get her," he yelled, for he
saw his friend's predicament.

The water was only thigh-deep, but the current pulled
and swirled. It had taken the girl off her feet, but she was
struggling pluckily not to be carried out by it. Half-
swimming, yet feeling mud under his feet, Lex lunged
toward her and grasped a handful of blue skirt and white
petticoat ruffles. Pulling her to him he threw the other arm
around her waist. As he did she turned up to him a small
pointed face with draggled red hair.

"Oh, Lex!" she cried joyfully. "Lex, you saved me from
drowning!"

In spite of the dirty water which was running down it,
that little triangular face was aglow with joy. But there
was no answering joy on Lex's face. He might have known
that Peggy would not come in a dirty boat—or come to

meet him in any other way. It was just like Fire to tag along with Toff and then upset the boat and nearly drown herself. He was so taken aback that he nearly let her go again, but she put out both hands and caught him by the shoulders.

"Hold onto me, Lex! I can't swim. But I want to learn. Will you teach me while you're here? I asked Toff, but he wouldn't."

"Why should a girl want to swim?" her brother shouted angrily. "I'll not only never teach you but I'll never again bring you out in a boat with me. Only an idiot would stand up in a dugout canoe. Now all three of us are wet and covered with this yellow mud."

"I was wet already," said Lex. "A little more water won't hurt me."

He pulled Sophia ashore, then helped Toff right the round-bottomed boat and bail it. They held it while the girl stepped in.

"Go sit forward," Toff told her. "You're just about witch's weight."

She looked so downcast that Lex was sorry for her. Although a half head taller than when he saw her last, she had been light to pull ashore and her waist felt amazingly small. He knew she was willful and hoydenish, and she was far from beautiful as she faced him from the bow thwart with wet clothes and hair and a face streaked with mud. He smiled at her.

"No harm's done. You didn't fall in water deep enough to drown you, and you'd probably have got ashore yourself, the way you were fighting."

"She's hardheaded," insisted Toff. "If you hadn't been here, I'd have had to let go the dugout in order to get her. The current would have taken it out and we'd have been marooned over here."

Fire cried: "That would have been fun! I've always wanted to spend a night out of doors."

"You always want to do wild, unladylike things. Lex, you better thank your stars you haven't got any sisters. I never know what Fire's going to do next, and Peggy thinks of nothing but beaux."

The word "beaux" sent a sharp pang deep under Lex Mourne's wet hunting shirt. He felt it was both appropriate and ladylike for Peggy to think of beaux. Doubtless they thronged the plantation and would give him no chance to see her. But, of course, it had never occurred to him that she was within his reach. She was as far above him as one of the stars he loved to watch. He had no thought of touching her, but he could admire and adore. Sal was the warm yellow lamp in the mill, always close by and calling him home.

But to his surprise and joy there were no beaux that evening. When he came downstairs Peggy stood in the drawing-room door, yellow roses in her dark hair and a long gown of yellow silk leaving her white shoulders bare. He knew that she was only fifteen and a few hours older than Fire; but between the leaves of the great mahogany folding door she was as poised and composed as any young lady, and her dark eyes said more to him than her few soft words of welcome. He was amazed and overjoyed at his luck in finding her alone, and at their half-hour *tête-à-tête* while supper was being delayed for Fire to be washed and dried and dressed. It never occurred to him that in his simple clothes he was the finest figure of a man Peggy Lane had ever seen or that she had purposely dressed early and come downstairs to coquet with him.

The full-length gilt-framed mirrors and the crystal candelabra did not awe him in the least. He was too much of a man for that. He was not only at ease, he was walking on air when Toff arrived. But his friend and host did not notice it.

"Oh, here you are," he said carelessly. "I went by your room, but you'd gone. It took me some time to convince Mother that Fire was neither drowned nor maimed for life."

Peggy's laughter was so sweet that Lex missed its note of scorn. "Fire enjoyed it. She loves that kind of thing. She told me all about it while Chloe was washing her hair."

There she stopped to glance sideways at Lex. "If I fall in the river will you rescue *me?*"

"No," said Toff disgustedly. "He's come to South Bank to visit me, not to be bothered by you girls."

Peggy's eyes grew darker and softer and her voice entreated and coaxed. "Oh, Toff, I'd hoped Lex would ride with me tomorrow. I won't keep him from you for more than an hour. I just want his advice about the new horse Father gave me."

"You don't need advice about the horse. Fire's is spirited, because she can handle it. Father bought you a 'lady's saddle horse,' which is horse trader's language for a cow."

"Toff, don't be mean to me! Don't listen to him, Lex! I've been riding just as long as Fire has."

"But not the kind of horses Fire rides," Toff told her.

Lex managed to get in a word there. He had not known Toff was so cruel.

"I think you ride beautifully, Peggy. I'd be glad—and honored—to go with you if you'll let me."

He was still feeling honored and glad when he set off with her next day. In her long skirt and tight bodice of hunting green, she was at once dashing and feminine. He watched her little hands in their doeskin gauntlets and her provocative profile under its three-cornered hat. He was recalling how considerately she had inquired of Fire whether Fire was going to use her horse or would lend it to Lex. Fire, he recalled, had not been so courteous in agreeing. For some reason her gray eyes had smoldered resentfully as she looked back at her twin. Then she had dropped her lashes over their gray fire, nodded curtly and turned away.

13

RIDES WITH PEGGY WERE FEW ENOUGH TO BE TREASURED
and hoped for. As a rule Lex saw her only at dinner or
supper and in the drawing room after the evening meal.
The river plantations were closer together than the farms
in the High Hills, and Peggy was always in demand by
friends at neighboring places. But she was unfailingly
sweet and cordial to him. More than once she managed
to give the impression that she would have preferred staying at home to talk or to ride with him, but that she felt
obliged to keep some engagement previously made.

Upon evenings when she was absent the great French
chandelier over the supper table seemed to Lex less brilliant. Peggy's presence made its long crystal teardrops
glitter with reflection of her bubbling joy in life. On evenings when she had gone to spend the night with some
girl friend, Lex would play chess with Mr. Lane until
Mr. Lane either checkmated him or fell asleep in his high-
backed chair and snored loudly and suddenly. Then the
older couple would retire, following after the butler, who
carried their candlesticks. This always happened early,
because the plantation started its day early. So their departure gave Toff and Lex an hour or more in the gun
room afterward. Fire, if allowed, would follow them there.

Lex did not object to her; he rather liked to have her
around. But her brother felt differently on the subject.

"Why do you tag after us? You don't even like guns."

"I do like guns—and I can shoot. I don't like killing birds or animals."

"Can she really shoot?" Lex asked in amusement.

Toff began: "Not a rifle, just—"

"A pistol," said Fire. "Father taught me." She looked at Lex with big troubled eyes. "Do you think it's unwomanly for a woman to shoot?"

"Of course not. My grandmother shot an Indian on the Catawba Path. He was sneaking up on the wagon where my father, a baby, was sleeping. The men had gone a little way off to hunt. My father told me about it and told me he had taught my mother to shoot."

"Oh, Lex, how brave and wonderful your grandmother must have been! If she hadn't shot that Indian and he had killed her and your father, it would have been perfectly awful—because *you* wouldn't be here."

They both laughed at her; but, being a man, Lex was pleased. The spring night was cool and Felix had lighted a wood fire in the enormous brick fireplace. Its light flickered on the cypress-paneled walls, and the metal of guns and pistols glinted in their forked racks. Fire had sunk down on the bare, polished floor boards with her back to the flame and her eyes lifted to Lex's face. It came to him suddenly that she made a charming picture, with Toff's bird dogs sprawled on either side of her and her slim hands stroking their coats of rusty red. But the picture had no appeal for Toff.

"Get up," he commanded with elder-brotherly indignation. "Mother has told you more than once that you are not to sit on the floor."

She obeyed, rising to her feet with one easy graceful movement before Lex could reach and hold out a hand to help her. It crossed his mind that neither Peggy nor Sal could have done it without assistance. But, he told himself, neither Peggy nor Sal would ever have sat on the floor and taken the heads of two dogs in her lap.

Fire seated herself in a chair. The red setters gazed reproachfully after her.

"It isn't my fault," she told them, and they thumped with their tails in response. "I like to sit on the floor with you, but my family won't let me."

"You'd better go to bed," said Toff. "You weigh five pounds less than Peggy, although you're an inch taller. Men don't like skinny women."

Lex remembered the feel of her slim waist in his arm. It had not seemed at all skinny, but rather, slender and lissome. He looked at her more carefully than he had ever done before. Being himself of fair coloring, he fancied dark women. But her hair was now tumbled and as bright as her nickname, and two small flames burned in her cheeks.

"I don't care about men," she told Toff angrily.

"But you like to dance. Why didn't you go with Peggy?"

"Because I don't like the Fortesques."

"Has Peggy gone to the house of those Tories?"

"Now don't you blame Peggy! She hates Tories as much as you and I do. Lionel Fortesque is crazy about her, and she doesn't like to hurt his feelings."

"Hurt his feelings, my eye!" jeered Toff. "Peggy flirts with every man she meets. But she must be hard up if she spends her time on Lionel. He's been walking with a cane ever since the governor began drafting militia."

"Peggy says he broke his leg on a fox hunt."

"He did—years ago. It healed perfectly, and he's been using it—until he saw he was going to have to fight."

"Well, that isn't Peggy's fault. She's kindhearted and sorry for him."

Toff turned to Lex who was listening. "Fire always takes up for Peggy and lets Peggy impose on her. The Fortesques are Tories at heart. Not long ago they entertained a British officer named Fay."

Fire cried: "Yes, and I saw his Red Doe! Toff, tell Lex about the Red Doe."

Lex's mind was on hunting. "Are you talking about a deer?"

"No. It's a horse. I saw it, and it's beautiful."

"It seems," Toff explained, "that these Fays raise horses somewhere in England, and this chap's grandfather developed and named the particular strain the Red Doe."

Lex was as eager as Fire now. "What's the type? Is it any good?"

"Fire saw it; I didn't. She describes it as a stallion, about fifteen hands and bright red bay in color."

Fire said: "It's the cavalry type, sturdily built but long-legged. It's neither especially large nor especially fast; but it has good speed, endurance, and a brave heart. I think this Major Fay rides it too hard. Elouise says he told them he needed a second mount and he was writing his father in England to send him the filly that belongs to his younger brother."

"Why can't he get a horse over here? Don't the British steal them from all the plantations, besides using marsh tackies?"

"Not Fay," said Toff. "He wouldn't ride a tacky."

"For cross-country work and getting through these swamps, I'd feel safer on a tacky than on a thoroughbred."

"You would be. But Fay doesn't do that kind of riding. He leads his column down the highroad, and he must be mounted on a breed of horse that is owned by no other man. He's sworn he'll shoot this stallion before he'll let it fall into the hands of any American rebel."

Fire sighed deeply. "I'd love to steal it. It wouldn't really be stealing, because we're at war with England."

"That's enough from you," said Toff. "When it comes to horse stealing—"

"Of course I won't do it. But I do want it, Toff."

"Well, you won't get it. You cut along to bed now, and let Lex and me talk in peace."

But Lex had not yet heard enough of the Red Doe. "Why did they give it that name?"

Fire welcomed the delay. "*Red* because of the color. They put in *Doe* because most of the foals are fillies. It's unusual for a mare to foal a colt."

She turned to her brother. "Please, Toff, let me ride to the east rice reserve with you and Lex tomorrow."

"No! We'll be gone all day—and we may swim in the river."

She looked her disappointment but did not beg any more. She stooped to pat the dogs, and they thumped with their tails more loudly. Lex replied to her good night, but he was not thinking of her or of Peggy or Sal. Thought of a horse could wipe all other subjects from his mind.

He was picturing to himself the Red Doe which he had not yet seen: a saddle horse, sturdy and speedy enough, bright of coat and brave of heart. . . .

14

ALTHOUGH FIRE HAD BEEN REFUSED PERMISSION TO JOIN THAT ride, both Lex and Toff were pleased and proud when they saw the plantation huntsman awaiting them in the stable yard.

Toff asked: "Are you going with us, Banjo?"

"Part way," said the half-Indian. He spat a stream of tobacco juice and threw a leg across his tobacco-colored marsh tacky.

He rode behind them on the plantation path, his smaller mount in a fox trot to keep up with the two long-legged thoroughbreds. Toff managed to speak softly from the side of his mouth to Lex.

"He's always liked you. That's the reason he came."

Lex was deeply gratified. He turned his head and called back: "Remember that coon hunt you took us on last time I was here, Banjo? I passed the lagoon where the varmint took to water when I was crossing the swamp on my way here."

"You did well to cross it. You could make a scout."

"So could Toff," said Lex generously. "He knows that swamp better than I do."

"He oughta know it. It's his own country. But he'll never make the huntsman you will."

Banjo had no inhibitions. Lex was embarrassed and Toff was indignant.

"I get just as many birds as Lex does."

"That ain't what I'm talkin' 'bout. You're lookin' for

62

birds then, and ready. What I'm talkin' 'bout is the way you carry your guns."

"Well, what's wrong with the way I carry my gun? You're the one who taught me how to carry it."

Banjo shook his head stubbornly as the pony jogged along.

"Ain't nothin' wrong with the way you carry it. But Lex's gun is part of Lex. And I ain't talkin' 'bout huntin' birds or deer."

"Then what are you talking about hunting?"

"Huntin' men," said Banjo—and spat on a pink wild orchid.

"You mean in war?" asked Lex.

"I mean this same war. Was we three in the swamp and I tryin' to hunt you two and you two huntin' me, I could slip up and kill Toff before he shot. But I reckon I'd have a hard time aslippin' up on Lex."

"Have you heard anything new about the war?" Lex demanded.

Banjo pulled his pony to a stop. "I hears a plenty, but I don't tell all I hears. I'm leavin' you now and headin' for the beeches on that rise."

Both boys knew that wild turkeys frequented a beech grove. Toff said: "Banjo, you oughtn't to kill even a gobbler in May."

"The missis tell me she fancy turkey meat for nex' Sunday. You got too many wild turkeys on this place, anyway."

He rode away from them, and left Lex laughing and Toff fuming.

"Mother has no regard for any seasons for game."

"I never saw a woman who knew or cared about them," said Lex.

"Banjo should know better. But he'll do anything on earth Mother tells him to. Father has reproved him for killing out of season, and he never changes his expression. All he says is: "Miss Hallie want birds to eat."

Lex knew Mrs. Lane's wiles. Without Peggy's coquetry, she could make any man do anything she wished. It flashed across his mind that of her two daughters Fire was perhaps the one more like her. Fire did not coquet; she was too independent for that and too young, he supposed. But there was something rather appealing about her slenderness and her steady eyes, even though she could hardly measure up to her sister.

He and Toff rode the banks of the east reserve and rice fields. Tiny sprouts tufted with jewel-green the black mud in which they grew. Lex sat his horse, gazing at them.

"I've never seen rice in flower."

"The blossoms are tiny insignificant bluets. But the effect is pretty when a whole field is in flower. Say, it must be midday by the look of the sun. Let's have a swim and then eat our lunch."

They swam in the yellow river, dried themselves in the sunshine, dressed and ate the sandwiches they had brought in saddlebags. For the return home they made their way by bridle paths out to the road that followed the Santee's southern shore, passing gates of the plantations on its way. As they came out on the road they saw a cloud of dust a half mile to the east. Shading their eyes with their hands, they drew to a stop and looked.

"Somebody's traveling fast on a hot day," remarked Toff.

Out of the dust cloud rolled a coach with its two horses galloping. Behind it they could distinguish a man on a tall black horse.

"It's the Fortesques'," Toff told Lex. "They sent to London for it. When I was small I thought it Cinderella's coach and pictured its horses turning into mice."

Lex cried out: "Fortesques? But isn't that where Peggy went?"

"Yes. Maybe she's learned some sense and is anxious to get home again. That's Lionel riding behind. He's going to need a bath after taking that dust."

The vehicle was now near them and a hand was waving from it. The Negro coachman pulled his sweating pair to a stop. Peggy's voice was crying: "Oh, Toff! Oh, Lex!"

As the young man on the black horse rode past the coach and up to them, Toff inquired: "What do you mean by bringing my sister home this way?"

The weakly handsome face flushed under its layer of gray dust. Lionel Fortesque removed his hat from his head and held it against his brocaded riding vest.

"We had news from Charles Town which disturbed Miss Margaret. She requested me to take her home as quickly as I could."

Another girl, whom Lex took to be Elouise Fortesque, was now leaning from the coach with Peggy. She beckoned to Toff. "You haven't yet presented your friend to me. Peggy has been telling me such nice things about him."

"He's Lexington Mourne," said Toff shortly. "Miss Fortesque, Mr. Mourne."

Elouise beamed at Lex and held out a hand, and he threw himself from his horse and walked to the coach door leading it. She was attractive, but both she and her brother spoke with an English accent which sounded artificial to the ears of a Back Countryman. He heard Toff inquiring: "What news did you get from Charles Town?" But Elouise was saying: "I've been hoping I'd see you. Peggy says Toff keeps you all to himself. You must both come over and dance at Madmarsh some evening."

"I don't dance, ma'am," said Lex, "—except a few country dances."

"I shall teach you the minuet. Peggy was right when she said—"

At that point Toff shouted in Lex's ear: "Charles Town has surrendered! That means the British will overrun the state! I beg your pardon for interrupting, Miss Elouise. But I wish my militia troop had been down there to help General Lincoln!"

Turning from Elouise to Toff, Lex saw Lionel's eyes gleam with a light which was unmistakably pleasure. It made him understand and share Toff's dislike of the young man.

Peggy wailed from her place in the coach: "I want to go home! I want to tell Father about Major Marion."

Lionel intervened smoothly. "There is no need for alarm. The war is now over, and His Gracious Majesty will pardon the mistakes of misled provincials."

Toff flared: "I'm not misled, and I'll have none of His Majesty. My country is South Carolina, not England."

Lionel shrugged his shoulders. "South Carolina is an English province." His eyes slid to Lex. "Where do you come from, sir?"

Lex looked him up and down. "The High Hills of Santee."

"Ah! A Back Countryman?" There was a tinge of scorn in the words, but Lionel continued: "The Back Country, although its people are less cultured, has many Loyalists."

"But I'm not one of them," said Lex. "And I don't believe the war's over." He turned to Peggy. "What do you know about Major Marion? I am interested because he is a friend of my father's."

Peggy cried: "He is wounded! They say he's broken his leg and is trying to escape into the Back Country."

Toff interrupted. "That's enough, Peggy. Lex and I will gallop ahead and send Sam back with a carriage for you."

He turned and bowed stiffly to Lionel Fortesque.

"You need not continue at such speed. Your horses are already worn out. Our head stableman will meet my sister, and when he does you can transfer her to our coach. She will be near home and quite safe, so you can then turn back. Lex and I will look after her."

15

AT THE LANE HOUSE THEY THOUGHT AND SPOKE OF NOTHING but the bad news.

Lex was deeply troubled. "I'd better start home tomorrow. If I could help anyways I'd stay."

Mr. Lane shook his head. "You cannot help us, and we don't need help so far. It may be, as Lionel said, that the war is over."

Lex and Toff spoke together. "The war isn't over."

"I hope it is," said Peggy, who seemed to have completely recovered from her earlier fright. "It would be so nice to be friends and dance again with the officers from—"

Fire stamped her foot. "How dare you say such a thing? It's *not* over. Lex and Toff are right."

Peggy pouted. "Don't be cross to me, Fire. I hate fighting—people killing each other—"

"So do we all," her father said. "But we hate injustice and tyranny even more. Now, you girls be quiet. The boys are the ones concerned."

He turned to Lex. "Have you any definite plans?"

"No, sir—except that if the war isn't over, I'll try to get up to North Carolina and join General Greene. I have a friend in the hills who's been wanting to do that."

"It's a good plan—if the war isn't over. Meanwhile, you'll get news here more quickly than you would in the hills. Why not stay with us until we hear something more? I've advised Toff to do just that. He should hear within twenty-four hours what his militia troop plans."

Toff urged: "It'll be our last holiday together for nobody knows how long."

Still Lex hesitated. It was in his mind that if the British knew the war was not over their most likely move would be to send a squad to the plantations to take prisoner any able-bodied young man. A fellow feeling caused Toff to read his mind.

"Banjo's got a grapevine to carry news up and down the river. If Redcoats are coming he'll be informed, and we'll have a chance to get away ahead of them."

Mrs. Lane leaned from her chair to put a hand on Lex's knee, thereby overturning her sewing basket and scattering dozens of small articles on the floor.

"Mr. Lane considers you a good influence on Toff," she told him—unperturbed by the fact that he and her son and daughters were scrambling on all fours to recover thimbles and scissors and bodkins and thread.

Lex stood up, flushed with pleasure and embarrassment. Mr. Lane—a small spare man as erect as a ramrod—came across the drawing room with his glass of port in his hand.

"What I meant, lad, in one short word, is that you are a man—which is more than I can say for some of the young blades around here."

Fire's eyes were fixed upon Lex and glowed like lamps in her small white face. But Lex was watching Peggy. Did Peggy want him to stay?

He said: "I hate to go, Mr. Lane. You've all been so kind to me. I'll be glad to stay a few days longer. But I want to get back to the hills by the time my father gets the news—and before Jeems Gaylord leaves to join General Greene."

Toff clapped him on the back and Peggy gave him a smile.

Mr. Lane said: "By that time I think you'll have more definite news to take to the hills."

Fire, rearranging her mother's tangled work, gave him

a glance between long smoke-dark lashes, then set the basket on the low table by Mrs. Lane's chair.

"Please, darling," she said, "try not to upset it again tonight. I'll turn into a monkey if I run around any more on my hands and knees."

"I'll try not to," answered Mrs. Lane obligingly. "But sometimes things just upset themselves. I really believe there's a mischievous ghost somewhere in this house. Oh, dear! There goes my shawl—and my fan—and smelling salts!"

Lex and Fire dived simultaneously for the Paisley shawl and vinaigrette and turkey-tail fan. Behind the back of her chair their heads came together with a crack which was audible across the room. In the general laughter talk of his going home was not resumed. But when Peggy and Fire rose to say good night and he walked with them to open the door, Fire looked anxiously up into his face.

"You'll stay—won't you, Lex?"

"I want to stay, but I've been here several weeks already, and as I told your father—"

Peggy was unpinning the yellow rosebud that she wore in her hair. "He'll stay," she said very softly—and held it out to him.

He slipped it into his breast pocket before he turned back to the others. That night in his room he stood a long time at the window, holding the flower between his hands. A warm breeze blew from the southwest, bringing the smell of river mud and of box from the garden.

The yellow rosebud emboldened him to ask Peggy to ride next day. She hesitated—but the glance she gave him before she dropped her dark eyes made his heart beat faster.

"Not today," she said regretfully. "I'm *so sorry*, Lex, but I've already promised somebody else."

"Could you—would you have—have time—any other day

between now and Sunday? I've got to go on Sunday. I've written Jeems to meet me."

"Of course! We'll ride on Saturday afternoon. It'll be sad—our last ride. . . . But you'll come back. . . ."

For the intervening days Lex lived in another world. He even lost his hearty appetite, causing Mrs. Lane such distress that at breakfast she managed to upset not only her own plate but the bowl of drawn butter that the butler was handing her.

"Perhaps you have country fever," she cried, while the disapproving servant mopped with a wet towel.

"I ain't got fever," the butler said; "but you sure gone and ruint this tablecloth, Miss Hallie."

"I'm so sorry, Felix. Please wipe it up for me. I meant Lex had fever, because the weather's so unseasonably warm. Toff, I think Lex should go to bed instead of going riding with you."

"He's strong as a horse," said Toff. "There's nothing the matter with him—unless he's fallen in love."

Lex felt himself flushing until his ears burned. Could Peggy's family suspect his feeling for her? He knew that it was hopeless, but he couldn't help—

Toff was going on. "I don't blame him if he has. Jeems Gaylord has a sister who looks like a ripe peach. Cheer up, Lex! You'll see her soon. Just don't spoil our last days of holiday by acting like a moonstruck calf."

They rode early and late, and Toff protested loudly when Lex revealed his engagement for Saturday afternoon.

"For goodness' sake, why did you let Peggy hook you?"

Lex was horrified. "I begged her to ride with me. It was kind of her, when she has so many invitations. Saturday afternoon was the only free time she had."

Peggy's brother gave a snort of derision.

"She hooked you all the same. Peggy knows just what

she's doing, and she never does anything she doesn't want
to do. Fire's a pest, of course; but at least she doesn't act
that way."

Although horrified by Toff's lack of understanding, Lex
seized upon the words "Peggy never does what she doesn't
want to do." He asked himself whether she could possibly
want to ride with him, instead of doing so out of courtesy
to a guest. Only the hope of that last ride kept him from
going home. He thought of his father and of Jeems, and
he longed for news from Charles Town. But Banjo assured
him and Toff that no British soldiers were in the vicinity,
and they had no more news of Major Marion. On Saturday he rode with Toff through the pine slashes and broom
fields which formed the western acres of the plantation,
inspecting them for poachers and forest fires. At three
o'clock, in spite of Toff's protests, he said: "I've got to
leave you now."

Against all horseman's instincts he galloped the four
miles back, and he threw his bridle to the head stableman.

"Please rub him down, Sam. I was late and rode fast."

Sam's eyes went from the sweated hunter to the two
matched mounts saddled and waiting, then his gaze came
to rest on Lex's retreating back. He knew all that went on
in the house, and sympathy made him forgive the sin of
hard riding on the home stretch.

As Lex ran upstairs he caught a glimpse of Fire coming
into the downstairs hall behind him; but, not wishing to
be delayed, he hurried to his room. He could not ride with
Peggy in his old clothes. Having only one pair of boots,
he set about cleaning them.

It was ten minutes of four when he looked into the
long wardrobe mirror. His boots shone, his new doeskin
breeches fitted his long lean legs and narrow hips like
gloves, his best dark blue coat showed off his broad shoul-

ders, and his hair was lighter than the sunburned face from which he had smacked it back with a wet brush.

He ran down the stairs as fast as he had run up, and Fire met him in the lower hall. Her eyes were unhappy.

"Lex—I tried to stop you before you went upstairs."

"Did you?" he asked, half-ashamed of dodging her, yet glad that he had not let her delay his dressing.

"Yes. I—I wanted to give you a message."

"Give it to me now—while I'm waiting for Peggy."

He added unnecessarily, for he knew that Peggy was always late: "She hasn't come down yet; has she?"

"No," said Fire, "—and she isn't coming. That's the message I have to give you. Laura Craigie came for her, with some other friends. Peggy told me to say she was so sorry, Lex, but she had halfway promised them before she promised you to—to go with them if they had the party."

16

LEX STOOD STARING AT HER. HE THOUGHT THERE MUST BE some mistake. Peggy had said she was sorry she couldn't ride with him earlier and had set this engagement for two days ahead.

He heard Fire saying: "I tried to stop you before you ran upstairs. I knew there wasn't any use for you to dress. Because I wondered, Lex—I mean—I mean would you ride with *me*?"

He knew exactly what she meant. She could not help his heartache, but she was trying to save his injured pride. Orders had been given for the horses to be saddled. The stablemen knew that he had planned to ride with Peggy. So far as servant gossip was concerned, the matter would be ended if he rode off on schedule with the other sister. He tried to smile at her.

"It's nice of you. I'll be glad if you'll ride with me, Fire."

She flew upstairs and was back again in ten minutes. "Let's walk to the stable," she said. "There's no use to make Sam lead the horses to the step."

He came out of his daze of disappointment enough to gaze approvingly at her. Her little tan boots danced under her long brown riding skirt. She wore neither hat nor coat —which Peggy always wore—and the close-fitting brown basque made her look taller and more slender than Peggy.

"Don't you want the saddles changed, so you can ride your own horse?"

"Oh, no!" she answered loudly for Sam's benefit. "I had

74

my horse saddled for you because you're accustomed to him when you ride with Peggy."

Lex was surprised at the spirit she put into the fat chestnut. When riding with Peggy he had let her set the pace, and had been obliged to curb his mount to keep back with her. He and Peggy had cantered slowly only now and then, walking the rest of the time through shady neighborhood roads while she alternately turned her profile for him to watch or tilted her head and smiled sideways at him.

But the memory of that was bittersweet. His heart was still sore with disappointment and anger. He and Toff had been comrades, in spite of Toff's advantages. Toff's family treated him as an equal, otherwise his Scottish pride would never have allowed him to visit them. Mr. Lane openly preferred him to Lionel Fortesque. Could Peggy look down on him? It was unfair. . . .

Fire said: "Let's go cross-country to the woodcock pond near the carriage road."

She kept Peggy's horse abreast of him in a smart canter until they left the road for the long fields of broom grass. Then she pulled to a trot in caution for burned-out stump holes. He admired her horsemanship for that—and he found himself admiring her. Stirrup-deep in the red-brown broom, she and the bright-coated horse were a picture. Her brown-red hair and her red-brown habit made her a part of the sepia landscape. At the woodcock pond they slackened gait and rode slowly around it.

"I love to come here alone, Lex—to read the writing left in the mud."

He pulled to a stop, surprised. "What do you mean, Fire?"

"I mean that all the wild things that come to the pond to drink write their names on its edges with their footprints."

He had never heard of a girl who could track—or who was interested enough to try. He challenged her.

"I don't believe you can really tell. What are those prints leading out from the tupelo?"

"Two raccoons—either young ones or small old ones. They came for the black gum berries as well as for water. You can see where they stopped to wash their food and lost some of the berries."

She began to laugh. "Toff had a young coon for a pet when he was a little boy. Felix used to give it chunks of rice cake left in the rice pot, and when the coon cub washed that, it disintegrated. The poor little thing would spend all day chasing individual grains of rice around in its water bucket."

Lex laughed with her. "Yes. They won't eat unwashed food."

But he was determined to investigate her wood lore. He swung down from his horse, and she did the same.

"All right. You know a coon print from a possum. But tell me what *that* is."

He was sure she would say "a deer," but she replied: "A wild hog."

He looked at her with new respect. "Who taught you?"

"Banjo. I slip off with him whenever I can. I love the woods and swamps. I hate to live in a house."

"Aren't you afraid of the wild animals?"

"Oh, no. The hogs aren't really wild. They are just razorbacks that have escaped from farms."

"There are black bear," he told her. "I still have scars from one."

"Then you must have meddled it to make it meddle you. The woods and swamps belong to them. They were here before we came."

"You're the strangest girl I ever saw. All the other girls

I know are scared to death of swamps and woods and the varmints that live in them."

"Don't call them 'varmints'! I hate the word. I love them all—from the little field mice to the deer."

"If you made your living on a farm and possums and bay lynx and foxes and bear came up and killed your chickens and hogs, maybe you'd think them *varmints* too."

"Maybe I would," she agreed slowly. "I wish I could see your farm, Lex. Whenever Toff comes back from a visit, I beg him to tell me all about it."

Lex told himself bitterly that Peggy would not have had time to listen while Toff talked of a dirt farm in the Santee hills. "What does Toff say about it?" he asked Fire.

"He says the fields are on red clay slopes and the gullies are deep and green as the swamps. He told me the white oaks stood taller than our live oaks, and the sycamore boles looked like frost in the moonlight. He said that from the top of a hill you could see stars that are below the horizon for us in the Low Country."

As slim and as still as a bronze nymph she stood there in the brown broom grass, her bridle rein hanging loosely over one arm and the other hand pulling a spray of honeysuckle from a myrtle bush where its vine was entangled. She broke it and smelled it and lifted her face to Lex.

"Toff said that on summer nights you could smell the honeysuckle—as sweet and as cool as moonlight—blowing from hill to hill."

"Did Toff say that the honeysuckle was like moonlight?"

"Oh, no! Toff never says things like that. He just said it was sweet. But it reminds me of moonlight. The way it looks and the way it smells make moonlight in the day." She added anxiously: "Do you think that's silly of me?"

"No. I asked you because I think the same thing myself."

"Oh, Lex, I'm glad you do! Of all the flowers I've ever seen I love the honeysuckle best in the world."

"It's nothing but a wild flower. Don't you like roses better?"

He thought of the curled yellow buds that Peggy wore in her hair.

"No," said Fire. "One reason I like the honeysuckle best is *because* it's wild. It seems more generous, somehow, to bloom in the fields where anybody can enjoy it than just to bloom in gardens as roses do."

She held the spray out shyly. "And smell how sweet it is, Lex."

He took it and smelled it, and drew its stem through a buttonhole of his best blue coat.

"I've always loved it—and I think it suits you. But the roses that grow in the hothouse are flowers that suit Peggy."

To his surprise she clenched both hands and stamped a narrow brown riding boot.

"Lex Mourne," she told him, "you're a fool!"

It startled him so that all he could say was: "Fire, girls don't talk that way."

"Oh, no," she raged at him, "—not the kind of girls *you* like. They pin yellow roses in their curls and talk sweet-mouth and make fools of men!"

"If you're talking of Peggy, she has a perfect right to do as she pleases. I know I'm not good enough for her—"

"And so have you a right to be an idiot if you choose! But I have a right to refuse to stay and listen to your stupidity. *No!* I don't want you to help me! I can mount a horse by myself."

She was away in a gallop before he could swing into his saddle; and, although she was riding the slower horse, she kept ahead of him until she drew to a walk in the laurel magnolia avenue that led to the stables.

17

there. "Fire," he began, "why did you—"

But they had reached the paddock fence, and she jumped from her saddle, called to Sam, and started toward the house. Lex overtook her at the steps, as Mr. Lane came out of the door.

"Where's Toff?" he demanded anxiously.

"I left him out in the west pine woods in early afternoon. I came back to ride with—"

"Me," said Fire.

"I'll go and fetch Toff," Lex offered. "I know which way he'll be riding in."

"No! For heaven's sake don't *you* go! I need help. Come into the house."

Mr. Lane closed the double doors of the drawing room behind them, then motioned with his head toward the sofa. A man was lying upon it—a man in a blue uniform.

"Francis," Mr. Lane said, "you already know my daughter Sophia. This is young Lexington Mourne from the High Hills of Santee."

With a cry of distress, Sophia ran to the sofa.

"Oh, Major Marion, we heard you had broken your leg!"

The thin, sharp-featured face contracted with pain.

"It's my ankle. I smashed it pretty badly several days ago. Even so, it would heal if I could just give it rest. But the British keep me on the jump. I've been hiding out with a family who have a cabin on the edge of the swamp.

79

But the Fortesques are having a ball tonight, and a half-dozen Redcoat officers with their orderlies stopped by the cabin to ask if they were on the right road."

Lex saw the anger on Mr. Lane's face. "Sophia, where has Peggy gone?"

"Why—why, Father—you know that Laura Craigie came for her to spend the day at Dunellen."

"She asked my permission to spend the day with Laura. It is now after sunset and she should be home. I cannot think she would dare—"

He was interrupted by a knock on the door. Lex jumped for it and seized the two knobs, holding them together and speaking through the crack.

"Who's there?"

"It's Felix, suh," said the butler's voice. "A note just come from Miss Peggy."

"Let him in," said Mr. Lane. "He knows Major Marion is here, and he's completely loyal to us."

Lex pulled the sliding doors apart, and the old butler entered with a note on a small silver tray. Mr. Lane opened it, read it—and crushed it in his hand.

"I cannot believe my own eyes! Peggy asks permission to spend the night with Laura and go with Laura to a neighborhood dance. I'll write her an answer that will bring her home at once!"

Fire caught his sleeve. "Father, let her stay! If you force her to come home, some of the men will escort her. It might be safer if nobody came here tonight."

"Much safer," said Marion. "Guests of Fortesques and Craigies are apt to be Tories. This ball, I am sure, celebrates the fall of Charles Town."

"Very well," said Mr. Lane. "I see it's the only thing to do. But when that young lady comes home again, she'll stay upstairs in her room for a week."

Lex's anxiety and excitement were so great that he forgot to feel disappointment at Peggy's absence or resentment about her threatened punishment. While Fire wrote he stood and gazed at the slender figure in blue lying on the sofa. Could this be the man who had served in the Indian wars—helped defeat the British at Johnson and Moultrie—fought his way stubbornly on the long retreat from Savannah—and, still refusing to accept defeat, recruited for the militia at Bacon's Bridge?

When the door closed on Felix Mr. Lane said: "Lex, we must get Major Marion upstairs at once. I'd rather Mrs. Lane knew nothing about this. She's true as steel, but she cannot keep a secret."

"I can carry him," Lex offered, "if you go ahead and show me the way."

Fire ran first, to make sure her mother was still dressing for supper and to pull the curtains in the bedroom chosen for Marion. Lex put his right arm around the thin hard shoulders and his left under the visitor's knees, then lifted carefully and slowly.

"Am I hurting you, sir?"

"No, boy. But let me get my left arm around your shoulder."

He winced as Lex laid him on the canopied four-poster, then glanced up at his tall bearer.

"I'm a fisherman. In your grip I felt like a minnow grabbed by a trout."

Lex shook his head gravely. "Nobody'd call *you* a minnow. You'd be the kind of fish that fights to the end."

"And slips off the hook if possible," Marion answered drily. "I see no heroism in fighting hopeless odds."

Sophia had lighted a candle behind a screen in a corner. "It won't be seen from outside," she said. "The curtains are heavy and long."

Lex was surprised at the change in her voice and her

manner. She suddenly seemed to have become a woman—
and to have forgotten her flare of temper at him.

"Lex," she ordered, "you go downstairs and ask Felix to
give you a kettle of hot water. If the cook or maids hear
you, say that you want it for shaving."

"And just what do you want it for?" asked her father.

"To soak Major Marion's ankle before I bandage it. I'm
going now to the medicine closet to get linen and lini-
ment."

When Lex came back with the hot water she was on her
knees by the bed, cutting away the soiled homespun which
wrapped the leg. Her father appeared amused by her
ministerings.

"You've been in dangerous places before. Perhaps you'll
live through this, Francis!"

It occurred to Lex, however, that Mr. Lane was protect-
ing his wife by keeping the secret from her and was not
willing to let his other daughter know it. Only Fire—who
had seemed to him half child and half wild bird—was being permitted to share its work and its danger.

The soldier appeared to be enjoying it, although his face
showed no emotion. He protested: "Let Felix do that—
or young Mourne. I'm not accustomed to the luxury of a
lovely young lady for nurse."

She flushed with pleasure, and her face was truly lovely
under bright disordered hair as she raised her earnest gray
eyes.

"I can do it better than either Lex or Felix. And I really
like to nurse people—or animals that are hurt."

As the last bandage came away she exclaimed in pity.
Lex leaned to look, and saw the swollen, discolored flesh.
He knew the pain this quiet man must have been enduring
underneath his expressionless mask.

"How did you manage to get here, sir?"

"The folks who were last sheltering me lent me a mule.

Both father and son wanted to ride here with me, but I wasn't willing to let them risk it. They lifted me up on the mule, and Sam and Felix lifted me off."

"Even so, I don't see how you managed to ride," said Lex.

He was watching Fire's hands as she bandaged, gently but tightly. Her long slender fingers were flexible and sure. He had admired Peggy's because they were short, with pointed tips; but Fire's had both strength and grace in motion. When she rose from her knees the ankle was cleanly and closely wrapped. Major Marion thanked her briefly.

"It feels better than it has since I broke it."

"You haven't yet told us how you broke it," Mr. Lane said.

"When I was recalled to Charles Town, a mutual friend of ours gave a party at his Tradd Street home."

Mr. Lane laughed. "I know who you mean—and I know the kind of party he gives."

"I should not have attended, since I'm temperance. But I went, and toward the end of the evening our host announced that he had locked all the doors and would permit no one to leave until they had drunk all the liquor and wine."

"I drink both in moderation, but I don't approve of that."

"Being the only sober man there, I was by that time very bored. But I did not wish to offend my host by insisting upon departure. I thought the easiest thing to do would be to find an open window and make my escape. I found one on the second story, and the drop was not as great as many a jump I've taken. But I happened to come down on an uneven cobblestone. I felt my ankle turn—and I heard it crack."

After supper Sophia was left with Mrs. Lane, while Mr.

Lane and Toff and Lex went upstairs. They found Marion sitting up in bed and eating from a tray that Felix had brought.

"Are you still keeping me a secret from your wife?"

"That isn't hard to do. Hallie believes anything she is told. We instructed Lex to make his farewells to her and say he wished to retire early because of his early start tomorrow. Then Toff and I came up with him."

"I, too, must go early," Marion said. "I must be away before day breaks."

"You must do nothing of the kind," his host told him decidedly. "You shall stay right here until that ankle is healed."

The dark eyes lit with pleasure, although the sallow face did not smile.

"My good friend, I know that you would give me shelter. But if I am found here you will suffer for it. Although the enemy do not even acknowledge my rank as an officer, they are eager to catch *Mister* Marion."

"Francis, you should neither ride nor walk."

"If you let me have a canoe I can work my way upriver. I must reach the Back Country. All hope lies now in that region."

"If you wish, you shall have a canoe—and Banjo to paddle it. But I implore you to rest for at least a few days."

"Let me see what news tomorrow brings."

"You may rest secure that Banjo will know if any hostile party is approaching."

"I know that. But I tell you that everything now depends upon arousing the Back Country. It will either be aroused and recruited by us or overrun and terrorized by the British."

"Sir," exclaimed Lex, "do you mean to recruit Back Countrymen for the defense of South Carolina?"

"I mean that: to recruit men who know the terrain, men

who will have an advantage over an enemy who does not
know it. That is now our only chance against superior
numbers and equipment. It is the chance the gray fox has
—his only advantage against men and horses and dogs."

Lex forgot to say *sir*. "I was planning to go with Jeems
to join General Greene. I'd rather join you if—if you'd
have me."

Marion said: "Go home and wait for word from me.
You are the type of man I shall need, young Mourne."

18

AT HOME AGAIN IN THE HILLS, LEX TOLD HIS FATHER ABOUT it all. News of Charles Town's surrender had arrived ahead of him, along with confused rumors of Marion's escape.

Yadkin Mourne took it philosophically. "If you're going I reckon you're going, and I'd rather see you with Francis Marion than with any other leader I know of."

"Jeems wanted to join General Greene, because he was a blacksmith too. But Edisto and I have been arguing with him. We'd like to go together, all three of us."

They kept on talking about it as spring went into summer. Lex recalled that Marion had said: "Go home and wait for word from me." But it was now hard to wait any longer. Echoes of what was happening in British-held sections were drifting into the hills like notes of a hunting horn.

Marion—although still unable to mount or dismount a horse without assistance—had joined Gates in North Carolina, carrying with him a small but hard-riding band.

Toff's militia troop had been sent to re-enforce the same command.

Cornwallis was using not only sword and gun but fire and hemp rope to subdue a rebel foe.

Cornwallis' right-hand man was Colonel Banastre Tarleton, an officer even more violent than his general.

And with Tarleton's cavalry rode Leftenant Evelyn Fay.

As those weeks went by, Lex became more restless. A Back Countryman with a long rifle stopped by one day to ask a drink. The Mournes insisted that he eat dinner and urged him to stay the night and rest.

"I take it kindly," he said, "but I'm lookin' for Marion. He's quit Gen'l Gates an' he's recruitin' in Williamsburg."

When he had finished the meal and gone on, Lex looked at his father.

"I'll not try to hold you any longer, son."

"I'll go tell Jeems this evening." He was thinking to himself that he would at the same time see Sal. To his surprise she had seemed to resent the idea of his enlisting.

She did resent it, and he came home depressed. Jeems was ready to leave any day, but Miller Hawkins forbade his son to go. Edisto was of the three the gentlest—and the least sure of himself.

"But I'm going with you," he told the others unhappily. "When you're starting I'm with you—if I have to run away."

Although certain he must go, Lex worried about his father.

"Pa, I'm doing all I can to leave the fields in good shape. It's a big place for one man. Can't you get help?"

"Don't you try to tell me how to run this farm, boy. And don't you fool yourself I can't get on without you. Little Adlai Johnston's coming for a half day every day. He'll do more work in that half day than you do in a whole one."

Lex felt the affection behind the rough words, and he knew it was his father's way of approving his departure, and of trying to make that departure easier.

"Two things I got to do before I leave are kill that wild-cat and build a new henhouse. The varmint tore off a couple of slats and got another hen last night."

"From the size of its tracks," said Yadkin Mourne, "it's the biggest cat I ever saw. How you figure to get it?"

"Soon as I build the new house I'll move all the poultry to it. Then I'll bait a trap in the old one where the cat's accustomed to prowl, and while the old house still has chicken scent. I'll kill the old rooster for bait. His head's sore, anyway. I figure to fix a piece of rope so that when the cat grabs him it'll not only spring the trap but shut the door on itself too."

He went to work on the project at once, carpentering by lantern light after a day's work on the soil. At twilight ten days later, he and his father removed the sleepy, squawking poultry from their roosts in the old henhouse to the new one. Then Lex baited his trap in the odoriferous former abode, and left its door closed but unlatched.

"That's right," approved Yadkin Mourne. "A cat's afraid of an open door, but he'll claw it open himself."

"I hope it's all right," said Lex. "I'll shut Vidette in the kitchen, the other side of the house."

"You better. Else he'll sure bark at the wrong time and scare the cat off—after letting it come more than once and get a hen."

"He might have been hunting, Pa. He's a good dog, but any dog's bound to roam and hunt some nights."

The two men sat together through that evening. Vidette did not bark, but neither did the cat come. At ten o'clock Yadkin went to bed, but Lex still kept vigil in the darkened house. About an hour later the silence seemed to explode. He heard the slam of the henhouse door, along with a snarling squall and the sound of fighting and thrashing. Vidette burst into baying, interspersed with screams of fury.

Lex was so sure his trap had caught that he did not even stop for his gun. Every bullet was precious, and one blow of an ax could kill a beast held in a trap. He took the steps with a leap and ran for the old chicken house. As he arrived outside it all movement stopped, but the animal inside snarled louder and more fiercely.

The setting moon was behind him and the darkness

almost complete as he turned toward the woodshed for the ax and a lantern. And as he did so a voice spoke close by.

"We-uns knows you's hidin' him, and we aims to take him."

He realized at once who it was, but he could not understand. Could they know he had the wildcat trapped and intend to take its hide? Hides were of no value at this time of year; but even so, he vowed to himself, they should not get it. He felt his hands clench with rage until his arms were taut muscle.

"Get off my land," he told them between his teeth. "You sneaking, thieving cowards, you belong in jail!"

"Talk don't break no bones, but bullets does," said the man. "We knows you got the black man hid. You an' yore pa helped him afore. But you can't help him no more. If you tries to, you'll be sorry."

So they were after Johnston again. Lex was thinking fast. They would try to search the house. It might be well to agree—then call and warn his father. Yadkin Mourne at a window with a rifle could . . .

Just then the wildcat, which had fallen silent at the sound of voices, moved stealthily in the dark chicken house. One of the Schofilites cried triumphantly: "So that's where you got him hid! You got him hid right here!"

Before he had time to think Lex exclaimed: "No!"

Then, as the two men prodded him backward with their long guns, an idea flashed into his mind. He gave way slowly, as if reluctant. He stood aside as they opened the door and yelled: "Come on out, man! We got you this time!"

The wildcat, terrified and at bay, kept silent—as Lex had guessed it would. Only a heavy breathing came from within the old chicken house.

"He ain't got no gun," said the first mountain man. "I'm goin' in. You hol' the door."

He stepped over the sill, and his comrade followed and leaned to look.

And at just that second Lex, who had been pushed aside, stepped up. He stepped up close enough to apply a foot to the nearer man's rear, sending him headlong and sprawling after his companion.

Then Lex stepped back and slammed the door and drove the peg through its staple—and listened to the inferno which had broken out within.

19

IT SEEMED TO LEX THAT THE SLATTED SIDES OF THE HEN-house shook and bulged. The man he had kicked had fallen against his companion and—he realized—one or both had fallen on top of the trapped wildcat. Shouts and curses and howls and snarls made bedlam of the quiet night, as the three fought it out in the small enclosure. Suddenly his father appeared beside him, rifle in hand.

"What's that you got in the henhouse, Lex? I never yet heard a wildcat swear."

Before Lex could explain, the flimsy door burst open and a man in full flight charged through it. But before he had cleared its sill something the size of a large terrier sprang upon his shoulders and head, raked them with cutting claws and held on, while the man fled screaming into the night.

"There goes the cat," yelled Lex. "He must have got loose from the trap!"

"Let him go," said Yadkin Mourne. "He'll never come near this place again."

"Here comes the other man," warned Lex. "Throw your gun on him, Pa!"

The second man staggered through the door, his empty hands above his head. His shirt was torn half from his back, and the blood running from his chest and face made black rivulets in the dim light.

"Stand where you are," Mourne ordered him. "What are you doing on my property?"

"Ask your youngun. He tole us the black man was in that house—then he shoved me in there and a painter tore me up."

"You lie," said Lex. "You came here chasing Johnston, and you heard the wildcat move in there and thought it was him. Your partner went in, I kicked you after him—and the cat made a good job of you both."

Yadkin Mourne began to laugh. "So that's how it was? And now instead of a wildcat to skin, we've got a polecat to hand in to the sheriff."

The man's whining voice was vindictive. "You turn me in an' your house'll burn—same as Johnston's."

They tied him in a chair for the rest of the night, and Lex and Jeems took him next day to the sheriff. After that one threat, the prisoner would not say any more. Lex told the sheriff about it.

"No matter how bold he is, seems like he'd have sense to know you wouldn't give him a chance to get back and burn any houses."

The sheriff, now riding back with them, shook his head and narrowed his eyes.

"There's only one thing can get him out of that jail and away from that deputy."

Lex and Jeems questioned him, but like the prisoner he refused to say any more about it.

"I want to talk with Johnston—and with your father too. These scoundrels know something we don't know."

Johnston's wife knew more than he did, for he had taken a load of corn after dark to Hawkins' mill, and—luckily for him—escaped an encounter. This time they had not only cursed and threatened her, they had knocked her down when they could not find her husband.

"I keep tellin' 'em I don't know, but they don't believe me."

"What made them come to my place then? Did you tell them he might be there?"

"Oh, no, Mr. Mourne! I wouldn't do nothin' to set 'em on you. They say they think you hidin' him 'cause you's a friend to us."

Sheriff Cebron asked intently: "What else did they say, Eunice? Did you hear them say anything else?"

She shook her head, but young Adlai spoke.

"Don't you 'member, Ma, they say the king's soldiers would be here any day now, and they was goin' to join 'em?"

"I 'members now, but I thought they was just tryin' to scare me."

Riding back to the Mourne farm, Lex asked: "Is that what you had in the back of your head, Sheriff?"

"Yes, there's a troop of Tories on the Georgetown road. I heard just yesterday that they were fifty miles east of us. These two devils have in some way been getting information. They've probably been hiding out with other Schofilites and that's the reason we couldn't run them down in the swamp."

"Do you think the troop you heard about is headed here?" asked Yadkin Mourne.

"I have no way of knowing that. I got my information from a couple of lads on their way to join Francis Marion. They hid in the swamp while the Tories rode by, then took a short cut in order to warn me."

"You think the man who got away from Lex has gone to join them?" asked Jeems.

"I'm sure of it. That's what they both expected to do after they had made Adlai sign his place over to them. They expect this section to fall into British hands. That's the only explanation of their daring to do what they did."

Sheriff Cebron stayed that night at the Mourne farm, and he and Mr. Mourne discussed the matter gravely.

"Until this happened, I was practically sure the Tories were bound for Williamsburg. They have it in for that section because its people sent for Marion to recruit. This part of the hills is so sparsely settled that it hasn't attracted their attention before."

"But you now think the Schofilite who got away the other night is on his way to join them and that he'll tell them something to bring them here?"

The high sheriff nodded. "I'm afraid so."

Yadkin Mourne told his son next morning: "You and Jeems and Edisto better be gone before night."

"But, Pa, the crop ain't in. Besides, if Tories are coming I need to be here with you."

"They got no reason to bother with an old man like me. I'll be safer without you. Do you want to join Colonel Marion, or do you want to be made to take parole?"

"They can't make me!"

"Then they'll hang you. Either way, Marion loses a good man. Don't be a young fool!"

Lex rode over to the Gaylords, to inform Jeems and to tell Sal good-by. "You'll wait until I come back?" he asked, his arms around her.

"I'll wait for you, Lex! Lex, I love you!"

Jeems and his father agreed with Yadkin Mourne and the sheriff; but Edisto begged them to wait until after dark.

"I want to be a good ways off before Pa finds I'm gone."

The sheriff knew just where Marion was, and he set them on their way. "Tell the colonel all you heard about that Tory troop."

When the thin moon set in red that night Jeems and Edisto and Lex made camp ten miles away, on a hammock of high ground in the heart of Santee Swamp.

20

A NIGHT IN THE SWAMP WAS NO NOVELTY TO THE THREE young men. Since childhood they had been accustomed to camping; and frequently, when a hunt took them far away and they found themselves benighted, they had built a fire of dry moss and bark and stretched out around it to sleep until dawn.

But they dared make no fire this night. They knew that a Tory troop was on the move nearby, and they realized that native-born Tories knew the country better than the British regulars did. They were in a sense three fugitives; and if captured they would be either jailed or paroled.

Unable to wait for breakfast, they ate half of the cold corn pones which Mistress Gaylord had given them, drank swamp water, and rolled each man his gun with him in the blanket he carried. Even on the hammock the ground was damp, and powder and metal had to be kept dry. At daybreak they woke rested and eager, finished the stale cornbread and took up their journey.

Sheriff Cebron had told them that Marion was at a farm-house east of Pocalla Springs, conferring with some of Sumter's officers. The latter half of the way was by road, so they reached the place before noon. It was a dirt farm, no larger than the Mourne place, its fields already plowed for second sowing and tall oaks growing in its stable yard. Into the trunks of these horseshoes were driven, and a dozen or more horses stood hitched to them. As the three walked up the dusty lane no human being was in sight.

But halfway to the second gate two men wearing butternut breeches with leather leggings, and shirts and leather caps with silver crescents, stepped from the chinquapin hedge and ordered them to stand.

They gave their names, and Jeems said: "We've come to join Colonel Marion."

"How you know Marion wants you?" asked the smaller of the two guards. His skinny legs bowed his leggings outward, his stomach hung over the waistband of his breeches, and the cast in his right eye gave him an evil expression.

Taken aback, Lex exclaimed: "Doesn't he want all the men he can get?"

"No," said the guard. "He's choosy. This here is a picked command. Just yesterday he said to me: 'Lovely,' he said, 'if all the chaps in my brigade were as handsome and bold as you, we'd have Cornwallis licked.'"

Lex realized that the man was a prankster, but Jeems was getting angry. "Marion wants any man can fight, and all three of us can do that. Get your big belly outa the way! We're going to see him."

"So you can fight?" asked the bowlegged man. His voice was almost tearful with joy. He leaned his rifle into a chinquapin bush, removed his cap and hung it on a twig, spat on his hands and squared off.

"Let's see just how long it'll take me, my young rooster, to throw you over my head into the hedge!"

Jeems handed his rifle to Edisto and slipped the straps of his pack from his shoulders. But the other sentry intervened.

"No, you don't, Lovely! All you say the Brigadier said is a lie. But I was there when he called you up last time and told you he'd send you back on stable duty for a month if you fit anybody but a Britisher."

He turned to the newcomers. "I'll take you up to the

house. Lovely here can throw Lord Tarleton over his head if he comes."

As he went with them he continued, "Lovely's a good man. Don't let his foolishment fool you. He can lick his weight in wildcats, and he ain't scared to try. We came across a big black b'ar in the swamp last month, and we needed meat. It stood taller than Lovely does, and not half so bowlegged. We was about to shoot it when he hollers: 'Save that bullet for a Tory, boys! I'll rassle the critter for practice, and kill it with my knife.'"

Recalling his own experience, Lex asked: "Did he?"

"He did, sho' nuff! He jumped in so quick and so close the b'ar couldn't claw him, and he stabbed it first try. But I never before seen a man fit a b'ar if he could shoot it instead."

Edisto inquired: "Is his real name 'Lovely'?"

Their guide looked surprised. He took off his cap and scratched his head.

"Must be," he answered thoughtfully. "I ain't never heard nobody call him nothin' else, and I don't see nothin' wrong with it."

After a short wait Lex and Jeems and Edisto were taken to Marion. He sat on a straight white-oak chair with one foot up on another chair, and he recognized Lex at once.

"So you came, young Mourne?"

"Yes, sir," said Lex, "—and I brought Jeems Gaylord and Edisto Hawkins."

"I know the names. Their people are builders of the Back Country. I'm glad to get all of you. I need men who know the swamps."

"We know the swamps, all right; but—" Lex added anxiously, "we haven't got horses, Colonel Marion."

"Others are in the same fix. You're supposed to get them yourselves."

Lex misunderstood. "Pa said I could have Blaze. But

he's a plow horse. He's too big-footed and clumsy to get through swamp country."

"I know," agreed Marion. "Draft horses are of small use. I have men on thoroughbreds, men on tackies and men on mules. We're beginning to hit back now, and we move fast and far. What I meant was that in every raid each man has a chance to get himself a horse."

Lex brightened at the thought of the Tory column advancing on the Georgetown-Camden road. He gave Marion the message from Sheriff Cebron.

"Do you think, Colonel, that the Schofilite who escaped would dare bring Tories to the High Hills to burn Adlai Johnston's house?"

"I think he would dare, knowing himself secure in the Tory regiments. The first question is whether or not it would be worth while for the Tories to march that way."

Lex waited, afraid to make any suggestions but hoping for some assurance that the Tories would be attacked.

"I've had reports on that column," Marion went on. "It's exactly four times as large as the force I can now muster. They're on their way to Williamsburg to capture me. When they get there they will be informed that I am here at Pocalla Springs. I can't fight and defeat them at present, but I can keep them marching all over the section. My scouts are following them now. If the column should for any reason divide, I will hear of it—and perhaps we can then strike at one of its halves."

Lex hid his disappointment. "Yes—yes, sir. Have you heard from the Lanes since you left South Bank?"

"No, but I left them all well—and Miss Fire bandaged my ankle again."

There was a spark of teasing in his eyes as he glanced at Lex and spoke Fire's name. But Lex was longing for news of Peggy. Time had dulled his resentment for what she had done, but it could not blur the picture of her loveliness. The cause for which he was enlisting said that a rich man was no better than a poor man. Toff and Fire certainly looked on him as an equal; but Peggy ranked him lower than a Tory in a red coat. He was only half-hearing what Marion said.

"She wanted to go along in the dugout with me and Banjo. She said a woman was needed to dress my ankle. A woman—" Marion paused to smile his rare slow smile. "It doesn't seem so long ago that, on my visits to South Bank, she used to sit on my knee and beg for stories of birds and animals."

"Yes, sir," said Lex. He was wondering whether Peggy had sat on the other knee. "Then you came upriver, as you planned to do?"

"Banjo got me as far as the house of some Patriots named Sellers. I rested there before I started for North Carolina."

Lovely appeared at the door and made a simian-like gesture which was evidently meant to be a salute.

"Gen'l Sumter's officers is ridin' up the road, sir."

"Very good. I'll see them here."

He turned back to Lex. "Lovely will find you quarters for the night, and I'll see you before you leave for camp in the morning."

"Lovely," he charged his hideous recruit, "I'll have no more of your escapades. You are in charge of these three new men, and you will guide them tomorrow." He frowned. "Do you understand what I mean?"

"I understands," said Lovely. His voice was disappointed, and the glance he turned on Jeems was speculative. But all he said to them was: "Git going now, you ring-tail raccoons, you!"

21

LOVELY SET HIS VICTIMS TO CLEANING STABLES AND RAKING straw for the farmer whose place was being used by the officers. At their work all afternoon, they saw messengers galloping in and out of the farmyard. At nightfall they were issued rice and hog meat, which they boiled in a tin bucket. They slept on hay in the barn and as soon as day broke were summoned by their commander.

"I have no uniforms for you," he told them; "but fasten these crescents securely in your caps. They are your only insignia, and if you're captured may save you from being hanged as guerrillas."

He put the three bright small sickles into Lex's hand.

"Mourne, do you know a swamp island on the east bank of the Santee, just a few miles south of the junction of the Congaree and the Wateree?"

"Yes, sir. I've hunted it with Toff Lane and Banjo."

"Captain Mouzon is there, receiving recruits. I want you three to start now. Lovely goes with you. I've released him from stable duty on the condition that he doesn't fight with his comrades. Will you see that he keeps his word?"

"I'll beat the tar out of him if he doesn't," said Jeems.

Lovely, in spite of his short bowlegs, walked as fast as they did. His conversation consisted of formidable warnings.

"Better not lose them crescents, whatever you do. If Tarleton ketches you he'll hang you, with or without 'em; but Peter Horry says he'll hang any man who *don't* wear 'em." He scowled at Lex. "And you—you long-legged strawhead—quit callin' Marion 'Cunnel.' He's been commissioned a Brigadier General."

They heard all about that when they arrived at Mouzon's camp. Veterans there had fought at Camden, Lynch's Creek and the Blue Savannah. But veterans at this rallying place were in the minority, and were getting more so every day. Every day they went out by twos and threes, and Lex noticed that they took with them the few new mounted men who arrived. These new men, some mere boys, poured in every day, most of them afoot but all with rifles and with hunting knives ground sharp. Many of them brought saws, and Lex wondered why. But Jeems knew and went to his commanding officer.

"I'm a blacksmith, as well as a farrier, Captain."

A forge was procured and he was set to reversing the work of Tubal Cain by grinding and hammering thin swords from the tools of toil. It gave him employment, and nothing perturbed Edisto; but Lex was growing restless as the time went by. He realized that lack of a horse was keeping him from taking part in the raids of which he was hearing. It seemed a vicious circle if no man who had to walk was given a chance to procure a horse from the foe. He went to Captain Mouzon and said so.

Mouzon smiled. "When you've had as much fighting as I have, you'll thank your stars, lad, for a rest in a good safe place. But don't worry. Sooner or later, any man who can shoot will find himself in action."

Lex had to be content with that, and about that time he got news from the High Hills north of them. A boy who had just come in went to Jeems with a message from Gavin Gaylord, of whom he was a friend. He assured them that no Tories had yet molested the neighborhood and that their homes and families were safe. He was as tall as

Jeems, but Jeems put down the hammer and stared at him, shaking his head.

"I've seen you with Gavin at the meetinghouse. You ain't any older than Gavin is."

The youngster frowned. "I'm fourteen and as good a man as you. So don't you go telling any tales."

They laughed at him but liked him for his spirit, and they let him make a fourth at the campfire where they cooked their scanty meals. But they teased him.

"Shame on you! Parson Dalzell's boy lying about his age. What's your pa going to say about it?"

"He better not say anything, or I'll tell him I been listening for fourteen years while he told folks at prayer meeting not to let their left hand know what their right hand was doing. Besides, he was willing for me to come soon as the British started burning Presbyterian churches."

That was news they had not yet heard, but others confirmed it. It was being claimed by the British commanders that sedition in the Back Country was started in Calvinist houses of worship. These volunteers who came steadily in were a cross section of the state. The surrender of Charles Town, the severity of its conquerors and the terrifying threats of Sir Henry Clinton's proclamation had at first frightened and fooled many into submission. Many believed the propaganda that their own congress had traded Georgia and South Carolina to the enemy in exchange for benefits to the other colonies. The men who defended Charles Town had been butchered or imprisoned in foul, crowded ships. The Tidewater was in British hands, and many others there were surrounded and helpless.

But severity proved a two-edged sword, and it was sharpened every day by Francis Marion and the blacksmiths who beat farm tools into weapons. Joy in the discovery that freedom was not completely lost gave a violent impetus to recruiting. Men who could not join him went north by hundreds to join General Greene. After every man hanged, every home or church burned, volunteers came faster to the hidden camps in the swamps.

One of the Tidewater recruits was a Charles Town man who had escaped, and he gave them details of siege and surrender. Lex liked him, but he and Jeems struck sparks from each other like hammer and hot iron. Jeems had by now practically adopted the minister's son as his younger brother. When talk of church burning occurred the man from Tidewater said: "Serves the High Hills right, for holding off since 'seventy-six and letting the Low Country fight for them."

"Say that again," said Jeems Gaylord, "and I'll hit you so hard you'll find yourself lodged in a cypress!"

There was a cry of *"Fight! Fight!"*—and a ring began to form. But the man from Tidewater looked Jeems up and down.

"No offense, young fellow; but I been told more than once that the folks in the V of the Broad and Saluda rivers were holding out for the king."

"They are," said Lex. "But that country ain't the High Hills. That's the stone hills of the Dutch Fork."

"And you three come from the Santee hills?"

"Yes—the red clay hills of the Santee."

"I come from Wassamassaw," Lovely put in. "I hear you can spell it backwards or forrards; but me, I can't spell it noways atall."

"It sounds foreign to me," said Jeems. "Whereabouts is it?"

"Hit's swamp country thirty miles inland from Charles Town. The British already bogged cannon down in Four Holes and Cypress close by it. I been there and helped drug out many as we could for Marion."

He paused to address Jeems tauntingly.

"I'm lookin' for you clumsy hillbillies to bog down same way on your first march."

Jeems laid down his hammer, muttering ominously; but an older man intervened.

"None o' that! We got work to do."

News continued to come in with each volunteer, and volunteers continued to come from swamps like Wassamassaw and highlands like the Santee hills. Sir Henry Clinton had amended his proclamation. Where he had at first said men must lay down their arms in order to obtain amnesty, he now said they should take up arms and fight against their own people. At this time he was Marion's best recruiting officer.

22

AS THE DAYS WENT BY LEX REALIZED THAT ANOTHER REASON than lack of horses was keeping able-bodied men in camp. No man ever arrived without a gun, for every man in the Back Country owned a rifle and knew how to shoot it. But ammunition was at a premium. On the farm Lex had been accustomed to mold his own bullets. He had helped his father with the task from the time he was six years old. These bullets were precious, and whenever possible they were recovered from targets, remolded and used again. More than once he himself had gone out to get a deer for its meat and carried no more than the one ball in his rifle. But a man could not hunt his fellow men with no reserve of ammunition. The pitiful minimum was three rounds for each soldier sent into action, but there was not enough to give every man in camp even this much. Some men had to be kept inactive, and Lex Mourne happened to be one of those.

With others, he was now put to molding bullets under supervision of the man from Wassamassaw. In this art Lovely was a perfectionist. He had brought with him a ladle of exactly the shape he preferred, and he demanded that the man who held it turn and tilt it at certain angles over the fire.

"Hit won't melt even 'less you does," he instructed them. "Pour it now—and shut that mold quick!"

When the mold was opened he found a half-dozen faults.

"See what I tole you? This-here bullet is rough an' t'other one's gone an' hardened lopsided. Lemme see that knife o' yourn, Mourne, 'fore you cuts the nib off. You cut a nib off a bullet with a knife ain't sharp an' you'll leave a little small piece will groove the bar'l of some rifle."

Lex's knife proved to be sharp, and he whittled from the bullets the tiny protuberance of lead always left on each. His instructor not only examined them with eyes and fingers, he put each in his mouth and felt it with his tongue.

Edisto said anxiously: "Ain't you scared you'll swallow it? I heard Colonel Horry telling a new recruit if he was careless and wasted a bullet he'd waste another to shoot him with."

In the damp heat of the late summer they worked around the fires, melting what little lead they could get and turning out a small number of bullets or balls every day. The smoke helped keep away gnats and mosquitoes, which pestered them along with red bugs and ticks. Some veterans appeared immune to these; others had patches of inflamed skin and even running sores. They were a wild-looking band, in all manner of dress and undress. New recruits like Lex and his companions wore the clothes in which they had lived and worked at home. But veterans who had escaped from the surrender of Charles Town and other Continental defeats were sometimes clothed in but a single garment, and occasionally only a loincloth.

Word of their necessity had gone out, and at this time women and boys began bringing clothing into camp. They brought shirts made of homespun cloth or leather, butternut breeches and coonskin caps. Some brought corn on the cob, bags of sweet potatoes or of meal. Infrequently someone would bring a bit of lead which was worth its weight in gold.

For reasons of safety Captain Mouzon gave orders that these friends who came afoot or in oxcarts should no longer beat a path to the camp. They were to bring their gifts to a spot on higher land just a few miles away, and there they were to be met by men from the camp who would transport the loads the rest of the way. It was a detail eagerly sought, for it gave lonely men a chance to meet women—women who had sympathy for them and their cause. Edisto was overjoyed when he was assigned to it, but Lex preferred the molding of ammunition. For several reasons he wished to keep close to headquarters. The Lane plantation was not too far downriver. It was possible Captain Mouzon might need a messenger someday. The Lanes were known to be Patriots. Peggy was merely frivolous. Surely in this hour of extremity she must have of her own choice stopped visiting Tories.

He wondered about that household as he watched the great river run east. Toff was probably engaged in actual fighting while he, Lex, was kept in a hidden camp. At times he almost wished he could have joined the militia. Then he thought of a thin swarthy-faced man with a wound so tortured that he could not mount a horse, who nevertheless insisted upon being lifted into a saddle in order that he might go about his business of arousing countrymen to fight for their own homes. If only he could get a horse! But how could he get one unless he rode in a raid? And how was he to ride in a raid when he had no horse to ride?

He thought about his father and Sal, and he got letters out when he could. Edisto said that some of the people who brought clothing and food offered too to take messages and letters. Edisto was enjoying his work, and he was wearing a new shirt. Jeems and Lex teased him and asked if he was trying to be a toff. But he only smiled happily, and stuck the blue blossom of a swamp flower through the crescent in his cap.

Summer dragged on, and to Lex's deep disappointment Marion did not even visit this recruiting camp. He and others of his band were busy harrying Barfield and Tarleton and fighting at Nelson's Ferry. Even the foe who called them "guerrillas" now knew better than to undervalue them. The Williamsburg Irish, whom Marion had recruited, formed a core of spirited resistance. Men were still rallying to the different camps—men who had learned that the war was not yet over. But many still thought that the Continental cause was lost. Many who were sincere in their sympathy for it had truly been persuaded there was no use to fight any longer.

Marion was combatting such defeatism by grapevine propaganda. Through woods and hills and lowlands, wherever his men went and wherever the women who loved them went, the word was secretly spread that the Back Country was just beginning to fight. News of Marion's successful raids was sent out. Men were beginning to call him the Swamp Fox and to call his band a brigade.

Lex longed to be directly under his command. He was thinking about it one afternoon when Lovely came and told him: "Cap'n Mouzon wants you."

Lex was startled. "Why?"

"All he tole me was you make bullets all wrong an' you eat so much he can't afford to feed you. Just you come 'long with me an' he'll tell you the rest hisself."

Other men were coming into the tiny clearing of dry ground where Mouzon had a shed of pine poles for a tent. He said: "You're Mourne from the Santee hills—the boy who's anxious to see a raid?"

"Yes, sir," said Lex.

"Colonel Hugh Horry is at a farm nearby, selecting men to ride tonight. Lovely seems to think you can hold your own. If you can with him I think you can with the British. He'll see that you have a mount and three rounds of ammunition. Go with him now—and report at once to Horry."

23

LOVELY RODE A LOP-EARED MULE, WHICH HE SAID HE PRE-
ferred to a horse. "Ain't so apt to fall down with you w'en
you run from Sir Henry Clinton."

Lex had the loan of a big black horse which belonged to
a man on leave from camp.

As they rode from the swamp trace he saw that their
small group was merging with a larger body of horsemen.
His companion told him: "That's Marion himself—leading
us—up ahead."

In the darkness Lex had not singled the leader out.
They were riding directly for the river, and they crossed
it and continued on the Nelson's Ferry Road. For as far as
he could see the way ahead was now full of shadowy
figures. Horses were moving in a walk and riders keeping
their voices down. It was mid-August, and from swamp
and ditches and grass came the chorus of insects and frogs.
The night and the whole world seemed full of its vibration.
It was so widespread and so loud that it did not even cease
as the slow hooves went by on the muddy causeway.

It took him back to a night of the spring past, when he
had sat with Sal underneath the black walnut tree. He
thought of her and of his father and Vidette. There would
be the clean smell of hay in the fields he used to cut. Was
young Adlai doing the work well? He could see in his
mind the pale sycamore trunks in the farmyard more
clearly than his eyes saw the dark cypresses that bordered
the way. The late honeysuckle would be cool and sweet

and sharp along the path he used to walk to the Gaylords'. Maybe Sal was now sitting on the piazza bench alone, thinking about him as he was thinking of her. Memory of her was warm and reassuring. He was sure that she cared for him and was ready to marry him. Her affection was solid substance compared to the deceit of Peggy Lane's coquetry. It seemed natural for a woman to wish to marry, to feel the need for a husband and home and children. He had at first thought it charming for Peggy to have a throng of beaux. But her treatment of him had made him realize that she was merely vain of her conquests and more in love with herself than she was with any man.

From her his thoughts went back to Sal and remained with her as they rode hour after hour in a silence broken by whispers. These drifted along the column and he and Lovely relayed them.

"Peter Horry's men are twenty or thirty miles ahead of us. Marion sent him to take command of the companies of LeNud and Mitchell and Benson and Bonneau."

"What are they doing?"

"Destroying enemy communications—sinking boats on the river from Jamestown to the Georgetown district."

Another horseman put in: "And getting ammunition. General Marion told Colonel Peter Horry not to come back without twenty-five weight of gunpowder, along with flints and bullets and buckshot. Hope we get some too—wherever we're going."

"Are we going to join them?" Lex inquired.

"More likely we're after Gainey or Barfield again. Here comes Marion now—and Hugh Horry with him."

The irregular column came to a halt as the two officers rode back along it. Marion was a slight figure, crouched like a jockey in his saddle, yet no man could have missed the fact that he was the ranking officer. He and his colonel stopped their horses near Lex.

"Sixteen men," said Marion. "They are all I can spare you, Hugh. Pick them now; for daybreak is near, and before it comes you must be in the Horse Creek pass."

Horry stood in his stirrups to look right and left.

"Last eight couples, fall out," he ordered, "—and follow me."

Lex looked back and, to his disappointment, saw behind him exactly fourteen men. It meant that he was detached from the main column to follow Hugh Horry instead of Francis Marion. Quick, low orders ran down the line, and it began to move forward with no sound except the creak of leather and the soft plop of hooves in mud. With it went the two men who had been riding in front of Lex, and Horry and Marion had already trotted away.

"It's just my luck to get left by one couple," he told Lovely bitterly. "I'd give anything I've got to go on with General Marion."

Lovely spoke from the side of his mouth. "We're going with him. Just you wait!"

He stuck his feet in the mule's ribs and galloped after the two officers between the moving column and the ditch that drained the causeway. In just a minute he was back where Lex waited with the other fourteen men.

"Come on, Mourne," he said loudly. "We're to go with the main body and send the last two men back."

As they overtook those two men he told them: "Gen'l Marion's compliments, and you git back with the Cunnel's men. Gen'l Marion needs a scout what is a scout—and that's me."

"He's lying," said one of the men.

But both reined back their horses.

"Orders is orders," Lovely told them firmly. "Ain't you just seen me talkin' to him like a brother?"

"I saw you talking to him, but I didn't hear what was said."

"Me and Mourne rides here, and you go back with the others."

The man who had been protesting started to speak again, but his companion said: "What's it matter? I'd as soon go with Horry. He's just as good a leader."

As they moved back to the waiting detachment, Lex heard him add: "That fellow's one of Marion's pet scouts. Marion thinks a lot of him—God knows why!"

He heard no more; and as he rode on at the tail end of the main column, he asked in joyful unbelief: "How'd you persuade the General? What did you tell him?"

"I tole him I heerd the British he's after tonight was at a tavern called the Blue House. He said he knowed it already an' for me to mine my business."

"Then—then you mean—you mean he didn't—"

"Shucks," said Lovely. "Neither he nor Horry will ever know the difference. Now, listen, boy—if you want to know what we're in for."

The men riding ahead of them turned their heads to listen too. Lovely had information the rest of them had not, in spite of his unorthodox ways of achieving what he wished.

"There's a detachment of British regulars and Tory volunteers just a few miles east of us on this bank of the Santee."

"Are you telling the truth this time?" inquired the rider just ahead.

The scout was offended. "Have it your own way—if you want to go into a fight not knowin' nothin' about it."

"How big is the detachment? And what's it doing there —just waiting for us to come along and tackle it?"

"It ain't so big—just two or three times as many men as we got. But they don't know we're comin'—an' they won't know lessen you an' that big-foot horse make too much noise."

The man addressed ignored the insult and asked: "How you come to find out all this?"

"Our scouts brought word in at sunset. I talked with ole Conway."

Lex listened—excited and eager. But for Lovely, he told himself, he would have missed the raid and been left behind with Hugh Horry and a handful of unlucky riders. He had always thought of attack in terms of running horses, shouting men and waving sabers. Most of these men had no swords at all; and except for a few officers the ones who carried such weapons were carrying filed saws. Lovely's mount was the only mule in the party. About half of them were riding marsh tackies. His borrowed horse was far above the average. Marion was up on his magnificent steed Roger.

For the next half hour Lex's heart thudded softly with anticipation, in rhythm with hooves thudding softly through the night.

24

THEN AGAIN THE WHISPERED WORD RAN BACK ALONG THE line: "Ride up—here where the road widens—and get the General's orders. Quit your braying there! The Tories are within hearing!"

"*I* ain't brayin'," said Lovely. "My mule was just talkin' to you—as one jackass to another."

He had silenced the mule by throwing himself on its neck and seizing its nostrils just as it commenced its first eerie notes. But he and the others hid their tension by rough badinage as they rode forward and pressed in a close circle around Francis Marion. In the darkness his features looked carved and completely expressionless. He wasted no words, but the ones he spoke went to their mark like bullets.

"Our objective is the Blue House Tavern. How many of you know it?"

A number of men said that they did. One asked: "Ain't we passed it?"

"We've passed its main approach. We don't ride up to front doors. We're going in by a roundabout path while Colonel Horry and his men cut off the enemy retreat on the Horse Creek pass."

Lex digested two pieces of information: one, that Horry's sixteen would be in action; two, that Marion seemed sure the British would be in retreat. He listened with both ears.

"I need not tell you that we will be outnumbered. You

114

are accustomed to that handicap, and I expect you to overcome it by surprising the foe and overcoming them before they can make use of their resources. You know as well as I how terrible is our need of ammunition. Get it. Get baggage wagons. If I see any of you merely riding down men and getting yourselves saddle horses—"

He paused. But what he did not say was as effective as any threat could have been.

"These enemy forces include both Tories and British Regulars. They have under guard two hundred Continental prisoners, bound for the prison hulks in Charles Town harbor."

A man asked the question which they all wished to know.

"Where'd they ketch these prisoners, Gen'ral?"

"General Gates has suffered a major defeat."

He had not told them before for fear of disheartening them. He realized shrewdly that on the eve of battle the news would arouse fighting rage.

"That is all. We are going in now."

He swung his splendid Roger around, and Lovely took advantage of the reforming of the line to swing himself and Lex near its front. They were not riding in couples now. At places the path was too narrow for that. In single file they moved as silently as Indians. Lex was thinking to himself that the British surprise would be complete, when the silence was suddenly shattered by the discharge of a musket ahead.

Lovely said: "That's from the Horse Creek side. Horry musta got too near them."

Marion called: "We're almost on them! Charge—straight ahead!"

Lex, now near the front of the line, was close behind him as they rode into the turmoil of the tavern yard.

Redcoats were pouring from the doors of the public

building. British in red and Tories in green were trying to mount in the yard or to escape on foot in the confusion. From the stables close by bugles repeated *to horse!* But there was no order—no design of defense. There was only uproar and hand-to-hand fighting.

There—in his first fight of the war—it came to Lex that this was the power of Marion's warfare. How could the foe at the Blue House know by how many they were attacked? They were in a strange land—in a hostile land which hated them. They were in the middle of a swamp where even in daylight they needed guides to march. In the war for which they had been trained, an enemy waited to attack with daylight. But they had been attacked in the night: sleeping or drinking, and unprepared. That first musket shot, fired by a sentry who had detected Horry's approach, had not given them time to arm and organize. The result was confusion. Men ran here and there, crying out unheard orders—or crying for direction. And in the meanwhile Marion's men made havoc while the sun did not shine.

But Lex was too busily occupied with the fight to think more. After that first clash of arms the men who ran out of the tavern had run back into it. Marion, who seemed able to be everywhere at once, ordered a squad to the back and himself started in the front door followed by a lieutenant.

He threw back over his shoulder: "Lovely, take a few who have the fastest horses and get to the stables!"

"Come on, Mourne," said Lovely. "Come on, Harley. Young Conway—you know this place."

They rode in a gallop around the building. Lanterns were now being lighted by the Continentals, but in the direction they were going was complete darkness and only curses and shouts.

Lex managed to ask: "Where are the prisoners?"

"Don't know. But somebody'll find 'em. We got the luck. We're after the horses and wagons."

The narrow road opened then for the stable yard of the tavern. Change from utter darkness allowed Lex to see buildings and several mounted men who were gesticulating and calling orders. As these caught sight of the squad riding down upon them on the only way of escape, they drew their swords and galloped at full speed to meet them.

Lex had no sword, only his rifle and a filed saw. He was at quarters too close for use of the former. An officer on a tall gray horse broke free of the group and tore on down the road. Lex wheeled his horse in pursuit—and as he did, heard Lovely's yell: "Heah comes a baggage wagon! Git it, Mourne!"

By this time Lex was at the house end of the short stable road. He had been gaining on the Tory riding the gray, and he wanted desperately to get the saddle horse. But Lovely's command stopped him in his tracks, for it was repetition of Francis Marion's order.

He pulled his borrowed steed back on its haunches, just as a wagon drawn by two mules broke from the tunnel of trees. They were in full gallop, and their driver was leaning over the doubletree and lashing them on. As Lex rode alongside, the wagoner uttered a yell of terror and threw himself from the wagon into the ditch beside the trace. Before Lex could catch the bridle of the near mule, the panicked animals swerved to the right. The off mule fell— the wagon's right wheels dropped in the ditch—the whole cumbersome body of the vehicle leaned and turned on its side.

Lex jumped from his saddle and began to unharness the kicking near mule from the wreck. He had a baggage wagon; but his heart was sore. In order to capture it and a sweating, frightened mule he had let an officer's saddle horse escape. He knew from the short chase in the stable road that he could have overtaken the Tory.

Lovely rode up. "Good work, boy! Where's the other mule?"

"Probably racing the wagoner through the swamp. It fell and tore loose, and the driver jumped."

"Our scouts'll beat the swamp until they ketch both."

He rode his own mule around the overturned wagon.

"Wait 'til the Gen'ral sees this. You done something in your first raid."

"I didn't do anything," Lex told him bitterly. "The wagon driver got away and the mules ran in the ditch and turned the wagon over. I could of had a saddle horse if you hadn't yelled at me and stopped me."

"Good thing for you I did yell. Marion woulda cut our ears off if we let a British baggage wagon git away. He wants this more'n he wants any saddle horse. Those fellows who fit aroun' the house got a lot of horses. But, so far's I know, you got the only wagon."

That only added fuel to Lex's wrath.

"Well, the General can have it and you can have the mule. And, the next raid we ride, don't you go yelling at me. I give you fair warning now, you can catch your own wagons. From now on what I'm after is to catch me a good saddle horse!"

25

LEX HID HIS DISAPPOINTMENT, AND ALMOST FORGOT IT IN THE general rejoicing over success. He and Lovely remained on guard by the baggage wagon until Marion had himself inspected it and discovered that it held the ammunition he was so anxious to procure. Then a detail was sent with lanterns to help Lovely get it again on its wheels, patch its broken harness, and substitute Lovely's riding mule for the mule which had escaped.

"I'm drivin' it," Lovely announced—and no one disputed his word.

Meanwhile, Marion had taken Lex back to the house with him.

"That was well done, young Mourne. Now I've other work for you. You look as if you could climb."

"I can climb, sir."

"Hugh Horry is now in charge of the search at the house. We have not yet found the commander of this force."

Lex was surprised, for the surrender appeared to be complete.

Marion was continuing. "He did not escape by the Horse Creek road. Colonel Horry and his men ran into a sentry there. The discharge of that sentry's musket was the gun we heard as we approached. Horry, very wisely, charged ahead after the fleeing sentry and reached the Blue House almost as soon as we did."

"I must have been at the stables, sir. I didn't see him and his men come in."

"At the stables? Did any officer escape you there?"

"Yes, sir. A Tory—on a big gray cavalry horse."

"A Tory wouldn't be in command. We're looking for a Regular."

As Marion got down from his saddle, Lex threw himself from his own horse and caught Roger's bridle. But the Swamp Fox called to a man on guard on the piazza.

"Hold both the horses. I need Mourne in the house with me."

There men were examining the walls from ceiling to floor, unhanging pictures in search of trap doors, and crawling under tables and benches in their hunt for any who might lie hidden. Horry came up.

"He just isn't in here."

"You've inspected this chimney where we found fresh soot on the hearth?"

"I stuck my own head and shoulders in there. I've ruined the only coat I own. I couldn't see past the bend of the chimney, so I had several men boost Little McGrath up there. He climbed fairly high—and thrust his sword ahead of him."

"Very well," said Marion. "Get me Little McGrath and Dargan."

He sent the two men with Lex up on the tavern roof. It was dark from overhanging trees as well as from night, and they slipped on damp shingles and slid on gable inclines. Where the huge chimney reared its top, Lex caught hold of the bricks and drew himself toward it. As he did so he was startled to feel under his grip the shape of a human hand as cold and as wet as the brick.

He clutched it and shouted to Dargan and McGrath. Together they drew from the chimney a young captain almost senseless with fright.

Downstairs Marion questioned him. He seemed a decent fellow, but his shaking legs could barely hold him upright.

"Do as you will with me," he implored. "But—but if it could be arranged so that my men do not know—"

"That you hid in a chimney?" Marion asked point-blank.

The boy's white face went as crimson as his torn smutty coat.

"But *why* did you hide instead of surrendering? Your men were in confusion. You must have realized that there was nothing to do but give up your prisoners. Is Cornwallis such an ogre that his officers dare not concede even when the situation is hopeless?"

"Not Cornwallis—sir, no," stammered the captain.

"*I*—then—am the ogre? It was *I* you feared?"

"Sir—after all that I have heard—"

"Go on! What did you hear? And from whom did you hear it?"

"I heard you waged Indian warfare—and burned men at the stake. The prisoners I am—I was—convoying have been telling my soldiers that you cut your own men's ears off if they didn't do just as you said."

The small, low-voiced French Huguenot frowned as he dropped into a chair and elevated his wounded ankle to the seat of another. He still favored that leg when circumstances permitted him to do so. Lex, watching and listening, recalled what Lovely had said. Legends were already shaping themselves around this Partisan leader. The scouts and Back Countrymen whom he led enjoyed tall tales and exaggeration.

"Is it possible anyone thinks I torture prisoners?"

"Sir, I was given to understand that you tortured officers to get from them information as to where you might strike next with greatest advantage."

"My scouts probably know more about Cornwallis' army and its movements than you do. No, sir; you may keep your sword."

Lex heard mockery in his voice although he did not smile.

"My band has more swords than we can use—and it may help you to sustain your prestige with Earl Cornwallis."

The young captain was stammering thanks as he replaced the blade in its sheath. Lex eyed it longingly. All he had was a filed saw, and he envied the long slender steel.

"Mourne," said Marion, "hand him over to the detail which has charge of the prisoners. It should be in front of the house, ready to start the return march."

He spoke again to the boyish officer, who was standing stiffly at attention.

"You will not be tortured; but, until exchanged, you'll enjoy the same fare that my men live on."

Outside in the tavern yard Lex found not only the British and Tories under guard but the two hundred Continentals who had been released by the Blue House raid. Horry was crying out orders.

"Get in line there! We want to be back where we started from before day breaks."

Somewhere in the confusion Lex discovered Lovely, sitting proudly as wagoner in the captured wagon and guarded by enthusiastic comrades. As they started he addressed his mules in language which was at once tender and profane.

When he saw Lex he called out: "I been tellin' the boys *you* got this. Hit's a long sight better thing to git than the horses they grabbed for themselves."

Lex said bitterly: "I wish I'd grabbed one for myself. I don't figure to go into the next raid mounted either on a mule or on top of a baggage wagon."

Then, ashamed of himself, he added: "I'm glad you fellows got mounts. And those two hundred Continentals Marion set free ought to more than double his band."

"Them?" inquired Lovely—and the word was loaded with scorn. "You just ought to hear what Hugh Horry said to 'em. He said if it was left to him he'd cut their ears off first, then hand 'em back to the British."

"But why did he say it? We made the raid to save them."

"We made the raid to get 'em—and we did what we set out to do. That in itself ought to show 'em what kind of a leader we have. But—"

He paused to pay his compliments to the off mule, which had stumbled.

"They been fightin' with Gates an' they got a bellyful of war. They say the war's over an' the British done won it. I heard Horry when he tole 'em the war won't be over long as there's a swamp fox—with two or four feet—loose in South Carolina. But they ain't havin' none of it. They're goin' home an' take parole. Out of two hundred only three of the yellow dogs are joinin' us!"

26

NEVERTHELESS, THE RESULTS OF THE NELSON'S FERRY RAID encouraged the Partisans and brought into their ranks a number of volunteers who had been hesitating. News of it was taken through the country by Marion's scouts, who were always on the move. They saw that it did not lose any size in the telling. Also, Lex came to find out, they took pride in describing their quiet but stern commander as a ferocious tyrant who did not hesitate to cut men's ears off.

Lex looked with envy at the new horses in camp. He prized that "well done" from Marion, but he longed for a mount.

Jeems was still working at his forge, and he refused to sympathize.

"Looks like they're going to keep me shoeing horses and grinding saws. I might as well have stayed home and worked, for all the fighting I'm seeing. Don't come belly-aching to me about not getting a horse of your own! At least you've ridden on a raid—and I haven't."

Bitterest of all to these two was the fact that Edisto had mysteriously acquired a marsh tacky. Quiet, shy Edisto, who had ridden on no raids, shod no horses, ground no swords, had suddenly appeared on a wiry brown pony. He had no saddle but rode bareback, with a headstall which had been part of a cart harness and a thin rope for reins. Lex and Jeems stood on either side of him, admiring and envious.

"His feet are as long as mine," said Jeems. "Bring him

over here where I can trim them, else he'll fall down with you when you start running from Tarleton."

Lex was busy combing sheep burs from the tacky's mane and tail.

"Go get your jar of bear grease and I'll rub it in his tail and mane. You got no right to have a horse if you don't know how to take sheep burs off him."

While Edisto went for the grease they speculated as to how he had come into possession of the animal.

"You ought to know," said Lex. "You been right in camp with him while I was off."

"I didn't see him all the time you were gone. I been working right here, long as daylight lasts. He was busy on that detail he's been assigned to, toting supplies the women bring to that new place a couple miles outside the swamp where Captain Mouzon ordered 'em to wait."

"I never did see Edisto so pigheaded. I asked him over and over how he got the tacky, but he just kind of smiled and said it was halfway his. That's all he'd say."

At that point Edisto came up with the bear grease and Lex showed him how to apply it, straighten the tangled hair and comb out the burs without pulling.

"You know all about horses, Lex. What you think of him?"

"He's a long way better than *no* horse," Lex said conservatively. "My feet'll pretty near drag on the ground when I'm up on him. But he'll be all right when Jeems trims his hooves and you brush his mane and tail."

He straightened from where he stooped, feeling the gaunt forelegs from knees to pasterns.

"At least he ain't got any splints. He's six or seven by his teeth. Unless it's a horse I've watched since it was foaled, I'd rather get it at that age than younger, because its legs are set by that time. He'll carry you. I'm glad you got him, Edisto."

"You and Jeems can use him whenever you want."

"Thanks—but I aim to get a horse of my own. Where'd this one come from? Did you buy him or steal him?"

But Edisto shook his head stubbornly and would not be teased into telling. "I didn't do neither one—and I just halfway own him."

They were mystified, but he would say no more.

It was a time when every day brought information of British strength and successes. Although Colonel Peter Horry had damaged enemy communications down the river and had brought back a supply of enemy ammunition, all other recent engagements had gone against the American cause. And success was making the enemy more and more savage. Cornwallis, after his defeat of Gates, had issued to his commanding officers orders even more severe than preceding ones. At Camden he arrested and hanged a number of boys too young and men too old to serve in the Continental militia. Among these were fathers and younger brothers of men in Marion's camps, and rage and grief were vocal around the campfires at night. Tarleton was even exceeding his general in brutality, as he pushed steadily inland with orders to get Marion at any cost.

All this was arousing the countryside and stimulating recruiting for the Partisans. But they were a strange band, never remaining long in the same place and varying in numbers from day to day. While men came steadily in, men were also going out. Their leader knew that they had come at great sacrifice to themselves from farms and lonely cabins, leaving wives and children or aged parents to protect those homes and to do the work required for livelihood. So he was wise enough not to refuse them leave to bring in the harvest needed for winter food, or to visit an ill wife or baby. He let them go, and in return they came back—almost to a man—to rejoin him and carry on the fight.

In that autumn Lovely's old father died, and he rode away on his mule toward the Wassamassaw. He returned at the end of two weeks with all the news of the Low Country. One thing he had heard was that Colonel Tarleton was headed for the Wateree.

Lex and Jeems and Edisto talked it over with him that night.

Jeems said: "Ed, you got a horse. Ask permission to go, and bring us back news."

"I'm scared to face Pa. You or Lex take the pony."

It was decided that Lex should be the messenger. He went at once to Marion, and found him in conference with the two Horrys. The officers gnawed on roasting ears of corn, upon which Lex and the other men had just made a meal and which he knew to be tough enough for horses' teeth. As he listened to Lex, Marion fingered the short sword which he always wore but which no man had ever seen him draw.

"Sickness at your place?" he asked. "Or does your father need you?"

"No, sir," Lex told him truthfully. "So far as I know Pa's all right, and he's got a boy to help him. But Jeems Gaylord and Edisto Hawkins and I been hearing talk that Tarleton was near the High Hills. The thing that worries me is that a couple of scoundrels there made threats about our place and the place of another farmer."

"How long would it take you to get there and back?"

"Not more than three days and two nights, sir."

"You're the boy who got the baggage wagon at Horse Creek pass?" enquired Peter Horry.

"Yes—yes, sir."

Peter Horry said: "You deserve something for that. But didn't Hugh tell me that you missed getting a horse?"

"Edisto Hawkins has a tacky. I could ride that."

"Very well," Marion said. "You may leave camp any

time you choose. But don't get yourself captured. Tarleton's idea of quarter is a rope thrown over a tree limb. And don't fail to be back by nightfall of the third day from now."

27

THE MARSH TACKY WAS SURE-FOOTED ENOUGH FOR LEX TO
avail himself of short cuts he knew through swamp and
bog and across gullies as he approached the High Hills.
He knew that his mount, although lightly built, was as
tough as hickory. The small hooves which Jeems had
trimmed to a sharp slope from shaggy pasterns showed
persistence of Arab blood. So did the long mane and tail,
now free of burs and tangles. Lex was recalling as he rode
stories he had heard or read about these native horses.
It was told that Spanish cavalry horses of Arabian strain
had either escaped from de Soto or been stolen from him,
and that these had mated with inferior horses allowed to
roam free by the pioneers.

The breed had deteriorated in size through the years,
until it standardized at last into a pony horse from twelve
to fourteen hands in height. Arabian characteristics other
than those shown in shape of feet and luxuriance of mane
and tail were present. The usual color was bay or brown—
prevalent in the Arab—and mane and tail and pointing on
knees and hocks were usually black. Some of the tackies
still showed the flat, powerful bone of the desert breed.
They had staying power for a long journey, intelligence
to take care of themselves, and were able to go longer
without food and water than the average horse.

Hour by hour Lex liked the pony better. He had left
camp shortly after midnight, so as to take advantage of
the waning moon. When he rode through his gate the sun

was still high in the west. Yadkin Mourne was not in sight, but young Adlai Johnston came running.

"Oh, Mr. Lex, I so glad to see you! I knowed you'd win the war and come home soon!"

Lex explained to him that the war was not won. He thought wryly to himself that most people thought it lost; but he had faith in Francis Marion and he did not wish to frighten the boy.

"Where's Pa, Adlai? I just got a little while to stay."

"He tuck a cartload of corn to the mill for grindin'. He say he'll be back 'fore sundown, and he tole me to stay till he came. I been feedin' the hogs when I seen you comin'.'"

Together they washed the pony down, rubbed his scratched and muddy legs, let him drink only a few quarts of water, and turned him into a big stall, where he rolled and rubbed himself on its deep bed of straw. Adlai climbed on the door to admire him.

"You say Mr. Edisto got him? I sure wisht I could git me one! You think Mr. Marion would let a black boy fight with him?"

"I know he would—but not until you're older. Now let's water Blaze and finish feeding the stock, so Pa won't have anything to do when he gets home."

He took joy in doing these tasks which had before been labor. Blaze whinnied at him as he forked hay into the stall. But he laid back his ears and bared his teeth in jealousy of the pony stabled next to him, which was now dry and cool enough to be watered and fed by Adlai. One by one the poultry were going to roost in the henhouse which Lex had built months before.

"Any more wildcats been coming up on the place, Adlai?"

"No. No cats. But a black bear took off a shoat last week."

The sycamore leaves were again green-gold and the

setting sun shone through them as Lex and Adlai ran to open the farm gate for Yadkin Mourne.

"I'm sure happy to see you, son! How come you got away, and how long can you stay home?"

"Just tonight and tomorrow and the next night, Pa. We got word in camp that Colonel Tarleton's force was pretty near and headed this way. Jeems and Edisto and I got worried and wanted news of you folks."

To hide the fact that he was touched, Yadkin Mourne began to scold.

"Never yet saw a young one thought his pa could take care of himself! You three better worry about taking care yourselves instead of thinking about the old folks."

"Adlai said a bear took a shoat. And how far are the British?"

"Yes, a bear took a shoat; but I'll shoot him sooner or later. How I know where the British are? I'm not going to meet them. Come on in and let's have supper now, since you and Adlai finished the evening chores."

Lex brought in a jug of hard cider and made batter bread and fried bacon. It was a happy meal. He told his father all that had transpired since his enlistment. After supper Yadkin began to yawn.

"Since you been away I got in the habit of going to bed soon as I ate supper. You'll be riding over to the Gaylords', anyway."

"I figured on walking over there. They'll want news of Jeems."

"Edisto's ma is fretting for news of him too, spite of all that old Hawkins says. Stop by and see her, son—or send her news by the young ones."

Lex reassured Mistress Hawkins and went on to the blacksmith's house. As he opened the garden gate, young Gavin yelled: "Here's Lex Mourne!"

The family crowded around him, in welcome as well as

in anxiety for news of Jeems. Sal's face was aglow, and she seemed to Lex prettier than ever. After Mistress Gaylord had forced him to eat a second supper and he had told them all about Jeems and given Jeems' messages, Sal rose to her feet.

"Me and Lex are going out in the swing now. Gavin built up that fire too big, and I want a little fresh air."

"Seems like Lex ought to have got enough fresh air in the swamp," her mother said in all seriousness. "I know they're living in the swamp—even if he won't tell me where."

"I can't tell you where, ma'am. We got orders not to tell anybody."

"Well then, I'll make a sweet shortbread tomorrow and send it over by Gavin for the three of you. Seems like Jeems can eat a meal sack of shortbread all by himself."

"I couldn't carry a meal sack of shortbread, Miz Gaylord. I'm riding a small tacky that's got to carry my weight more'n twenty miles in a day."

Sal pulled his arm impatiently. "Come on—or Ma'll talk all night and make shortbread all tomorrow!"

The scent of the moonflowers seemed to Lex even sweeter and heavier than he recalled. Sal's face, since his arrival, had turned to follow his every movement. As they sat in the home-built swing, he reached and pulled her to him. When he raised his mouth from hers he asked: "Miss me a little bit, Sal?"

Her arms were still around his neck, and she snuggled even closer.

"I miss you something terrible, Lex. I miss you more'n you miss me."

"How you figure that? I think about you in camp. I don't take up with any of those women come in and out."

"You been gone six months, and you ain't come back once in that time. People been askin' me where you was and if you left me. The fellow was courtin' Serenius Brown's sister came back—and married her before he went off again."

"We'll get married soon as the war is over."

"You askin' a lot when you ask a girl to wait. S'pose I wait—and then, after all, you get killed or something."

That had not even occurred to him, and he puzzled over it. It seemed to him that if a woman loved a man, waiting would be no harder for sweetheart than for wedded wife.

"You got a good home, Sal. You better off here with your pa and ma than you would be if I married you and took you to Pa's place or—or anywhere else."

He stopped to ask himself where else he could take her. Then he added honestly: "Besides, I ain't got any money yet to take care of you with."

"Married men don't have to fight. Lots of 'em make excuses."

His arms slackened around her soft plumpness.

"Sal," he told her earnestly, "I don't *have* to fight. I joined Francis Marion because I *wanted* to."

She sat up and pushed his arms away. "Then you're a fool," she said shrilly. "There's always some as fights for others, and there's others smart enough to sit back and not fight."

"Sal!" he cried, appalled and yet reaching for her. He felt her soft body against him as she came into his arms, bursting into tears as she threw herself upon him. "Lex, can't you see I love you and want to keep you?"

Those words brought him back to her. He was still hearing them and feeling her in his arms when he rode Edisto's tacky back to the camp that third day.

28

REMEMBERING SAL'S WARM ARMS AND EAGER LIPS AS HE RODE back to camp, Lex felt regret that he could not marry her. Before, he had not been anxious. He had realized that he was young and could not support a wife. When he started going to see her on those honeysuckle-scented nights of a summer past, he had been only seeking the romance of a girl's companionship. From the first she had been in earnest, but he had not. Now his enlistment and her ardor made him desire marriage as much as she did. He had made that plain to her, and she had promised to wait.

"There ain't any other boy in the hills I care for like I care for you, Lex!"

Perhaps he would get not only a horse but a share of gold and fine cloth and provisions from a raid on some British convoy. When the war ended and he went home, his father would be glad for a woman in the house.

He dismounted to lead the pony through a bog, taking care not to lose the small box of shortcake slung by a strap across his shoulder. Mistress Gaylord had told him to eat of it on the way, but although hungry he wished to hand it unopened to Jeems.

As soon as he rode into camp he felt the excitement. Tension ran like drawn catgut from man to man. News had come in that the hated Wemyss, in command of the 63rd Regiment and re-enforced by Major Harrison's Tories, was cutting a swath through South Carolina. Tarleton was also on the move. These combined forces far outnumbered the small band which Marion had so far assembled and which he was trying day by day to increase. His immediate need was for reconnaissance: to discover the location of the enemy, and to ascertain its numbers before his Partisans dared strike again.

The men in camp knew all about it, and talk of it was putting them at one another's throats. Some wished to attack at any odds; others thought they should hide or disband, to form again and fight when they had a chance of victory.

While they argued and quarreled, Francis Marion and his officers conferred. The result of this conference was to send out a small force of picked men under Major James. Word went around the camp that those had to be scouts who knew the terrain, as well as the boldest and most resourceful horsemen.

A few days later Lovely came to Lex.

"Major James' scouts are starting tonight. They are all volunteers."

"Of course I want to go. But what can I ride?"

"I'll get you a horse for this—and you can catch you another one."

This time they did not dare ride the road as they had ridden to Nelson's Ferry. They moved in single file through forest paths or were led by scouts through pathless swamps. At the first hint of daylight they stopped and made camp, while two scouts went ahead on foot.

Ahead was the highroad supposed to be the British line of march. But they waited daylong in cover of the woods, taking care not to show themselves upon it or any other road. As soon as one of the scouts came back next day, he reported the enemy column to be on that road ten miles away, and to be doing just what Major James was doing: moving by night and resting by day.

Lex could hazard a guess as to their own distance from the road, and Harley confirmed it.

"Tonight they'll have to pass less than three miles from here."

For fear of Tory scouts, they did not begin to move until after dark. Their progress was then even more stealthy than it had been two nights before. The moonlight hardly penetrated the canopy of treetops above them as Lex held his horse to a walk exactly twenty feet behind the man ahead of him. They had been ordered not to speak, and they knew how to keep bit rings from jingling. Only the sound of their horses' feet beat out the slow minutes of that hour's ride. When they reached a thickly wooded spot about a hundred feet off the road, Major James halted and stationed them. His whispered orders ran from one to the other.

"Dismount and stand at your horses' heads. If one of them whinnies I'll skin you alive. Watch for everything through chinks between the trees. Don't let me hear a word or a sound from any of you—but be in readiness to carry out a command if I give it."

Woodsmen and hunters to a man, they kept such silence that the small things of grove and thicket began to cry again. Lex could distinguish their different voices and almost understand what they said to one another. Sal had disliked them, he recalled; but he liked to hear them. Some sang for the joy of singing and others against loneliness; some were calling for their mates.

His sharp ears heard the approach of mounted troops even before a scout appeared like a shadow from his post down the road. Thousands of horses' hooves—he had never heard so many at once—were thudding toward his station.

The sound grew louder and louder. He kept his hand upon the soft nose of his own mount, ready to close his fingers upon the nostrils if it tried to whinny to its fellows.

But it had been cavalry-trained by horsemen it now was serving against, and it stood in quiet without lifting a foot to stamp. Now the vanguard of the force was in sight. Colors were indistinguishable, but the moonlight glinted on the helmets of the dragoons.

Lex had never before seen as a unit a regiment of British cavalry. Men and horses moved steadily, with assurance and precision, as they rode the rutted, unfamiliar way. Moonbeams flashed from the metal of their accouterments as they proceeded without halt and wordlessly. File by file they passed the ambuscade where Major James' scouts, even more silent than they, were upon the watch. Column by column the main force went by. Once a charger snorted and a trooper cursed in a whisper, swinging his nervous steed back into line. Lex realized that the animal had sensed the presence of horses hidden to one side of the road. But human beings of duller perception and instinct had no idea that eyes were upon them as they passed. Lex felt the silk-soft nostrils of his horse begin to quiver, and he closed his fingers upon them to shut off any reply. In the unreal moonlight the procession went on: thousands of soldiers and horses, well-armed, well-fed, well-trained. Under the eyes of that ragged, small band they rode—and Lex Mourne saw why Marion fought like a swamp fox.

Then of a sudden the last ranks passed. The moonlight lay on the empty road and gilded the dust that hung over it. The crickets and late cicadas and frogs took up their nocturnal refrain.

Lex had never seen a play, but he realized he had been watching one. The might of the English king had just passed in display. What were a few hundred woodsmen in a swamp to this? To join in battle against such odds would be both hopeless and foolish. Why was Major James still waiting? No order had been given. Why were his scouts still standing like statues at their horses' heads?

Then his ears, keen as those of a fox, caught the approaching rhythm again. . . .

A rear guard, he realized, was following the regulars.

No word was spoken by the waiting scouts—but the whisper of a little breeze ran like a murmur from man to man.

As the head of this column came in sight Lex realized they were Tories. Their green uniforms were black in the night, as were the woods alongside the road. But they lacked the magnificent co-ordination of the British regulars. They lolled in their saddles, not keeping stirrup to stirrup. However, they were a large force. By now several hundred of them had passed.

Now the road in the moonlight was empty again. But a hundred yards behind that last rank another column straggled. Lex, trying to notice everything he could, estimated it at fifty men. He realized that it was only the tag end of the large force Wemyss was leading, but he knew it was three or four times as large as James' band.

Just as it came abreast of them Major James stood in his stirrups so every scout could see him. He drew his sword and raised it and the moonlight met its steel.

"Charge!" he shouted. "Take prisoners—and retreat the way we came!"

29

LEX FELT HIS TRAINED CHARGER RESPOND AS HE THREW HIM-
self into the saddle. He was suddenly in the midst of a mob
of struggling, swearing men and rearing horses. The Tory
rear guard, taken completely by surprise, had no idea of
the numbers by which they were being attacked. They
offered no resistance but tried to escape and reach the
main force ahead of them. Not a shot sounded. The partisans were obeying their leader's order to "take prisoners"
rather than kill. The cavalrymen upon whom they had
fallen as if from the moon did not stop to draw swords or
strike back; they spurred their mounts in panic to reach
their comrades ahead of them. Two horses were over-
thrown and with their riders rolled in the road.

Lex was one of the attackers who had collided with
them. As one mount rose he leaned and caught its bridle
line; but it pulled back, snapping the leather, and tore on
after the column. As it did so there came from that column
ahead shouted orders and a trumpet call.

At the sound Major James shouted again: "Retreat—
bringing your prisoners!"

Lex leapt from his saddle upon a trooper scrambling in
the road. He seized the man's weapons and with his saber
urged him into the woods where his comrades were with-
drawing. As he did so a volley of musketry from the ranks
ahead whistled through the air above them.

"Hold my stirrup," he told his man, "and trot alongside my horse. If I feel you let go I swear I'll shoot you."

As he mounted, the terrified captive seized his stirrup and moved with him. Around them the woods rustled with the Partisans' withdrawal. Although Lex was walking his horse, the man at his stirrup stumbled as he was dragged through bushes and over logs. Another volley of lead sang overhead. But its only effect was to speed the raiders' departure; for the British were not risking firing into the woods and killing their own men as well as the enemy.

A mile from the road they stopped on a small hammock to take stock of what had been achieved. The prisoners were not many. Major James had allowed only a few moments between his order to strike and his order to withdraw. But he now had something more tangible than mere information to carry to his chief. The uniforms and insignia of the captured men would confirm what he had to tell. A Continental soldier could be exchanged for each. Besides which, prisoners often talked—either accidentally or purposely.

The Partisans were in high spirits. They had seen the glitter of moonlight upon the might of the English king. Yet, in spite of the strength of that display, their small band had fallen upon and routed and taken captives from the rear guard of an army of thousands.

The fellow whom Lex had caught was begging a ride.

"I'll fall if you make me walk. I can't keep my feet in this jungle. When I do you'll think I'm trying to get away and you'll shoot me."

Lex glared at him. "I ought to shoot you anyway. I was hoping to come out of this with a horse to ride for the rest of the war. Instead of that I got something calls itself a man but can't even stand on its own feet."

But in order to hasten the return the prisoners were taken up. Behind each horse carrying double rode an unhampered trooper with rifle ready, in order to foil any attempt at escape.

Their meeting with Marion took place before dawn two
days later. Lex found Jeems and Edisto and young Dalzell,
and they waited together through that day. Lovely was
for once serious. He brought them information.

"Officers still talkin'. But I kin tell you now what the
Gen'ral's goin' to do. He's got to withdraw."

Lex demanded angrily: "Why? Our raid was successful."

"You seen that column," said Lovely. "You know well as
I do what'll happen to his Brigade if we tangle with it."

All day they waited in suspense. Then at sunset a bugle
lined them up to hear the decision. Marion walked from
his tent, limping slightly but with thin shoulders thrown
back. He stopped in front of them, his eyes going from
face to face.

"Your command finds it necessary—for the present—to
abandon our defense of this section. Men who wish to go
to their homes may do so—and join us again when we return. Men who are staying, be ready to start in an hour
for Lynch's Creek."

Of the four friends, only Jeems was undismayed.

"We must be going to join Nat Greene. I've always
wanted to fight with him, because he's a blacksmith too."

"Well, I don't," said Edisto. "I enlisted to fight for my
own people. If Marion's deserting them I'll accept the
leave he offered."

In that hour decisions were swiftly made. Lex and Service Dalzell—although unhappy and puzzled—were riding
with the Brigade. The Dalzell boy had his own mount and
Jeems would have Edisto's tacky. When he protested,
Edisto said: "Keep it. I ain't going far."

"How you figure that? It's a long way to the hills."

"I ain't going to any hills. I'm just going to the river.
I got friends there—and I don't hanker to see Pa."

They bade him good-by and charged him to have news

from home ready for them on their return. Lovely said that return would be soon.

"Gen'ral's doin' the right thing. He's fixin' to ketch Tarleton with his lordship's shirttail out. I got a horse for you, Mourne. Hit ain't purty as the black, but it's got four legs."

They were a small band assembled by the bugle "to horse." As Marion rode to the head of the little column, Lex noticed that his once handsome red vest was shabby and faded to brown. But his orders were just as sharp and assured as they were in victory. He had heard from Major James the strength and size of the force being sent against him. He knew they could not only surround and inactivate his small band, but that he would lose many of that band by death or capture if he remained.

But hearts were sore in the line behind him. A trooper asked sullenly: "How come the Gen'ral keep on wearin' that red vest? He tole us not to wear green or our own men would shoot us for Tories."

Lovely answered him. "He wears it because he's cold, you fool, and he ain't got nothin' else to wear."

Lex's heart was sore too, although he believed in his leader. He knew as well as his comrades that they were on the road to North Carolina. Beyond that he knew nothing —but he trusted Francis Marion. He—Lex—had had a small taste of victory. This ride in the night was a retreat and was more bitter by contrast. He let his mind go back to Sal, and he found reassurance there. When the war was over she would be his wife ... in his home always. . . .

Then a picture of Peggy slid like a lovely phantom between them—Peggy with rosebuds in her dark hair and dark lashes lifting and falling. He tried not to think of her—to recall Fire by the woodcock pond—Fire in an old brown riding skirt with a spray of honeysuckle—

But Sal Gaylord was his own girl. She belonged to him

and he to her. She came of the same sturdy stock he did, and he could count upon her. He had been foolish, he told himself, even to let himself dream about a planter's daughter. But why? Toff was his friend—and so was Fire. Was there really a difference of social degree, or was that difference only of individual belief and behavior?

He could not find the answer, and he would not try. He would go back to the hills he loved and to Sal Gaylord. She would be true to him, and he would be fighting for her—no matter where General Marion led the Brigade next.

His horse threw its head restlessly to loosen the rein and drink from a swamp branch that crossed the road. While he sat in the saddle, stroking its coarse mane and listening to the long gasping swallows with which it sucked up the water thirstily, he forgot about all three girls in a more immediate thought.

For the second time now he had had a chance and had failed to get from the enemy a horse of his own.

30

THEY WERE SIXTY MEN WHEN THEY REACHED THEIR DESTINA-
tion of Amy's Mill. All along that secret march small parties of scouts had been detached to station themselves at
strategic places and from there to keep Marion informed.
For part of the way the main force had dragged two small
field pieces, which they were determined not to leave to
the enemy. Before they reached Drowning Creek these
had to be abandoned. They were pulled as far as possible
off the road and into the swamp and left to sink of their
own weight in black mud. Then the Swamp Fox and his
few followers rode on in the despondency of retreat, knowing that they were turning their backs upon their own
people, taking small comfort in the fact that it was wisdom
to "live to fight another day," yet holding by what they
realized was their only chance of helping the Patriot
cause.

Lex's thoughts were unhappy, both about the retreat
and about the people he loved and was leaving unde-
fended. Jeems and young Service Dalzell remained with
the main body of men, but Lovely and others were left at
White Marsh. From that small hidden camp it was possible both to keep in touch with Tory activity along the
North Carolina border and to receive news from the scouts
southwest of them.

This news whetted their anger to razor edge. When the
tale of Adam Cusack came in, it was hard for their officers
to hold them from return. Tears were running down the

leathery face of the backwoodsman who brought it. He interrupted his own narrative with harsh curses, and the men listening cursed with him.

"I seen Missis Cusack and her young ones. That is, all but the next to littlest one."

Jeems swore and drove his hunting knife to the hilt in the wooden block he used in his work.

"Cusack had a right to enlist and fight on our side. You just wait till I catch me a Tory soldier!"

"Shut up," said a man named Harley, "and let Conway tell the rest."

"They came in the night," said Conway, "and dragged Cusack out and tied his hands behind his back and put a rope 'round his neck. While one squad was doing this, another was going 'round the house setting fire to curtains and beds with candles they took off the tables. They was putting anything they liked in their pockets too."

Lex asked: "Were Missis Cusack and the young ones still in the house?"

"The missis ran out after her man with the baby in her arms, and the other children come screaming after her. When she sees what they're doing to Cusack, she runs and kneels down in front of that dog of a Wemyss. She begins begging him not to hang her man, and the children come kneel down by her and cry and beg him too."

"Didn't he give her any answer?" asked Lex.

"He give her this much answer. He say, 'Woman, get out my way, or I'll ride over you and your brats!' He put spurs to his horse and he woulda done it too, if a couple of his own officers didn't ride up and grab his bridle. They tell him, 'Pardon, Colonel, but you can't do that. That ain't the kind of thing the king's officer would do.'"

Service Dalzell swore, and Jeems turned on him.

"Quit it, Service! You're a preacher's boy. I'll do all your swearing for you."

"They pull Wemyss to one side, but he shouts to the men holding Adam Cusack, 'Go ahead and swing the traitor up!'"

"You mean they hanged him with his children looking?"

"That's what I mean. Missis Cusack and the children seen that on one side and the house blazing on the other. And it was just that time—one of the servants told me—her oldest gal begins hollering, 'Ma, where's Jamie?'"

"How old was this Jamie?"

"Little more'n two years old. Seems like when his ma grabs the baby, she seen him holding his sister's hand. But his sister says now he broke loose and run after his ma."

"What they do?"

"Miz Cusack give her gal the baby and she run back to the house and try to git inside. But the soldiers pulls her back, and the roof falls in just then. Next morning they find what was left of Jamie. Poor little fellow was so scared he run and hid underneath a bed."

Francis Marion came up to the group, and Jeems Gaylord turned on him.

"When I get in a fight, Gen'ral, I don't figure to take any Tory prisoners."

Marion's voice was lower than his and Marion was not as tall by half a head, but Marion's answer came back like a lash.

"You'd better figure on doing just what I order, Gaylord, so long as you are in my Brigade."

"You heard about the Cusacks—sir?"

"Certainly. Conway brought me the report. If we ever catch Wemyss we'll deal with him as he deserves. But all the British aren't butchers."

"I'm talking about Tories. They're worse than the Regulars."

"Tories, then. All of them, I repeat, aren't like Wemyss. I heard Conway tell you that two officers defied Wemyss when he tried to ride a woman and children down. The servants told him that several soldiers tried to get into the house when they heard a child was inside."

"That's right," said Conway grudgingly. "But me, I feels like Gaylord."

"You may feel as you choose—but you'll both obey my orders."

A little silence fell on the group as their minds dwelt on the horror of which Conway had told. Every man of them had left loved ones farther south. They had chosen to march northward with Marion because they believed he would lead them back when the right time came to strike again. But what had been done to the Cusacks could be done to other families. Every man of them was picturing his own home in flames, his old father or young son hanged, and no telling what other atrocities committed.

Marion spoke slowly. "You shall avenge Adam Cusack and little Jamie. I had not meant to tell you, for plans are not yet completed. But I have had news from General Sumter and from Williamsburg. I think we will march soon."

Several men spoke together. "Back into South Carolina?"

"Back into South Carolina to strike again—and harder. I know how you feel about this retreat, and I'd like to tell you now that I do not blame you."

They were hanging on his words, for he was reticent. Never before had he talked with them so, and none of them ever heard him say so much again.

"Were I in your place—not knowing the over-all plan of South Carolina warfare as I do—I am not sure that I would have stuck by a leader as you have stuck by me. I wish to tell you I thank you."

Jeems Gaylord swore to hide his feelings, as he worked

his knife free of the wooden shoeing block where he had driven it in his rage.

"I'm staying with you, Gen'ral, so long as you got a half-starved, spavined, swayback nag for me to shoe. But I'm asking you, when we get back in South Carolina—just for a change—to take me along on a raid where you're after *Tories.*"

31

THE NEXT DAY GAVIN WITHERSPOON BROUGHT IN A FEW GUNS and prisoners from an almost single-handed raid. It was not much, but it cheered them. They said to one another that perhaps the tide was turning. They reminded one another of Marion's promise that they would ride soon and would ride south.

Jeems shod the horses, Marion's Roger among them. The slow days passed—and suddenly orders were given to march. It was a forced march, riding night and day; but men and horses were by now accustomed to hardship. Their scouts warned that on Little Peedee the enemy hopelessly outnumbered them. They passed through that section during the night, and at Lynch's Creek were joined by Captain James and Captain Mouzon with small re-enforcements. A conference was held as to the possibility of attacking Wemyss; but that hangman had taken refuge in the defenses of Georgetown, a strong British post. Orders were given to ride on toward Shepherd's Ferry.

Scouts from that section of the state were now leading the band, and they told of a large enemy force camped so as to command approach by the navigable stream. Some advised an attempt to land in small boats from that stream under cover of night, but Francis Marion shook his head.

"I was on Sullivan's Island when the British tried to cross Breach Inlet and land from Long Island. Small boats and men floundering in the current were targets as helpless as sitting ducks for our riflemen on the beach."

Hugh Horry agreed with him. "Young Conway here knows a swamp road a mile north of the ferry."

"I can ride it blindfolded," the boy told them; "but it's boggy causeway, and we'll have to cross a plank bridge."

He led them on another night ride through swamp. The horses' feet made loud sucking sounds in mud that was ankle-deep, and the frogs in lagoons on either side hushed singing as they passed. Lex was thinking to himself that, were he encamped in such terrain, the silencing of those voices of night would give him warning of someone's approach.

At midnight they reached the bridge, and the whispered order ran down the line: "One at a time—ride in a walk—and keep the middle of the way."

They knew all about loose-plank bridges where a board rose like a seesaw if horse or man walked to one side. But in spite of all precautions the drum of hooves upon wood gave warning to the sentries ahead of them. Half of the Partisan force was across when a gun boomed out from the camp which they had hoped to surprise.

Francis Marion did not waste a second for his decision. He shouted, *"Full gallop ahead!"* and he spurred his own horse to a run in the lead.

Lex Mourne found himself with Colonel Hugh Horry's command, dismounted for the attack on the Dollard house. It was a frame building of considerable size used by the enemy for headquarters, and Marion's scouts had reported most of the Tory troops camped in its yard. They could not know that at sound of the alarm gun these troops had moved swiftly to a field nearby—the very field across which Horry was approaching.

The double surprise of that meeting in darkness caused a turmoil of confusion and death. Lex, moving carefully

with his rifle at ready, was unhurt by the first volley, but
men fell all around him. He fired—threw himself flat to
reload—rose to a knee and fired again into the flashes of
red flame ahead. Some of the Partisans did the same,
others broke in retreat. The night was a bedlam of gun-
shots, screams of agony, curses of anger and commands of
officers. The British, who outnumbered them two to one,
were mowing down Hugh Horry's companies with their
fire. But Horry's voice rang out over the noise in time to
stop a recoil which could have been a retreat. He ordered
a charge. They rallied and obeyed to a man. And as they
charged it happened that the small advance guard which
had been sent ahead under Captain Waties discovered the
enemy's rear and struck at the same time.

Hand to hand, and with gun butts and knives as well as
fire, they fought it out. But Waties' thrust was too much
for the foe. Caught between the two attacks, they broke
and retreated to the even deeper darkness of Black Mingo
Swamp.

And then as the starlight paled to dawn Marion's men
on the Dollard field sought out the wounded from the
dead and knew how terrible was their loss.

One third of all combatants were either killed or dis-
abled. Since the Tories had two men to every partisan, the
British loss was greater in numbers. But it was not so in
proportion, and the Swamp Fox's little band realized in
that daybreak what they had paid for the victory. Captain
Logan had been killed; Captain Mouzon was so terribly
wounded that he never recovered enough to fight again.
Lieutenant Scott was another casualty.

Lex, busied with carrying water and lifting wounded
men, finally came upon Jeems Gaylord lying on a heap of
pine straw. He opened his eyes as Lex leaned over him,
and he remarked: "You look as if you're worse off than
I am."

"I'm not hurt. What can I do for you?"

"Nothing. The Dalzell young one has been bringing me water, and I'm just waiting my turn with the sawbones."

"I can see it's your leg, Jeems. How long you been here?"

"Seems like I been here all night. I caught a bullet in my thigh just after the fighting began, and I managed to drag over here so as not to get trampled."

Service Dalzell hurried up with a tin cup of water, and the soldier-surgeon came at the same time. Lex appealed to him: "He's my best friend! What can I do?"

"Hold him down, the two of you, while I get the ball out of his thigh."

Lex and the parson's son performed that dreadful task while the surgeon probed. He finally dug out the British bullet with procedure that reminded Lex of digging lead from a tree trunk. He poured raw turpentine into the deep wound and then bound it tightly with strips of unbleached linen.

"This will get you two or three months of leave, lad," he told Jeems. "If you have a sweetheart at home, that may be worth the wound."

"I ain't got a sweetheart," Jeems told him; "but I got a hound-dog I'll be glad to see again."

The doctor handed the turpentine to young Dalzell.

"Pour some on Mourne's head, he's got a scalp wound. Then bring it on to me."

"I'd just about forgot it," said Lex. "A Tory broke his gunstock over my head last night." He felt carefully of his bloody, matted hair. "But I did more than that to him—and I'm glad of it."

The effects of that victory at Black Mingo were to make other men as bitter as he was. They had come to actual hand grip with the enemy, and every man of Horry's companies had lost a personal friend or seen one wounded.

Now they were not only willing but anxious to fight. The news of the successful battle brought back their men on leave and numbers of Whig recruits, and many Tories turned sides and came over to fight with them. During the next few days, while Lex and Service Dalzell cared for Jeems in the old frame house, volunteers came steadily by twos and threes into camp. And among them came Edisto Hawkins in an oxcart with a long-legged, shy-faced boy who looked even younger than Service.

32

THEY SAW AT ONCE THAT EDISTO HAD GROWN STOUTER. HIS voice and his manner seemed happier and more assured.

"Soon as we heard the Brigade was on its way back, me and Sonny here started out to find it."

"You've come to join us again?" Lex asked.

" 'Course we have. We're fighting for our own people now. Besides"—his face tightened as he looked at the boy —"Adam Cusack was a kinsman of his pa."

"Who's his pa?" asked Jeems. "He looks to me too young to fight."

"I ain't too young to fight Tories," said the boy. He had a thick shock of soot-black hair, and he stammered slightly as he went on. "Pa fit with General Gates. He was killed at Camden."

Jeems always fathered the young, although he kept them in order. "It's a hard thing to lose your pa, but you got a right to take pride in him."

"I t-take pride in him," said the boy. "All three of us takes pride in him."

They were interested as well as sympathetic. Lex prompted: "Who you mean by all three of you?"

"I mean my ma an' me an' my new pa."

"You got a new pa?"

"Yes—him," said the boy—and he threw back his mane of hair and looked at Edisto.

That very nearly brought Jeems to his feet from his mattress on the floor. He forgot his wound and started to rise, and lay back with an exclamation. Young Dalzell stared, big-eyed, while Lex beat Edisto on the back and all three cried out questions.

"Who is she?"

"Where'd you find her?"

"What she look like?"

"What's her name?"

"Samantha," said Edisto happily. "Was Samantha Sellers, is Samantha Hawkins now."

"What you mean by sneaking off and getting a wife while we were away?"

"Seemed like there weren't any use to wait, and I couldn't get word to you up on Drowning Creek. Samantha's got a farm too big for her and Sonny to work it alone, and I told you I wasn't going home to my folks."

"So that's where you went when you and Jake Harley left us?"

Sonny spoke. "Yes, he come to us. Ma and me makes welcome any men fights for General Marion."

"How'd you come to meet up with her and Sonny in the first place?"

"They used to bring corn and potatoes to the first camp we were at after you and me and Jeems enlisted."

Jeems lifted his head from the mattress. "I recall about that. You were on duty bringing in provisions while I was shoeing horses and grinding saws."

"Ma and me hauled the stuff in that same cart," said the boy. "Only we had the tacky then, so we got 'long faster."

"You mean the tacky I've been riding?" Jeems asked him.

Edisto nodded. "Samantha and Sonny said they could do without him since they had the ox. The tacky's too light to put in a plow, and they wanted to do all they could to help on account of Sonny's pa."

Sonny was gazing anxiously at Jeems. "Did the tacky get shot when you did?"

"No. He's all right. We left the horses in the woods and went into this fight on foot. You can go now and see him if you want to. Lex says they got the horse pens out in that scrub pine grove."

Sonny went with alacrity, and Jeems turned on Edisto. "You ain't much older than he is. How come you married a woman old enough for your ma?"

"She's just sixteen years older than Sonny. I don't want any girl flirtin' and flutterin' 'round me. I seen enough of my sisters—and of yours, too."

"I wouldn't blame you for that," said Jeems. "But—a widow woman—with a son taller than Service—"

"She's the kind of woman I wanted to marry," Edisto told them placidly. "She suits me. You'll understand when you see her."

Jeems rolled over on his mattress and groaned aloud. "Maybe so," he agreed; "but I'd rather be shot in the leg."

Lex tried to fill the awkward pause. "How far do you live from here?"

"Less than fifteen miles. It's on this side the river and on the way to the hills. Soon as we can get Jeems there, she'll nurse him till he can go on home."

Jeems began to raise objections. "She's got no call to let me in. In a day or two I'll be able to ride. Besides, with you and Sonny gone, she'll have all she can do."

All his life Edisto had been dominated by Jeems and Lex; but he overrode them now with a calm and sure insistence.

"Samantha never yet turned anybody away. Besides, somebody's got to carry the oxcart back to her."

"Then you go along with us, and tell her who we are," said Lex. "Or else I'll stay and you can take Jeems."

Edisto told them, with his new-found dignity: "Saman-

tha was willing for Sonny to come. She said other women
were sending boys as young. But she wouldn't want me to
leave him soon as he joined the Brigade. We got some
rough ones in this crowd, and she's taught Sonny to be
God-fearing."

Although recruits were coming in, battle-weary men
were asking leave. Lex and Jeems obeyed Edisto and
started next day in the swaying cart. Lex had talked with
Colonel Hugh Horry, to whose command he had been
assigned on the eve of the battle near Shepherd's Ferry,
and Horry had told him plans for the immediate future
were in abeyance.

"I'm still advising against joining General Greene, and
so is my brother."

Lex was disturbed. "I thought General Marion had decided against that when he brought us back here."

"Nothing is ever decided. We are such a mobile brigade
that we can be sent here and there. The high command is
for one large force and is always urging that we join it.
General Marion believes in the kind of warfare he's wag-
ing, and General Sumter and other South Carolina leaders
are anxious to keep him in this section."

"I hope they do," said Lex. "But of course I'll go wherever the Brigade goes."

"That's the spirit. A victory like ours at Black Mingo
means more to the Continental cause than any fighting we
could do along with General Greene."

"You think it's all right for me to leave then, Colonel?
If plans change and you're riding in the next few days,
could you get me word to the Sellers place?"

Horry had agreed to do so, Lex now recalled, as the ox
swayed on, pulling the cart wheels crookedly against the
walls of the deep sand ruts. Lex was walking alongside,
guiding it with his voice; and of its own accord the beast
turned into the side road which Edisto and Sonny had

described. Wagon tracks led on through a stubble field, and ahead they saw a two-room cabin connected by a dog-trot with a lean-to kitchen.

As they caught sight of it a woman came to the door and stood for a moment shading her eyes with a hand from the low sun. Then she came down the steps and crossed the field to meet them, and they saw she was not tall but amply built, with silk-soft hair as black and as thick as Sonny's. Without words she raised steady hazel eyes to Lex's face ... then her look went slowly over Jeems who was propped in the cart and plainly in pain from the journey....

"You be Lex Mourne and Jeems Gaylord," she told them in her deep sweet voice. "Time and again Ed has told Sonny and me about you. I got Sonny's feather bed made with clean sheets, and I'll take the ox, Lex, while you put Jeems to bed."

In that moment both Lex and Jeems understood—as their friend had said they would. Jeems stammered: "You got no call to put yourself out for me."

Lex was lifting him from the cart. "You leave the ox for me, ma'am. Soon's I get Jeems in bed I'll do the yard work for you."

"I'll be grateful," she said—and she smiled at him and then at Jeems. "I hold we all got a call to help each other. Ain't you been wounded in the same war I just sent my baby to fight?"

"I'll say one thing," said Jeems. "Edisto's got more sense than I ever knew he had."

Samantha laughed—and as she did they saw a long dimple appear at one corner of her wide, sweet mouth.

"Light now, and come in. You're Edisto's friends, and you're welcome. You'll be favoring him and me and Sonny if you'll feel the house belongs just as much to you as it does to us."

33

SAMANTHA WAS NOT BEAUTIFUL AND SHE WAS THIRTEEN
years older than Edisto, but her heart was so full of kindness and love for others that it seemed obliged to overflow
in deeds of goodness for them.

She had cooked supper while Lex did the farmyard tasks
outside, homesick as he went about them for his father's
farm in the hills. He washed his hands in the basin outside
the door, then went into the kitchen.

"Bring that-there bench," she told him. "I'm taking the
vittles in Jeems' room, so he won't have to eat in there by
himself."

There was corn bread and shortbread, collard greens,
and a platter heaped high with small fresh-water fish fried
golden-brown.

"Sonny used to ketch them in that creek makes off from
the river. I ain't much of a fisherman, but I figure a body
can do most anything if they ain't too lazy."

"Seems like you can," Jeems told her admiringly, as he
accepted a fourth helping.

She was too genuine to protest. "I try. That's all a body
can do. Now you tell me all about Sonny and Ed."

They told her, while she asked the questions a wife and
mother would ask.

"It was hard to let Sonny go; but he kept begging and
I had a feeling his pa woulda let him. Even so I couldn't
have stood it if I hadn't known Ed would look after him."

"Edisto's looking after Sonny," they told her. "That's

159

the only reason he didn't come back. There's no fighting going on now, and anybody can get leave. But Edisto said you wouldn't want him to leave Sonny in camp."

She nodded. "Ed's a good Christian man. When I first saw him hauling the provisions we brought, he seemed to me just a boy 'round Sonny's age. I know how much younger he is than I am. But, maybe—"

She paused to fetch hot corn bread and serve them both.

"Maybe the kind of woman I am just *has* to mother a man. I knows some as does nothing but squeeze a husband half to death to keep 'em, while they do nothing. But I figure you get more happiness if you pull your half of the load."

The long uncomfortable journey had jarred Jeems' wound and it had become inflamed. Samantha dressed it and gave him hot tea of herbs which cooled his fever and reduced the swelling. When at the end of a week he was able to travel again, she suggested that Lex take him on home in the oxcart.

"I'm not doing any plowing now, and I can spare it until you come back this way."

But Lex's message from Hugh Horry came before they could start. Marion was marching again into Williamsburg, and was calling every man to return to him.

Samantha said in her slow, soft voice. "Go on, Lex. I'll drive Jeems."

"I can drive myself, if you lend me the ox. I already been too much trouble to you."

"If folks are true friends there's no such thing as trouble. When the day comes I need your help, I'll take it and thank you, Jeems."

So Lex started for Williamsburg with Hugh Horry's courier, and found that most of his old comrades were rallying there too.

"We're after Harrison this time," young Conway told

him. "He's over by Lynch's Creek. My pa's gone that way now, with several other scouts."

But these scouts brought Francis Marion news of an even greater opportunity. Colonel Tynes and his recruiting officers were active on the Black River. Not only were they arousing all who still had Tory sympathies, they were forcing men of other opinion to take the oath of loyalty to King George and the king's shilling along with it. Also— Conway and his fellow scouts reported—they had stored at Tarcote generous supplies of arms, ammunition, food and clothing.

Marion's men rode and rode fast. They struck without warning this time, capturing men and officers and Colonel Tynes himself, in addition to the supplies they needed desperately.

After that raid there was jubilation in the Swamp Fox camp. Weary, ragged men sat around fires, eating good food to which they were unaccustomed and listening to good news which the scouts were still bringing in. Young Conway told it all to Lex, for both he and his father took part in the scouting.

"We got thirty more men. They always come in after a successful fight."

Lex spoke between mouthfuls of well-salted beef which he was grilling in gobbets on the end of a forked green stick.

"Some of 'em come in after defeats too—or when the Tories have been on a hanging spree."

"I know. I asked Pa how come that was. He says there's folks will always want to be with the winners, and there's other folks will always feel for the underdog."

Conway chewed his own meat reflectively. "Hit's lucky for us it's that way. But all I can think about now is how glad I am to get some salt on my meat again.

"I'm glad the General's got a blanket too," he went on.

"He's been sleeping without one ever since his burned up. Several men offered him theirs, but he wouldn't take 'em. Said it was his own carelessness, and he'd sleep without until the British gave him one."

"How'd it happen?" asked Lex.

"Must have been when you were off with Colonel Horry. It was one night after we'd been riding for twenty-four hours. Marion made him a good soft bed of dry pine straw and went fast asleep on it. A spark from his fire must have crawled or been blown that way. Anyhow he was so dead-tired that the straw and the blanket burned under him."

"His cap's charred too, and somebody said his back was singed."

"It was. He let Pa put bear grease on it. Pa says it was burned bad enough for him to say a few cuss words."

"I didn't know Marion ever cussed."

"He doesn't—but he did that time. Pa says he sat on a log with that water bottle in his hand, taking a swig of it like it was medicine."

"Conway, why does he put vinegar in his drinking water?"

"Pa says it's because he's French. Pa says Frenchmen hold plain water ain't good for your stomach. Most all of 'em cut it with wine, but since the Gen'ral ain't a drinkin' man he uses vinegar instead."

"Did your pa ever see him draw that sword?"

"No—and nobody else ain't."

"Jeems Gaylord knows all about iron. Jeems says by this time, with all the rain and mud it's caught, it must be stuck so hard with rust in the scabbard that Marion couldn't pull it out if he needed to."

"He won't need to long as he has his pistol. Lovely says he's the best shot in the whole Brigade," put in Service.

"He's the best rider too," said young Conway.

Service Dalzell disagreed with that. "Colonel Horry and his brother both look better on a horse."

"I ain't talkin' about *looks*. They may sit up straighter and pull a sword and wave it. But Pa told me about a jump General Marion took on Roger. He was cornered, and he took a seven-foot fence and a four-foot ditch."

Lex shook his head. "That's too high and too far. Did your pa have time to measure?"

"No—but Pa was hid in the woods close by and he saw it. Afterwards he asked the man who owned the field how high was the fence."

"Well, go on and tell us. How come the General was cornered?"

"He was cut off by a squad of dragoons. Not knowing the field, he rode for the corner near the woods. But the farmer'd just dug a ditch four feet wide to drain it, and he had a fence on top of the bank made by the dried mud of the ditch. Pa says he thought the Gen'ral was a goner that time. The dragoons were riding down on him, whooping like a fox hunt. But he just leaned forward in the saddle like he does and put spurs to Roger and gave him his head. Pa says Roger flew the fence and cleared the ditch on the other side, and the dragoons pulled up swearing so loud he heard 'em clear to the woods."

They thought about that: of a small thin man leaning in his saddle and taking an improbable jump rather than be captured. Service broke the silence by saying: "Here's Edisto."

Lex took one look at Edisto's face and got to his feet. "What is it?"

"I been looking for you—all 'round the camp—Lex."

"Anything wrong?" asked Lex.

A minute before they had been eating and laughing and exchanging stories. Now he felt a formless and wordless premonition.

"It's Samantha," Edisto said. "She's—she's just come into camp."

"Is Samantha hurt? Why'd she come?"

The gentle days at the Sellers farm rushed back upon Lex. If the Tories had hurt Samantha . . .

"Samantha ain't hurt, Lex. You know she's been to the hills with Jeems. She came here to bring you a message."

"To bring me a message?" Lex's brain was alarmed and reacting slowly. He repeated: "Where's she? What's she got to tell me?"

"She's with General Marion, and he sent me to fetch you. But—but I got to warn you, Lex—it's bad news she's brought you!"

34

BOTH FRANCIS MARION AND HUGH HORRY WERE WAITING
with Samantha. She was as calm and at ease with the two
officers as she had been with the boys who were Edisto's
friends, but her eyes were full of pity as they came to rest
on Lex.

He asked her anxiously: "You been to the High Hills
with Jeems?"

"Yes, Lex. That's what I did."

"And you brought me news from home?"

"News I'm sorry to bring, Lex; but I had to bring it."

His throat felt so tight that it was hard to speak.

"Edisto just told me it—it was bad news."

"That's why I come to tell you myself. I couldn't let you
hear it from strangers."

"Tell me, Samantha," he begged her.

"The Tories came through the High Hills just before
Jeems and I got there. They burned your house and the
Johnston house."

Before his eyes came a vision of the low farmhouse
where he had been born ... green-gold of the sycamore
leaves as they fell ... the time when his mother had sung
him to sleep ... his own room under the slanting roof,
from which he had watched the wheeling stars ...

Never again would he see it—except in memory. And
then an even more terrible thought flashed across his mind.

"Samantha, did they—did they hurt my father?"

"Not except they turned him out in the driving rain and

the cold. He stayed 'round the place trying to save what he could. He's sick now with the pleurisy, Lex."

Marion spoke. "You'll want to leave at once, Mourne—and, of course, you may take Roger."

Lex's heart was beating so fast he could hardly say: "I'll thank you for him, sir."

He turned again to Samantha. "Where's Pa? Is he much sick?"

"I'm 'fraid he's mighty sick, Lex. He's over at the Gaylords', and Miz Gaylord is nursing him. He's getting care."

Lex rode Roger that night as fast as the charger had ever been ridden in his wildest raids. But all along the way he remembered to pause to let the animal breathe and drink small amounts of water from streams that crossed the roads. A weary man and a weary horse stumbled into the Gaylord yard just twenty-four hours after their start.

Yadkin Mourne was in desperate straits, but he knew his son.

"I—was hoping—you'd get here, boy."

He caught himself as he saw Lex's face contract with grief, and the old-time roughness crept back into his faint voice.

"All I mean is—I wondered—if General Marion could spare you."

"He lent me his own horse, Pa."

Stories of Marion's war horse as well as of Marion were already circulating through the Back Country. The sick man whispered: "You mean *Roger?*"

"I mean Roger. Gavin's rubbing him down out there by the barn right now. Last thing the General told me was to ride the tail off him if I needed to."

"Looks like he thinks a lot—of a no-count boy like you."

"He think a lot of *you*, Pa. He sent you his respects—and his hope for a full recovery."

Yadkin Mourne was pleased, and he tried to answer.

The effort sent him into paroxysms of coughing and brought Mrs. Gaylord into the room.

"You do the talking, Lex. Don't let him. Now hold up his head high enough for him to swallow this medicine the doctor left."

She administered from a cup the dose of pine syrup and narcotic. Then she brought more feathers to replenish the pan which burned slowly in a corner, giving forth evil-smelling fumes.

"Doctor says he don't believe burning feathers helps lung sickness. But he's young and new-fangled. The old doctor always used to tell me to burn 'em. I pulled Jeems' pa out of pleurisy by keeping him breathing feather smoke."

Yadkin Mourne was growing more drowsy, and his questions came lower and farther apart. Lex tried to prevent them by talking steadily.

"Yes, Pa, General Marion's got another horse—one he took from a Tory—but Roger's the best. No; I ain't got one for myself yet. I been in several raids, but I had hard luck that way.

"Yes, sir. I been up to the North Carolina line with him. We marched back just in time for the fight at the Dollard house. That's where Jeems was wounded in the leg. He's been red-hot to get in a raid ever since he joined, and the first one he rode in he got shot.

"You say Mr. Hawkins raised Cain about Edisto marrying? You might of known he would—but Edisto's lucky. I knew you'd like Samantha. She's the one brought me the news."

He leaned closer to his father, for although Yadkin Mourne's eyes were closing, his lips were trying to shape words.

"You'll—be—lucky—boy—if you get one like her."

Lex fell silent, thinking that over. Why should his father

say it when his father knew he was going to marry Sal? Before his eyes rose a picture of Samantha's sweet placid face. And for some reason there appeared beside her the images of three girls—black hair and brown and red. . . .

"Yes, Pa. We're going to win—no matter what the Tories do."

He clenched his hands as he leaned down and saw what they had done written on his father's sleeping face. Mrs. Gaylord came to the door and beckoned to him.

"You ain't yet had a bite to eat. You got to eat now, Lex. Gavin can sit in Mr. Mourne's room while I'm feeding you."

Lex looked around. "Where's Sal?"

Distress for his father had so filled his mind that he had not really thought of her until Yadkin Mourne spoke of Samantha. A sickroom was woman's work, and surely Sal—

Mrs. Gaylord broke in by setting a plate of hot food before him. "Sal happens to be off now. You eat—else you'll get sick and be no help to your pa."

He did not ask for Sal again. He was in no mood for love-making and was, in a way, relieved by her absence. But while he ate he asked Mr. Gaylord and Jeems exactly what had happened at the Mourne farm.

"It was one of Tarleton's columns," said Jeems. "He's said to be sick down in Charles Town. But they say Cornwallis told him, sick or not, to get out of bed and catch *Mister* Marion."

"Did they hurt any of the Johnston family?"

"No. Pa says they just turned them out like they did your father. It happened before I got home. He'll tell you."

"I not only saw it," the smith said, "I talked to the officer in command. I told him your father hadn't raised a hand against the British."

Lex dropped his face in his hands. "But *I* had. I'm the cause of it."

"No, you ain't, boy; and I'll tell you how I know. That officer I talked to was a captain dressed like a monkey in a red coat. But, all the same, he didn't like the work he was sent to do. He sat there on a reddish-brown stallion in his red coat, and he said to me: "Mind your business, fellow!"

"Then how come you know he didn't like what he was doing?"

"Because he turns to one of his leftenants, and I heard him plain as he said: 'Get on with this nasty business! I don't like to make war on civilians any more than you do; but we've our orders to destroy the two houses pointed out by that filthy turncoat who guided us here.'"

"Turncoat?" Lex's mind flew back. "Mr. Gaylord, you mean—"

"I mean it was the Schofilite the sheriff had in jail. The British took that section months ago and let out all prisoners who enlisted with them. I surely wish Cebron had hanged that skunk when he had the chance, instead of just locking him up."

It all fell into place for Lex: the Mourne house and the Johnston house had been marked for destruction by the men he had met in the swamp. It had been an act of revenge on the part of a renegade. At least the British officer had stopped short of hanging and had not liked his work. Nevertheless, by burning the Mourne home he had caused—

"You had courage, Mr. Gaylord, to say what you did. I wish you'd heard the name of that British captain. It ain't unlikely I'll meet him yet."

"I heard it all right," Gaylord told him grimly. "He had a fancy name to match his fancy red monkey coat."

Lex's eyes looked his question, and the blacksmith said: "*Evelyn Fay.*"

35

YADKIN MOURNE DIED THAT NIGHT, AND THE NEXT AFTERNOON was buried in the churchyard seven miles away beside Lex's mother. When he rode back to the Gaylord place, Lex fell into bed and slept the sleep which he had lacked for three nights. Jeems was limping into the room as he awoke in full daylight.

"What time is it? Why didn't you call me early?"

"It's high noon, and Ma's getting dinner ready. She said to let you sleep long as you could. Wasn't no reason to wake you."

"I want to see the—the place—before I start back. What happened to the animals? I haven't had time to ask you that. I was thinking of nothing but Pa."

"The Tories took the horses and turned loose the hogs and cow. Gavin and Adlai and some other boys rounded up most of those the next day. Here's Vidette. I brought him over here, but Ma told me to keep him out of Mr. Mourne's room."

The hound, now full-grown, pulled loose from Jeems' grip on his collar and rushed upon Lex in a passion of welcome. It broke him down—as nothing else had yet done. He sat on the side of the bed, with a hand on each long, softy, tawny ear, fighting to regain his composure.

"He can stay on here," said Jeems. "Gavin's plumb crazy to hunt him. Gavin says he's a better trailer than old Bell Mouth."

In days gone by, the favorable comparison of any other

170

dog to Bell Mouth would have caused a challenge, if not a fight, from Jeems. Lex recalled that, and was grateful for the concealed tenderness.

"He'll never be what old Bell is, but I'll thank Gavin for keeping him. There's some dogs around the camp. A 'gator got one since you been away. General Marion says the men who own them got to get rid of them, because they'll howl when the moon is full and a Tory scout might locate the camp. I wouldn't take Vidette there, even if I could. I'll be grateful for him to have a good home."

He choked on the word *home*. "Jeems, I want to go—go over there. I got to see the place, sooner or later. I got to arrange some way about the stock. Soon as I do that, I want to get back to camp—and the sooner we ride a raid the better pleased I'll be."

He and Jeems went to the Mourne farm that afternoon. From a mile away he caught sight of two lonely chimneys on the home hill. The sycamore trunks were dark with smoke, but the barn had not been destroyed. The Johnston family emerged from it to meet him.

"We been sleepin' here, Mr. Lex. I knew you an' your pa wouldn't mind. I been feedin' and waterin' your stock."

"Pa'd have been glad to let you. Did you lose your stock?"

"Yes. You know how close my barn was to my house. It burned, and the soldiers shot all my hogs. Only reason they didn't bother to kill yourn is they got mine fust and had all the pork they could eat."

Lex shook his head. "I sure feel for you, Adlai."

Young Adlai put in: "Mr. Lex, Bubba and me got the last one of your shoats run down and penned today."

Lex put a hand on the boy's shoulder and squeezed it hard. But words would not come to him ... and of what use would they be if they did? Of what use to him was the shoat? Or the rest of the stock? His grieved mind had no place for such matters, but they must be met and adjusted. Animals could not be left to starve. The only thing to do was to give them . . .

He looked from the wreckage which marked the house site to fields in stubble which now had no one to plow and sow them.

Johnston said: "The boys and me goin' to raise a cabin right off. We look after things for you long as we stays here. What I was wonderin' was—after we gets the cabin built and goes back to our place—how 'bout me takin' the stock on half shares?"

"You might as well take them. There'll be nobody here to feed them."

"If you thinks it's fair, I'll take the cow and the poultry and hogs home with me. I'll feed 'em and raise all I can get from 'em; and I'll use the milk and eggs and as much pork and poultry as if they was my own. But I'll raise plenty more. You knows I'm a good man with stock. When you come home I'll turn half what I got over to you—and lessen the Tories come and butcher 'em again, I'll guarantee that half'll be more than you got now, Mr. Lex."

When Lex agreed and thanked him, Adlai said simply: "You're helpin' me much as I'm helpin' you. That's the only way I sees to get a start again."

Lex's mind was less disturbed and his heart a little eased as he drove back with Jeems and helped unharness and stable the horse. Only one thing remained now to be done before he rejoined the Brigade.

"Jeems, is Sal visiting any one of the girls in the hills nearby? I'd like to see her before I leave. But if she's with friends too far off, I'll just leave her a letter."

Jeems slammed the trace chains over the harness peg and turned to Lex a face that startled him.

"Sal ain't visiting any girl. If she *is* my own sister, she's nothing but a—"

"Hold on, now! What do you mean? Sal's a nice girl, and you know she's waiting for me."

"She ain't a nice girl and she ain't waiting. She's married to that Serenius Brown who's hiding out from fighting."

It jolted Lex so that he took a grip on the stable door beside him. But he felt neither the grief nor the rage occasioned by his father's death and the loss of his home. He was able to feel only a dull wonder. . . .

"I hate to tell you now, on top of all you gone through. But I tell you this: 'stead of her doing you wrong, it's the best piece of luck yet come your way."

"I—I ain't blaming her. But"—he was recalling her ardor that last night in the swing—"it's just that she said she'd wait."

"Sal wouldn't wait for nobody. All she wants is a man—any man."

"How'd it happen Serenius wasn't called in the militia?"

"It didn't happen. Serenius fixed it. Soon as he knew he was going to be called, he said he had a call from God to preach. I told him: 'I think too much of God to believe He'd go hog-calling.'"

"What did Sal think about that?"

"She thinks the sneaking coward is doing the smart thing. She thinks you and I are fools to feel we ought to fight."

"She did say something like that the last time I talked to her. But I couldn't think she meant it. When did she marry Serenius?"

"Day after Samantha brought me home. First thing she asked was why you hadn't come too if you got far as the Sellers place with me. Both Samantha and I told her Colonel Horry had sent young Conway by to tell you to meet him in Williamsburg."

"Didn't she understand I had to do that?"

"No. She flew up in the air like that little old bantam

hen does when she's setting. She said so much and said it so loud that Ma hauled off and slapped her 'side the head."

"What did she say, Jeems? What *could* she say?"

"She jumped on Samantha. Samantha was just looking at her—but she was looking a plenty. Sal screams, 'Don't you look at me that way! You, a widow woman, grabbed off a boy could be your son. Lex had a right to come back here with Jeems! I'm going to marry Serenius now if it's the last thing I do—and it's all Lex's fault! You stop looking at me like I'd done him wrong!' "

"What did Samantha say to that?"

"Samantha says, 'Don't put words in my mouth because you got guilt in your own heart. Besides, I don't think you'll be doing Lex Mourne wrong. I think you'll be doing him a big favor.'

"Sal squalled louder at that, and Ma slapped her sideways. Pa came in then—he and Gavin had heard her yelling clear out to the forge. Pa stands up in the door and says, 'Let her marry Serenius and go. I'm glad to be shut of her—and if Lex ain't glad at first, he'll sure be glad later on.' "

36

IT SEEMED TO LEX THAT THERE WAS NO ROOM FOR ANYTHING but hatred in his heart: hatred for the enemy who had caused this disaster. He knew that the land would wait for him and that he would someday go back to build a small house on the hill and break the fallow fields. But his father's death, while less horrible than hanging, had been caused by the enemy just as surely as if they had hanged him. He even blamed them—unfairly—for Sal's dereliction. His brain had told him all along that she only wanted a man—any man—and her own brother had confirmed it. But his heart and his injured pride argued that she would have been his wife if war had not called him from her.

Both that thought and the real grief for his father were transmuted into hatred for the British. He came back to Marion thin-faced and hard-eyed.

"Lexington Mourne, sir, reporting for duty. I rode your horse hard; but I've rubbed him down and he's all right."

"Your father?"

"He died three days ago."

"I'm sorry, Mourne. He was my friend."

"I'd like to get into action as soon as I can."

"I've already spoken to Hugh Horry and his regimental officers. You are a sergeant and will have several men under your orders. The Brigade is dividing into small bands for new assignments."

The work ahead was a hide-and-seek game with Tarleton, who—hurried from a sickbed by Earl Cornwallis—was

175

endeavoring to rejoin his legion in the Back Country. After missing him at Nelson's Ferry, Marion stalked and was in turn stalked by him. Prisoners were taken upon both sides, although no battle of any importance was joined.

Sergeant Lexington Mourne, detached for reconnaissance, brought his squad of two men into camp one night when these captures were being discussed. Several men taken by the Partisans from the Tories were of American birth and claimed they had not enlisted but been impressed. According to their story, they would, if not captured, sooner or later have escaped and joined the Continentals. It could have been true. Such things were happening.

"I wouldn't trust them," said young Dalzell. "A liar is always a liar. If they lied to the Tories they'll lie to us too."

"I reckon you're right. A liar kind of cuts the ground from under your feet."

But Lex was not especially interested in the news of the prisoners. He was wondering what effect his report to Marion would have on the activities of the Brigade. He had been sent to contact General Sumter, and he knew that gamecock to be ready and willing for attack.

"Just by looking at him," young Service was saying, "you'd know that man with the clawed-up face was a liar and a traitor."

But Lex and his small squad were sent out again immediately, and he never had a chance to see the traitor or to judge of his lying.

The work was exciting and dangerous, and he and the men with him were furnished the fastest and surest-footed mounts available. They covered the whole section between Marion's and Sumter's camps, keeping both Swamp Fox and Game Cock informed of all hostile activity in it. They worked singly, being deployed by Lex so as to cover the ground most advantageously. More than one of them only escaped capture by the speed of his horse and its ability to dash directly into the swamp at a spot where boggy footing and jungle growth slowed up even the most enthusiastic pursuer. Every one of them knew that capture meant certain hanging; for they were spying on the enemy. As autumn came on, Lex had the satisfaction of carrying word to his commander that Tarleton had gone after Sumter and been defeated on the Tyger River.

In that October occurred also the major British defeat of King's Mountain. It caused rejoicing all through the Back Country. But Partisan leaders realized that the foe, although losing now whenever they joined in battle, still held a line of fortified posts which controlled South Carolina and northern Georgia. Georgetown, Camden, Winnsboro, Ninety-Six and Augusta formed a great circle, reaching back to Charles Town. Within this was an arc with troops at Fort Watson, the Motte house and Granby. Besides these lines there were British strongholds at Dorchester-on-the-Ashley, Monck's Corner, Biggin and Orangeburg, as well as at Nelson's Ferry and Scott's Lake.

And after bringing good news from several reconnaissance trips, Lex was now obliged to bring the news of General Sumter's desperate illness. Critically wounded in the chest, he had been taken by some of his men—swung in an oxhide for litter—to a secret place where the enemy could not find him.

That put an end to Lex's work in the Back Country. But he had been in camp only two days when the older Conway came to him.

"General says you know a place called South Bank on the Santee."

Lex pricked up his ears. "I do. What about it?"

"Seems like a half-Injun there gets news up and down

the river. A lot of those fancy planters is friends with Red-coat officers."

"Well, these people ain't. I know them. They're Patriots."

"That's why we're goin' there," said Conway, unperturbed.

"When? Why?" demanded Lex.

"We're startin' now, so's you kin tell this Injun I'm Marion's scout an' he's to tell me all he finds out. Seems like, if he don't know who you is, he's liable to put a knife in you before you kin tell him."

It sounded just like Banjo, and Lex asked no more questions. He accepted his good luck gratefully and started at once with Conway. The old scout said that the way was clear, so they traveled the highroad following the south shore. Lex straightened his leather cap and wished he had been able to dress less shabbily as they rode the back approach of the laurel avenue. Fire, in the old brown riding skirt, was talking to Sam in the stable yard.

For just a moment she stood staring—then she cried out and ran toward him. Lex jumped from his saddle and met her with open arms. She threw her own arms around his neck, burying her face against his doeskin shirt—and before he realized it he had dropped his head and was kissing her soft burnished-copper hair.

37

WITH THE REALIZATION OF WHAT HE WAS DOING, HORROR swept over Lex. He had kissed Sal with an enjoyment spoiled by no misgivings, even before he had any serious intentions. But to kiss Toff's little sister—a girl who made a man think of sunshine on broom fields or of moonlight on honeysuckle...

He lifted his head and pulled away, almost pushing her from him. But she clung to him, lifting eyes that were darker gray with tears.

"Oh, Lex! Lex, we've heard about your home and your father!"

So that was why she had run into his arms. Her sympathy had carried her away, and he had taken advantage of it.

His face burned with shame, but it was too deeply tanned to betray the flush. Fire saw the distress of his expression. She put both hands on his shoulders.

"Poor Lex! Don't look like that! We're all your friends, and we love you. I'd do anything to help you. I'm so glad you came to us."

Lex saw old Conway's sharp little eyes fixed upon him with the brightness of interest. It made him more self-conscious, and he spoke abruptly.

"I was glad of the chance to get here and see—see all of you. But I came on business for General Marion. Mr. Conway is one of his scouts and wants to talk to Banjo."

That did not seem to surprise her.

179

"Do you want Sam to call Banjo—or would you rather go to his cabin?"

"We'll go to his cabin."

"Then you'll come on to the house? You'll be able to stay with us, Lex?"

"I'll come to the house while Conway and Banjo are talking. But we've got to ride back to camp tonight."

She accepted that without protest, although she looked disappointed. It struck him that her manner was more mature and responsible, although she moved as swiftly and lightly as the childish Fire he had first met. As she started for the big house and he and Conway for the river, he glanced back and told himself it might be the way she now wore her hair. It was piled high on her head—as Peggy had worn hers—but was less formally arranged, with looser curls. Perhaps he had rumpled it by his ill-mannered behavior. But his face began to burn again at memory of its silkiness and its faint scent of rose water.

He left Conway with Banjo, having agreed to meet the old scout in an hour at the stables. Felix awaited him at the front door, and as he talked with the butler he glanced at the drawing room, half expecting to see Peggy—Peggy in her picture frame of yellow-gold silk and rosebuds. She was not there. But another girl was running down the great staircase: a tall slender girl in a pale-green dress, soft lips parted and big eyes bright, and hair even more burnished gold than the roses that Peggy wore.

"Mother told me to bring you up to her sitting room," Fire said. "She hasn't been well and seldom comes downstairs."

He expressed regret as he followed her, glancing around at the spacious plantation house where he had been happy. It seemed even more beautiful by contrast with the hardship in which he lived now with the Swamp Fox band. The mahogany stair rail was satiny under his hand, and steps were soundless in the deep-piled carpets. Mrs. Lane's boudoir was paneled and upholstered in gray silk, and an open fire struck gleams from its dull-gold curtains. She lay in a chaise longue, and she took Lex's hand and drew him down and kissed his cheek.

"We have been grieving for you, my dear boy, ever since Banjo heard the bad news and told us."

"Thank you, ma'am. I'm sorry you're sick."

"I'm quite well again, but I worry about Fire. The child is working too hard. She has taken on all my duties, and she helps her father too."

"Now, darling," said Fire, "it was worrying made you ill." She turned to Lex. "We had news that Toff was wounded."

As he exclaimed, she added quickly: "It was only a slight wound, and we've heard that it's healing fast. But now that mother has no excuse to worry over him, she insists upon worrying over me."

Mrs. Lane said: "Because she rides alone all over the plantation. Her father says she's safe, but I do not feel she is."

Lex smiled. "She used to do that when I first came here."

"I remember. You helped Toff hunt for me when I ran away, and once you brought me back on the horse behind your saddle."

She adjusted the gray and gold pillows under her mother's head, stroking the beautiful white hair and scolding gently.

"Did you hear what Lex said? Since I rode alone safely as a little girl, I must be even safer now that I'm grown up."

Lex looked at the piquant face, not so perfect as Peggy's face, but by turns wistful, sparkling or grave. He thought of deserters from both sides who hid in the woods and sneaked up on farms to steal food. He was suddenly troubled, and he spoke gravely.

"I'm not saying that. Why do you ride alone?"

"In order to carry messages and do errands for Father. Our overseer left to join the Tories. We never liked him, and we're trying to get on without a white overseer. But it puts too much work on Father, and somebody has to help him. He rode to Jamestown today, on business."

"I'm sorry to miss him. Will you tell him I sent my respects?"

"I will—and I know he'll be sorry not to have seen you, Lex."

"So will Peggy," said Mrs. Lane. "She's spending a few weeks with friends in the Winyah district." She added: "Peggy's so accustomed to gaiety that she finds it dreary with only Tory families around us."

It pleased Lex to think that Peggy was no longer associating with Tories. It helped him lull to sleep a questioning in his mind as to why she could not have stayed at home and nursed her mother and kept the house while Fire helped Mr. Lane. At least she had turned her back upon Lionel Fortesque and the people against whom her brother was fighting. As for Fire, although she looked willow-slender in the green gown, she had a radiance which belied her mother's fears about overwork. She continued to laugh at those fears, and she did not tell him of many real difficulties which war had brought to South Bank. She gave him details about Toff's wounded arm, and she read Toff's latest letter to him while he ate a supper brought by Felix.

"I've already told Felix to give Mr. Conway a meal in the dining room."

"There's no need for that," Lex assured her and the butler. "Banjo had sweet potatoes roasting in the ashes and a shoulder of venison on the spit by his fire. They'll eat while they're talking, and"—his voice grew regretful—"I'll have to ride as soon as they get through."

And on that ride he carried with him the cheer and warmth of the gray-gold room, and the kindness and sympathy which had welcomed him to it. He even forgave himself for daring to kiss Fire's hair. The happy thought occurred to him that, since she could not see out of the top of her head, she was quite unaware he had done so.

He frowned as he looked at old Conway, jogging beside him in silence and chewing leaf tobacco. It might be well to tell the scout that he, Lex, was looked upon like a brother by his friend Toff Lane's sisters. But memory of the gleam in two shrewd little eyes kept him silent.

The visit had made him happier than he had been since his father's death. The two women, although externally a contrast to Samantha, had given him the same feeling of comfort and contentment she did. He saw it all again in his mind: the laurel avenue—the house—Mrs. Lane's boudoir. . . .

And the picture that was clearest and stayed longest with him was not the picture of a dark-haired girl in yellow at the drawing-room doors.

It was that of a slim girl with hair like flame from pine wood, running down the stairs in a dress the pale green of young oak leaves.

38

BEFORE THE NEW YEAR MARION MOVED HIS CAMP TO WHAT
was probably the most famous of the Swamp Fox dens.

Snow Island lay in a loop of creek on the east bank of
the Peedee, just below the place where Lynch's River
flowed into it. Moated by nature and surrounded by miles
of swamp, it was both a safe retreat and a formidable
stronghold. Only a scout could find his way to it. There
were neither bridges nor roads to cross its jungles and bogs
and lagoons. The Partisans had secret paths by which they
emerged unexpectedly to strike the foe—then disappear
again. They needed no roads or bridges for their horses
trained to the country. Their sentries, posted around the
camp in the tops of the tallest trees, kept watch in case of
enemy penetration.

The sixth sense which made Francis Marion a great
leader caused him at this time to abandon caution and
take the offensive in a way he had not done before. His
raids cut communication between Cornwallis and his
colonels. His raiders captured supplies bound for the British at Georgetown and Charles Town. In desperation the
high commander sent his favorite—the bold and cruel
Banastre Tarleton—to seek out and destroy the Swamp
Fox's camp and his men. This expedition failed even to
find Snow Island.

And Marion continued to strike harder than ever before.
He was now commandeering Negro laborers and horses
from Patriots as well as seizing them from Tories. He be-

gan to arrest those men who had so far refused to identify themselves with either side and give them the choice of remaining enemy prisoners or declaring openly for and aiding the Continental cause.

Snow Island, ringed about on all sides by British forces, continued to act as a thorn of swordlike proportions in British flesh. Superior numbers of Tories and Regulars, better armed and better trained than the men they hunted, still failed to locate it. But from it sallied small swift-riding groups, to plunder a convoy or throw a column into confusion.

One of the best-known leaders of these sally parties was Captain Conyers, who made a joust of war. A man of heroic figure and romantic mind, he appeared to enjoy his tilting with death. Sometimes he ventured alone close to an enemy camp and, hurling insults at its commanding officer, dared him to ride out alone and engage in single-handed combat. These invitations were never accepted. On the contrary—and naturally—the whole opposing force was called to horse to chase him. Because of his speedy and well-trained charger, he was never captured, but disappeared in the swamp laughing loudly over his shoulder at them. The men of his company loved him, boasted of his exploits, and sympathized with him in his attachment to a young lady by name of Witherspoon.

The two Conways, father and son, knew that part of South Carolina as Lex knew the High Hills. It was young Conway who brought to Francis Marion the news of his nephew's murder.

The scout walked tight-lipped through the camp and to his commander's tent. Watching him, Lex and Edisto saw that the news he carried was bad. When he came out of the shelter Marion followed him and stood alone for a moment—hand on his rusty sword hilt and eyes staring as if beyond the swamp. His Negro servant just then approached with a tray of food. Lex heard the Swamp Fox say harshly: "Take that away!" Then he turned on his heel and began pacing to and fro.

Lex and Edisto hurried after young Conway and, when they were a safe distance away, demanded: "What's happened?"

"The British have killed the General's nephew, young Gabriel Marion. He was an officer wearing a lieutenant's uniform when they captured him. They had taken away his arms and he was standing helpless with other prisoners. As soon as they found out his name they shot him in cold blood—on the spot, without a trial and without a prayer."

Captain Conyers came up in time to overhear. He began to rave like a man gone berserk.

"Who did it? By the heavens above, I'll get the man who did it and hang him right here in the swamp!"

Conway said: "I haven't yet found out the name of the officer in charge of the prisoners. He's the man responsible, whoever fired the gun."

The angry circle was widening. Men clenched their fists and cursed and demanded the names of the dastards.

Captain Conyers had his own sword in his hand. He gestured so violently with it that even the men who admired him most moved beyond his reach.

"The officer's responsible—but the whole troop should be hanged along with him."

Conway nodded. "A farmer told me he was watching from behind his fence. He said they grabbed Gabriel Marion and pulled him out of line, and when the boy saw what they were going to do he called to the officer in command: 'I'm a prisoner of war! Aren't you going to protect me?'

"The man who was watching said the officer turned his back while they shot young Gabriel down."

A yell of rage went up from the men assembled. Captain

Conyers and other officers started toward the place where Marion paced alone. The rest of the camp waited, talking excitedly, hoping for orders to ride at once on a raid of revenge.

But when their officers came back Captain Conyers shook his head.

"I know what you want to do," he told them with the understanding which endeared him to them, "and I want to do it as badly as you do. But the General's orders are *no reprisals*. He says he's going to keep the rules of war."

An inarticulate growl of rage and curses told him that they read his mind and agreed with what he was thinking. He translated it and replied before he turned away: "All I hope is that you and I will have the luck to catch that officer and the swine he calls his 'men.' If we do, all I can say is that when I'm fighting mad I'm liable to forget a few of the rules of war."

They broke into groups as he left them; but although they were weary they could not settle to sleep for long hours yet. They moved as close as they dared, to watch that silent man who paced, his thin shoulders bowed slightly and his set face expressionless.

"God knows I'd like to help him," said Lex. "But I don't dare go near him."

"You better not dare," young Conway said. "He wants to be alone."

"Then can't you tell us any other news? Didn't you hear anything else—anything that can cheer us up?"

Young Conway reflected. "I'd forgot. I was so mad about this fool thing. But it seems like the younger Witherspoon gal—the one that's Cap'n Conyers' gal—knocked the devil out of a British officer."

They were pleased to hear it and urged the scout to continue.

"A British column that used to be under Tarleton is

camped close by the Witherspoon place. The Witherspoons are Patriots, but naturally they do all they can to
keep from getting burned out. The British officers hang
'round and try to beau the young ladies. 'Sides the two
daughters, they got a pretty visiting gal. Seems like a Redcoat named Fay is sweet on her."

Lex pricked up his ears. "Conway, you said *Fay?*"

"Yes. Sounds like a fancy name—name for a gal and not
a man. Anyway, this visiting gal lets him come to see her.
The Witherspoons don't like it; but same as I told you,
they don't want to do anything to get their house burned.
One day this Britisher comes in and says in his fancy voice,
'I am informed that the ruffian Conyers is somewhere in
this vicinity.'

"The gal he came to see just listens and smiles, but the
Witherspoon gal jerks her shoe off her foot. The Negro
who's butler told me the story, and he saw it all. He said
it warn't any soft shoe but a hard one she wore walking,
and it was covered with mud besides.

"She says, 'You coward, you, why don't you go out and
meet him then?'

"And she hits him so hard in the face that she breaks the
round glass he wears in one eye."

"Glory," exclaimed a voice from the shadows beyond
the campfire, "he will burn the plantation house now!"

"He might have," said Conway, "except for the other
girl. She ketches him by the arm and begs him, for her
sake, to forgive her friend. The butler says she's so pretty
and Fay's so crazy about her that he promises to forget it
all."

They shook their heads in wonder and they praised the
Witherspoon girl. They thought her a fit sweetheart for
the captain they followed.

Only Lex sat silent. It must be Evelyn Fay. Mr. Gaylord
had remembered his "fancy name." It must be the officer

who had sat his tall red horse while the Mourne farm-house burned on a Santee hill. Oh, for a chance to meet him in battle! The Witherspoon place was not far away, and perhaps Francis Marion would allow him . . .

He turned to the young scout with an abruptness that matched his thoughts.

"Do you know the name of the visiting girl that the Britisher is sweet on?"

"I never saw her," said Conway. "I was hid out in the barn. The butler told me the story and he spoke of her as 'Miss Lane.'"

39

SINCE THE BRIGADE HAD ENTRENCHED ITSELF AT SNOW ISLAND, Lex Mourne had been told by Colonel Hugh Horry to go to the corral and take his choice of the commandeered horses. He had selected a powerful roan, tall enough for his long legs. It carried him well but showed wicked white in its eye and was apt to kick other horses that came too near. Although assigned to him, it was not his personal property, and every sally that he rode aroused new hope for the capture of a real cavalry charger.

The day after hearing about the Witherspoon girl and Fay, he went to Marion and asked leave to scout at the Witherspoon place. His commander stared for seconds with black eyes which seemed to bore through him.

"For what reason would you go? This is not your section and you do not know it as the Conways do."

"No, sir. But I can find my way to the Witherspoons."

"Are they friends of yours?"

The piercing look caused him to hesitate.

"No—no, sir. But a young lady I know is visiting there."

"I am aware that Miss Peggy Lane is their guest. Are you asking permission to go to see her?"

That had not been Lex's idea. His only desire was to get information about the officer described by Mr. Gaylord—perhaps by some chance in a hundred to meet him and force him to fight. After Peggy's rebuff he would not have cared to visit her. The very suggestion aroused his stubborn Scottish pride and he blurted: "I'm not going to

190

see any girl. Major Fay is the man who burned my home."

The dark eyes in the haggard face made him drop his own angry gray ones.

"Request refused," said Marion. "What you need to learn, young Mourne, is to put personal feelings aside while you are in the service of South Carolina."

As Lex raised a hand to his cap and turned, his commander added: "Wait! Do not go away thinking you are the only one. It's a bitter lesson which I have been trying to teach myself all the long night past."

He kept his word and refused to allow reprisals, and his officers saluted and withdrew—as Lex had done. But every man in camp was doing all he could to find out who and where were Gabriel Marion's killers. Within a few days old Conway brought them the information. To the last man they memorized it and prayed for a meeting. They said nothing to the General, but they discussed their plans with one another.

At just this time General Greene wrote General Marion a letter which expressed his appreciation of the Partisans' achievements. After General Gates' unco-operative attitude, the letter was encouraging. But Nathaniel Greene did more than write: he detached Lieutenant Colonel Lee to effect a junction with the Swamp Fox and to co-operate with him in every way. The Continental Regulars and the Robin Hood band which saved South Carolina were at long last accomplishing a union.

It was from Light Horse Harry Lee's men that Lex received his next news of Evelyn Fay. These men and their commander were at first labeled as "fancy" by the hard-living Back Countrymen whom they had joined. But the Virginians were born cavalrymen, as were Marion's raiders, and the fellowship of courage and mutual purpose soon smoothed out difficulties. Sitting around campfires and cursing the scanty fare, they talked of many things—but mostly of horses.

"We saw the strangest thing coming down here," a man named Page confided to Lex. "It was back of a big country house on the last day's ride."

"Next to a camp the British had just abandoned," put in another newcomer.

Page laughed. "Yes, they abandoned it soon as they knew we were coming. But, although the redbirds had flown, we saw another kind of bird—kind you call vulture."

"We call 'em turkey buzzards," corrected Edisto.

"Well, whatever you call 'em," Page went on, "Colonel Lee told Smith and me to ride over and see what was attracting 'em."

Lex and his comrades listened, wondering if the buzzards had collected because of some human being shot or hanged.

"It was a horse," said Lee's cavalryman. "Your buzzards had been busy, but enough of him was left to know that he had been red bay and a stallion."

Lex was incredulous. "Could you tell how he was killed? There's been no fighting along that road. Anyway, we shoot men—not horses."

"He wasn't killed in battle." Lee's cavalryman grimaced as he chewed his leathery beef. "Ain't you poor fellows got any salt around here?"

"Only when we get out and take it from a British convoy. Go on and tell us about the horse!"

"The officer owned him killed him so your crowd couldn't get him. The Negro butler told me, and the Witherspoon ladies told Colonel Lee. He was some special breed of horse raised by the family of that officer over in England."

These men who killed other men in battle looked at each other, utterly aghast.

"The butler seemed to know all about it. He said a courier galloped into the British camp in the night to bring the commander word that Lee's Legion was approaching. The major in charge wanted to stay and fight, but the messenger had orders for him to break camp at once, since we outnumbered them. Butler said that in the hurry and confusion some of the horses broke loose and tore around the pasture in the dark. Troopers recaptured all except this stallion. He was especially strong and swift."

"Seems like they would have let him go rather than have killed him."

"Not this Major Fay. Time and again the Witherspoon ladies and the servants had heard him brag nobody except the Fay family owned a Red Doe, and that he'd shoot his own charger before he'd let any damned rebel get the strain."

Marion's men swore softly as they chewed their unsalted beef. To a man they loved horses, no matter who rode them. Horses were not only innocent tools of war, they were desperately needed by the Partisans.

Some practical soul inquired: "What did the major figure to ride after he shot his own mount?"

"He's got another: a young mare is full sister to the stallion. He rides so hard that he needs two, and he sent to England for the filly not long ago."

"Even so . . ." Lex said, speaking half to himself. For his thoughts had gone back to what Fire and Toff had told him. The stallion was surely the same mount that Fire had described, but he had not known of the filly.

"Even so, it sounds crazy," he said hotly. "One thing you've got to grant the British is that they love horses. I wonder the troopers obeyed an order to shoot a horse."

"They didn't. The butler said they were shooting in the air. He said it looked like what he thought hell was, with running horses neighing and screaming in torchlight and muskets being discharged and Fay yelling orders and cursing. When all the other horses were caught and the column was drawn up and waiting, this major swings his mare from its head and rides to the pasture gate.

" 'Open it for me, you fools,' he says, 'and mount your own horses and fall in.'

"They can see him ride across to where the stallion was standing, throwing his head down to paw, then throwing it high again.

"He stands that way, watching, and lets his master ride up near him. Then he rears nervously and screams—and as he wheels to run again Fay drops him with the first bullet."

For minutes there was dead silence around the campfire. Then a man said devoutly: "He oughta have his neck broke."

The Virginian said: "Well, it ain't broke yet. It's just as stiff as ever. They say he's a handsome scoundrel—but mean as they ever come. They say he rode to the head of his column without a look back at the horse.

" 'I'd rather have him dead,' he said out loud, 'than loose to get foals for rebel Americans! *March!*' "

40

WHEN LEX RETURNED FROM HIS NEXT SALLY HE FOUND JEEMS in camp. That night, with Edisto and Sonny and Service and others, they sat around a fire and exchanged news. Jeems had brought a home-cured ham, as well as a large box of shortbread.

"Gavin drove me with the mule; so I told Ma I could bring all she made. Gavin had an idea he'd enlist, but he's too young and I ran him back."

"Ain't he 'most as old as Service and Sonny?" asked Lex.

He looked at the two youngsters, who instead of meeting his eyes stuffed their mouths with shortbread and gazed off at the Spanish moss. It hung all around them like curtains enclosing a firelit room, and the moving light from the flames streaked it rose-to-carmine.

"He's already turned fourteen," said Jeems, "but he's small for his age. If he was long-legged like them, then he could lie like them."

He paused to frown at the two offenders, who looked away as they chewed on hunks of the sweet pink ham. Then he turned back to Lex.

"Johnston told me to tell you his second boy was plowing an acre of your land with the ox. He said to tell you the stock was doing so well he needed to plant more land than his own to feed them."

"I'm willing for him to do it. The woods take back a field quick if you let it lie. Has Adlai got his house built?"

"He's got a two-room cabin, and he figures on adding to

it. His three biggest boys still stay in your barn with the cat."

Lex thought of the old yellow cat, whose name was Pumpkin. . . . He thought of his father weeding the gourds and pumpkins and squashes . . . of moonlit nights and the specter-white sycamore boles. . . .

"How's Vidette?"

"He's fine. He runs at night, so he'll never get fat."

Nights in the hills when the poignant scent of the honeysuckle was everywhere. . . . Like the moonlight it had no favorites. . . . It belonged to anybody who loved it. . . . Fire loved it, and Fire had said . . .

He turned abruptly to young Conway, who made one of their group.

"Did you ever find out where that horse-killer Fay marched to?"

"Yes. He marched directly south and crossed the Santee. Then he turned west on the south shore road. Pa sent me back to tell Marion while he stayed on their tail."

Lex pictured Fay's column of Redcoats crawling like a bright snake along the southern bank of the Santee. They would have to pass the Lane plantation. Was Toff still in North Carolina, or had he been detached like Colonel Lee's men? How were Mr. and Mrs. Lane? Had Peggy returned from the Witherspoons? What of Fire?

Led by Captain Conyers, they rode out before the next daybreak in the direction of Indian Town. They were not told where they were going or what the business was; but soon after they cleared the swamp, whispers ran like wisps of smoke among them.

"Cap'n says we're in for a skirmish."

"Skirmish with Tories or Regulars?"

They hated the Tories more than they hated the British-born, and consequently a fight against them was even more welcome.

"Cap'n didn't say—but he says *take prisoners.*"

They surprised the foe in a farmyard, eating the noon meal. The fight was brief and decisive. Only a few escaped. The others threw down their arms and were rounded up by the raiders while Captain Conyers rode off to talk with the farmer nearby. When he came back to his party, his face was dangerous.

"If one of these prisoners escapes between here and Snow Island," he told them, "the man who lets him escape will get what that prisoner would have got."

They started back at once, with Lex and Jeems riding in the vanguard. Behind them the prisoners rode in a single line with a Partisan on guard to right and left of each. Dusk fell before they entered the swamp, and the whispers began again.

"We've got the ones who murdered the General's nephew."

"What makes you think so?"

"Are you sure?"

"Any fool would know it. Didn't you see Cap'n Conyers talking with the farmer—the same one that told Conway?"

"Besides that, one of the prisoners told his commanding officer's name."

"Think Marion'll hang him?"

"No—I'm sure he won't."

"Wish Cap'n Conyers would let us stop and do it right now."

"Better keep your mouth shut, or Conyers'll hang *you.*"

Lex, still riding in the lead, explained the matter to Jeems. The swamp slowed them, and they rode single file —except for where the prisoners were surrounded by their guards. They were halfway in to the island when a commotion broke out behind Lex and Jeems. There were confused noises—several shots—and then shouts. Conyers on his huge horse plowed through bog to the front of the line.

"Halt!" he ordered. "Who did that? Some of you must have seen him."

"Seen who?" they asked him. "Who did what, Cap'n?"

"You know as well as I do. An officer rode this way."

It was dark in the swamp. All that the vanguard had seen was a Continental officer's back as he galloped off in the trees to one side. That back had looked familiar, but they could not identify . . .

Conyers was swearing. "The General will have my hide for this!"

"For what, Cap'n?" Jeems asked him. "We don't yet know what it is."

"I was a quarter mile behind with a couple of scouts. You know I always cover my party that way, so that nobody can sneak in and see the way we go."

"Yes, sir. We know," chorused Jeems and Lex.

Whispers along the column had told them what had occurred.

"When I heard those shots I galloped up. All anybody can tell me is that one of our own officers rode alongside in the darkness, shot our captured officer and dashed off again."

"That's go—I mean bad," said Jeems. "Is the skunk dead?"

"Dead and in hell by now," said Captain Conyers. "I'm not worried about him. What I'm worried about is the officer who shot him."

But he need not have worried. By some strange chance, even the men who guarded the prisoner had not recognized his killer. The officer who dashed off into the swamp had evidently circled around and joined the column behind Conyers when he rode forward. The knowledge that he stood among them while Marion questioned them, helped them to endure the ordeal.

After an hour the Swamp Fox turned, enraged but helpless, toward his tent. He knew when he was beaten, and he saw that no torture could draw from a man of that party the name of the executioner.

41

MARION'S WORDS WERE FEW, BUT HIS ANGER WAS GENUINE. Stalwart Captain Conyers squared his broad shoulders and took it. Too late, realization came to the band that with the guilty officer dead there was even less chance of identifying the guilty troopers. Most of the scouts agreed that the only fair thing to do would be to hang them all. But Marion, grim-faced, ordered that they be treated like any other prisoners.

Young Gabriel was dead, and the killing of his murderer had done nothing to make his death less horrible. It dwelt continually on Lex's mind. He knew—as did everyone else in the band except Marion—the officer who had done the deed in the swamp. But, like everyone else, he would have both lied and died before revealing it.

And then something happened to turn his thoughts elsewhere. Young Conway shook him out of his blanket before dawn.

"Pa's just got in camp, and he's brought a gal with him. The General says for you to come—and to come fast!"

The general had spread his newly acquired blanket on a bit of high ground before his tent. His campfire still burned, for it was damply cold and day had not yet broken. The red light of the flames played on Fire's hair, which spread over her shoulders and hung past her waist. She was trying to push it back and pin it up on her head; but when she saw Lex she let it fall and held out both hands to him. As he gripped them and looked down at her,

he saw that her face was scratched and as dirty as it had
been on the afternoon she fell in the river. She was blink-
ing the tears from her eyes and trying to steady her voice.
All she could say was: *"Lex! Oh, Lex!"*

Marion patted her shoulder. "My dear, you must sit
down. You have been walking all night. Come over here
on my blanket."

He led her to it as if he had been leading a queen to a
throne. As she crossed her ankles and dropped to a seat
as easily as a child, her copper-gold hair trailed behind
her.

"Fire—are you hurt? You *couldn't* walk all that way!
Fire, tell me what has happened!"

"I didn't walk all the way," she said—but he heard the
weariness in her voice. "I've had Toff's dugout hidden in
the willows ever since he went away." She smiled faintly.
"The same dugout I turned over when we went to meet
you, Lex."

"But if you crossed the river there you had several miles
of swamp between you and the Georgetown road. And the
road—and the country between there and here—is full of
raiding parties. Fire—you—alone . . ."

"I wasn't alone. But I would have come alone if I'd had
no other way. Banjo got me across the river and through
the swamp. He got me to the place near the road where
he always meets Mr. Conway. Yesterday Mr. Conway got
me a ride for miles in a farm cart."

Several officers who tented near their commander had
been awakened, and they began to approach. Lex was so
intent upon Fire that he did not notice them or turn. He
went down on one knee beside her on the blanket.

"But why did you leave South Bank?"

"Because I couldn't stand that Major Fay."

Lex's voice rose to a shout. "Major Fay? At your home?"

"He occupied it almost a week ago. Several companies

of cavalry are camped around the stables, and he and his officers quartered themselves in the house."

"Do you mean he turned you and your family out?"

"No—and, to be truthful, he's treating us better than most British officers would. He is acting under orders from Earl Cornwallis; and he says that under a new decree Father has either to take parole or be sent to prison in Charles Town."

"Has Peggy come home?"

"Yes. Why do you ask?"

"Because I know this infernal Fay has lost his head over her."

The big gray eyes in the small, pale, dirty face seemed to flash sparks at him.

"Oh, you know that, do you? Well—you take a whole lot for granted!"

At that point Lex heard Conyers' voice, eager but pitched low and ingratiating. "General, can I assist you and this lovely young lady in any way?"

Lex rose to his feet, glowering. He knew that Captain Conyers could woo as enthusiastically as he could fight. But this was a case where Lex ranked his superiors. It was his prerogative to protect Toff's little sister from romantic Continentals, as well as from villainous Redcoats. Had it been Peggy, she might have turned from him to the newest suitor. Fire did not coquet, and men did not seek her as they sought Peggy. But to his amazement she was smiling up at Conyers, and in spite of stains and scratches that smile made her entrancing.

"I thank you, Captain, but I am in General Marion's hands. Your offer honors me. I have often longed to see an officer of whose bravery the whole Low Country is talking."

Conyers' face lit with joy. He swept the muddy ground

with his cap, took a step toward her—stumped the toe of his boot on a cypress knee and nearly fell.

Lex stood his ground with folded arms, not yielding an inch and not putting out a hand to help his superior. As Conyers recovered, Marion spoke.

"I thank you, gentlemen, but I do not need you. The young lady is a daughter of one of my oldest friends, and Sergeant Mourne is her brother's friend."

It was by now light enough for Lex to see disappointment on the faces of Conyers and Postell and the Horrys as they turned away. But he had no sympathy for them. They were old men, he told himself—some of them more than thirty—and they had no business to come and grin that way at a young girl. Fire must resent it—in spite of the silly way she had smiled at Conyers and flattered him. She was probably too tired to know what she was doing. That was the reason she snapped at him, Lex, when he told her he knew that Fay had lost his head over Peggy.

Marion's Negro servant came up just then with a wooden shingle serving as tray for three bowls of lye hominy. Marion sat on the blanket on Fire's other side and beckoned to Lex to seat himself.

"We'll have breakfast together while we make our plans. There's only one piece of bacon, so it goes to the lady."

He insisted that she eat the unappetizing boiled corn before he allowed her to talk any more. Then he said quietly: "Do you realize, Sophia, that you cannot return to your home?"

She flashed: "*I would not if I could*—so long as Major Fay is there."

Marion's eyes seemed to be reading her mind, so intent was their gaze. Fire dropped her own eyes and a faint flush spread from her throat over her face.

"I think I understand," said the general in his low, steady voice. "But there is another and even more dangerous angle to this affair. I know all about Fay. He is a second Tarleton. He is bound to guess that you have escaped to his enemies, and he knows you have knowledge of both his location and his strength. He may—as Tarleton would—treat you as a spy if he can find you."

Fire started: "I'd rather that than—"

She stopped in midsentence.

"No," said Marion. "You would not rather. You would die if thrown in a filthy prison crowded with rough and evil women. I shall send you to some safe place—and you will do as I say."

"I'll do whatever you say. Could—could Mr. Conway get word to Mother and Father that I'm safe?"

"I will see to that. Have you any friends in the Back Country?"

She shook her head. "I've never been there. My friends are in Charles Town—or on plantations near the coast."

"That section is British-occupied. Mourne, have you any suggestions?"

"Yes, sir," said Lex. "If she wants to go to the High Hills I know Miz Gaylord would take her in. Otherwise, there's Edisto's wife, Samantha."

"Samantha!" said Marion softly. "You've got the answer, boy!"

42

EDISTO WAS SENT FOR.

He said: "Samantha's lonesome, and she'll be glad to have Miss Lane. Anyway, Gen'l Marion, you know she'd take in anybody *you* asked her to."

"None of us can tell for how long it'll be," warned Marion. He added gravely: "Besides that, the British may be looking for her."

"Then we better get her there quick as we can. You want me to carry her?"

Lex broke in. "No! I'll carry her."

Marion stared him down. "If I give you permission."

"Yes, that's—that's what I mean, sir. I was just thinking . . ."

"I'm thinking too. Perhaps you're the one to do it—since she knows you best of us. You'll have to travel by night, and it's a full night's ride."

"Fire can ride, sir—just as well as any man in your Brigade."

"Perhaps so. But she doesn't look as tough as my scouts, and she'll have to ride a man's saddle and go by secret ways."

Lex promised: "I'll get her there safe."

"You'd better—or I'll know the reason why. Now she can have my tent to rest in until sunset."

At sunset they started, with Fire sitting sideways in a cross saddle. All the officers were back to watch their departure, and more than one offered to relieve Lex of the task. Marion smiled his faint and infrequent smile.

"Sergeant Mourne is a qualified scout, and he knows the way to his objective."

When they cleared the swamp the night was black and the spirited horses were eager to run. Lex knew how precarious is a sideways seat on a Somerset saddle. To reach the Sellers place before day they would have to go full gallop at any places where footing was safe enough.

"Fire, when I first knew you you used to ride astraddle."

"When you first knew me I was a little girl—and you still treat me like a little girl."

"You always seemed to me like one—'til you talked like you did to Conyers. That fellow's a lady-killer. You didn't use to flirt."

"Maybe I'm learning better sense," she told him briefly.

He was completely baffled. This was another and a strange Fire. He told himself that he had done nothing to provoke her. Girls were hard to understand. Horses were much more reasonable. Maybe if he brought the talk back to riding...

"All I meant was that we've got fifteen miles of open road before we take our next short cut. That's a good horse, but he's moon-eyed and likely to shy at night. If you'll fling your right—your right foot over and ride that way, we could make much better time."

"All right," she agreed. "It's too dark for anybody to see."

He was praying that they would not meet anybody as they took that fifteen miles at a steady canter. He had in his belt two pistols that Marion had handed him.

"Leave your rifle," the general had said. "If you encounter a patrol, it will be a case of shooting your way through and outriding them."

He knew the next wood path would bring them out on

the Georgetown road and that for ten miles on it they would be in their greatest danger.

"Now, Fire, listen!" He described the turn from the highroad to the Sellers farm. "If anybody tries to stop us, I'll hold them while you ride on."

"You think I'd do that and leave you?"

"For heaven's sake be sensible," he said in exasperation. "My horse is faster than yours, and I can overtake you."

"You're just saying that to make me go on. Captain Conyers said this was the best mount in the Brigade, except for his and the General's."

"You seem to listen to everything that fellow said. The General sent *me* to take you, not Captain Conyers. The only reason I'm making this ride is to get you safe to Samantha."

She interrupted furiously. "You needn't have bothered. Captain Conyers and Colonel Horry both offered to do it."

"Fire, what's the matter with you? I never called it a bother. You heard me ask the General to let me do it. You know I'd do anything for Toff's family. Not only that, but I've got orders and I'm trying to do my duty."

Her voice was resentful. "At any rate, Major Fay never told me he was trying to do his duty when he—"

"When he what?"

"Oh, never mind! Isn't this the Georgetown road? Hadn't we better gallop again?"

They met no patrols on the Georgetown road, and they reached the Sellers farm just as day was breaking. Samantha put both arms around Fire while she was listening to Lex.

"I'd have been mad at you and Ed if you hadn't brought her. This is a small place and out of the way. They'll never find her here. I just finished milking and I'm making bread. Soon as you eat I'll put her to bed in Sonny's room.

And you'd better get some rest, Lex. You can't start back 'til nightfall."

Both on account of safety and of the horses, he could not. He slept all that day on a bed of quilts in the kitchen. When Samantha woke him she gave him fat letters for Sonny and Edisto.

"Your girl's still sleeping. You want me to wake her?"

"Of course not. And she ain't my girl. She's my friend's little sister. You'll find her the helpful, homey kind. She ain't the kind to make eyes at men."

"Is that the way it is? She's the purtiest thing I ever saw, sleeping there with that hair like gold silk spread all around her. You tell the general I'm proud to have her here and he can count on my taking care of her."

He was disappointed not to have told Fire good-by. But he had needed his own rest, and she needed rest even more. She had washed her face in a bucket before they left the camp. He reckoned she would look pretty with that long, bright hair all around her. . . .

But what he must now think about was getting himself and the two horses back. For half of the way he rode one and led the other, then changed. They were not hot when he turned them into the corral, for he had been obliged to ride in a walk through the swamp. Daylight was beginning to filter through the trees and men were rolling out of their blankets as he started to report to Marion.

Captain Conyers stopped him. "You're a lucky devil, Mourne. That girl's what I call a beauty."

"I don't know what you're talking about, sir."

"Oh, don't you? Well, at least you knew enough to get yourself appointed her escort and to get her hidden safely away from Major Fay's attentions."

"From Major Fay's *attentions?* You're joking, sir. The General said that scoundrel might hang her as a spy."

"Oh no he wouldn't! No man would hang her—so long as she'd smile at him."

"You made a mistake between the sisters, Captain. This Major Fay is sweet on the other one."

"He was before he saw her. I know all about that, son. Her sister stayed with the Witherspoons: a little coquette with a pretty moonface and brown curls that she knows how to toss. No man would give her a second look after he saw that redhead."

Lex stumbled as he went on to Marion's tent. He had hated Fay before, but he was now half-blind with rage. It was bad enough for the Britisher to have been sweet on Peggy, but it was sacrilege for him to think of little Fire.

It came to him in a sudden flash of illumination that little Fire, although slim as a wand, was now half a head taller than Peggy. He had thought a redhead a subject for teasing—but Captain Conyers had dwelt on the word with an unmistakable note in his voice. Samantha had said, "She's the prettiest thing I ever saw, sleeping there with that hair like gold silk spread all around her."

Marion said: "Mourne, you look as if you're walking in your sleep. I expected you to rest yesterday. I have a mission for you."

"I did rest, sir; and I'm ready for it. I'm reporting that Fire—Miss Lane—is safe with Edisto Hawkins' wife."

"That's good news. Now, about this other business. . . . I met you first at the Lane plantation."

"Yes, sir. I remember."

"Just how well do you know South Bank?"

"Almost as well as I know the hills around my home. I've visited Toff several times, and we either rode or shot over every acre of it."

"Now, while it is occupied, could you slip in there and talk with Banjo?"

"I could, sir."

"You are north of the Santee. The British are camped upon and patrolling the south shore road. How would you reach the place?"

"I know my way through the swamp from the George-town road to the north shore. Toff and I used to swim the river, just for fun."

"There'll be no fun about this, Mourne, if you get caught."

"I realize that, sir."

"Young Conway is scouting around Georgetown, and last night I had to send old Conway after a deserter. You and old Conway are the only men to whom Banjo will talk."

"I know, sir—and I can reach Banjo."

"When old Conway brought Miss Fire in, they told me that Major Fay had mentioned he expected re-enforce-ments. If I could know just when and where to ambush that party ..."

Lex said nothing. He had hoped he would be scouting for an attack on Major Fay's command.

"If they once effect a junction with Fay they'll be too strong for us. But if I knew exactly how many are now at South Bank and how many are approaching ..."

"I'll try to get all that, sir. Anything else?"

"Yes. Leave word with Banjo that Miss Fire is safe. Don't go near the big house—or Major Fay. That's all. Start on foot at sunset."

43

BY MIDAFTERNOON OF THE NEXT DAY LEX WAS IN SIGHT OF
the north shore of the Santee River, at a point a quarter
mile upriver from the plantation. Every foot of the journey had brought back to his mind his happy visit to the
Lanes' two years before. He tried to recall the grounds in
perfect detail now, for he knew the success of his mission
was dependent on that. Marion had chosen him because
he believed that Lex knew South Bank well enough to get
into its grounds and obtain firsthand information.

He could not risk swimming the river until after midnight when the half-moon had set. He told himself, too,
that sentries were less alert between that hour and daybreak. So he made a bed of dry leaves between two cypress
knees and curled himself upon it. When he woke the
crooked red moon was gone, and he could tell by the stars
that the night was half past.

He swam the river with long silent strokes, letting the
current take him seaward and across at the same time.
When he felt mud under his feet and waded ashore he
knew that he was at the eastern end of the gardens. Willows fringed the south bank as well as the north one, and
an alley of cedar trees led up to the house. But he avoided
that thoroughfare, crouching deep in the willows, and
waiting to be sure there were no sentries around before he
began to creep toward Banjo's cabin.

When he reached its door and gave the knock that he
and Toff were accustomed to use, there was no sound in

reply. He had expected none. He knew that Banjo would be looking from some hidden peephole to make sure who the visitor was. He also knew that had Banjo seen an enemy there, that enemy would have got a knife in his back before he got a sight of Banjo. But the cabin door opened before him like a shadow moved by moonlight, and he stepped in just as noiselessly.

All the next day he hid in the huntsman's house. Banjo had gone out before dawn to make sure that all traces of footprints were obliterated. Banjo fed him, and showed him how—if anyone came—he could climb the wall by means of two spikes where clothes hung, and lie flat along a broad beam above. Banjo told him all he knew.

But Lex realized that Felix and Sam would know more. Banjo had not been allowed for days to talk with the other two. Mr. and Mrs. Lane and Peggy had been sent to Charles Town when the British learned of Sophia's escape. Felix, the old butler, had been hung up by his thumbs in a vain effort to make him tell where Sophia had gone. Since all this, Major Fay had become more savage, and neither Sam nor Felix dared communicate with Banjo. In fact Banjo was being watched, and Lex decided that he must leave the huntsman as a decoy and himself get at least as far as the stables in order to find out what Sam and Felix knew.

From the stables a quarter mile away came bugle calls and the shouted orders of sergeants. At intervals a sentry walked the path to the cabin, stared woodenly at Banjo who sat on its step mending a fish net, wheeled and paced away.

So the long day had passed, and after dark Lex had descended from the beam and eaten dried venison while he and the huntsman made plans.

"I hates to see you go to Sam and Felix's house. It too near the stables, and sentries walks there all night."

"But I've got to do it," Lex said. "The British have taken your gun and ordered you off the yard and they're watching you besides. The minute that sentry doesn't see you at your house he'll start an alarm and a search. If you stay here with a lantern burning—so anybody can see you through the window—it will help keep them off my track."

Banjo realized the sense in the plan and trailed the sentry while Lex started out that night. He had waited until late, both for cover of darkness and because he wished to find the butler through with his work and at the house he shared with the head stableman.

Avoiding paths, Lex moved through woods and shrubbery. The rustle of every leaf sounded to him like thunder. He was thankful when he at last emerged at the back of the two-room house which was set in a well-swept space at the head of the street of slave cabins. The house was unlighted, but one window shutter was bowed. He recognized it as belonging to Sam's room, and he was glad because he knew that Felix was deaf. For long enough to look and listen for any approach from any side, he stood waiting and watching behind a tree trunk. Then he lay flat on his stomach and for fifty feet dragged himself by inches to the half-open window. As he rose to his feet, trying to merge himself with the cabin wall, he whispered through the shutters: "*Sam—it's me—Lex Mourne.*"

Sam must have been near the window, for his terrified whisper came back. "*Oh, lawd, Mr. Lex! Why you come here? They gwine ketch you!*"

"*Let me in—without making any noise.*"

By the time he had crawled through the window, Felix was in the room too. Lex gripped each man by an arm and drew them close in the darkness.

"Just answer my questions in whispers. If we hurry we're safe. Nobody is anywhere near the house. I looked all around from the yard."

Sam was able to give him the number of cavalrymen, where their sentries were posted, which way rode their patrols. He knew that other troops were expected, but did not know from what command or when or why. Felix supplied that.

"Major Fay tole me at dinner tonight to save the best brandy for Major Wemyss, else I'd get hanged w'en he come next Saturday."

Lex longed to whistle his satisfaction aloud. By this stroke of good fortune the archenemy was delivered into his hands. For he knew approximately where Wemyss was and that there was only one road he could march to the Lane place. With this information, Marion's raiders could wait in ambush upon either side. Scouts could plash the timber ahead and behind to impede retreat and add confusion. He was thinking to himself of what Marion would do as he made his way back to Banjo's cabin.

He found the huntsman troubled. "More soldiers been comin' by here. Don't try to get to the river tonight. They're on the watch, Lex."

"How would they know? You destroyed all my tracks. None of them saw or heard me go to Sam's house."

"I tell you they're watchin' for somethin'. If you're set on goin', I'm goin' ahead of you. That way, if they lays for you I kills 'em with my knife."

"No," said Lex. "This is my job. I told you that before. Besides, if two of us go it gives them two chances to catch us."

He felt surer of himself since his successful trip to Sam's house. He knew that the troops occupying the place were not native Tories but British Regulars, and that they did not know the terrain as he did. He followed the deep garden shrubbery west, knowing the river would carry him east.

He had almost reached the willows, and their leaves were water-pale. As he slipped from the yew border a figure loomed before him and a voice ordered: *"Halt! Stand where you are!"*

44

LEX HURLED HIMSELF TO ONE SIDE INTO THE PALE-LEAVED willows. Even if the sentry shot, shooting was better than hanging. But he hurled himself practically into the arms of two other British soldiers. He fought them like a wildcat, and for a few seconds the three rolled together in the mud. Before he even had a chance, others were upon him. Hands seized his arms and legs; he was dragged to his feet and his wrists twisted behind his back and tied with a neckcloth. Somebody lighted a lantern, and as its light flashed in his face he saw that he was surrounded by about twenty Redcoats. The one who held the lantern high spoke with a Cockney accent.

"The blasted renegade wasn't lying about the footprints, after all."

Lex thought about that as he was pulled along, a soldier grasping each elbow and the others forming a circle around him. He thought to himself that Banjo would not have left footprints in the garden to betray him. But he knew that he was betrayed—and he saw no chance to escape.

When he stood in the stable yard with his ring of guards around him, he caught sight of old Sam among the frightened Negroes gathering in the background. He hoped that none of them would do anything to betray the fact that they knew and cared for him; for he knew they could not help him and would only bring punishment upon themselves if they dared show sympathy. He felt sure that Banjo, too, was watching from the shadows; but he was

just as sure that the British would not get a glimpse of
that woodsman.

From the house four officers were now approaching,
with two slaves carrying lightwood torches before them.
Lex drew the sweet pine smoke deep into his lungs, and
stared back at the tall arrogant man in a major's uniform
who had come close and was staring at him.

"A guerrilla—and a spy!" said Major Fay.

Lex was thinking fast. Life seemed very sweet to him
then—even when cold bit at night through a ragged blanket and when he sometimes got no more than one meal of
corn or sweet potatoes in a day. He knew that his errand
made him a spy; but he was still wearing his cavalry spurs,
and the hat with the silver crescent was—or had been—on
his head.

"I was trying to cross the river to rejoin my command.
If you think me a spy, let your men search me for papers."

Fay drew a small box from the tail of his coat. He took
snuff slowly, and his Roman nose twitched like a rabbit's.
He cast another scornful glance at the lean figure, as tall
as he, but whose homespun breeches and doeskin shirt
were smeared with rust-colored mud in contrast to his
brilliant and perfect dress.

"I do not need to find papers to convict you as a spy.
You are caught within His Majesty's lines, and you are not
in uniform."

"I'm in the uniform most of Marion's men wear into a
fight. The crescent on my cap is his insignia."

Fay's voice was scornful too. "I see no cap—and no
insignia."

Lex's heart was like a lump of ice inside him. Even with
the crescent, hope was forlorn; without it hope was non-
existent. He turned slowly, for they were not now holding
him, and his eyes went from man to man of the soldiers
closing him in.

"I had my cap on when you caught me. Did any man of you find it?"

For a second there was dead silence—then a scuffle and whisper. A soldier detached himself from the guard and walked toward Fay. He stopped and saluted.

"This is the hat, sir, that the prisoner dropped when we took him."

Major Fay frowned. "Leftenant Saunders, take the hat. Is that half-moon on it the Swamp Fox's insignia?"

A slender man just as young as Lex saluted as he stepped closer to the torchlight. He turned the muddy cap in his hands, and then raised his head.

"It is the insignia of Francis Marion's Brigade, sir."

"A band of guerrillas," said Major Fay. "They should be hanged as soon as caught—and this one is going to hang."

Lex's voice was hard.

"We are Partisans, Major Fay, and not guerrillas. Our officers hold their commissions from the South Carolina Assembly. The only difference between us and the Continental forces is that they are paid and uniformed and we are not."

That was a mistake. Fay was weak and vain and arrogant, but he did not enjoy hanging these forlorn rebels as Wemyss did. However, this rebel's voice had been defiant, and had contradicted him before officers and men. Also, Tarleton—rebuked by Earl Cornwallis—had in turn rebuked his underofficers for being too lenient. Wemyss would arrive in three days at the plantation. To tell his brother officer how he had caught and hanged a spy— while they were both drinking Mr. Lane's best brandy —might well put him in line for promotion.

"I need no more proof than I have that you are both a spy and a guerrilla. But I have proof."

He turned to the young leftenant who still held Lex's cap. "Have the deserter brought here to face him."

Lex heart was beating so hard that he hoped it would not be heard. Marion had sent old Conway after a deserter. He stood in tortured uncertainty until two soldiers led forward a man with his hands also bound behind his back: a man whose sullen, mean face was scored by deep scars which looked as if they had been made by a wild beast's claws.

For a long moment the two prisoners stared at each other. Then Lex caught his breath with an audible gasp. He recognized the Schofilite, and he knew the man recognized him and wished to do him harm. Fay had said "the deserter." Had the man truly dared to join Marion's band? It was possible. Many men changed sides in this war. Lex had not seen him in camp. The man would of course have avoided both him and Jeems. But Lex recalled having heard in camp someone speak of a new recruit with a "clawed-up face."

Major Fay broke the silence. His face was red with anger and his voice was harsh. He was soldier enough to dislike this man far more than the boy caught spying.

"Well, renegade—what have you got to say? You came in this morning with a story that you wished to report a spy in camp. Maybe those footprints you said you saw on the river's north bank were made by you and you are the spy."

So the man had found his footprints where he took off to swim. He might have known Banjo would never leave a trace. The Schofilite was trying to speak but was half-insane with terror. Scorn for him made Lex throw his own shoulders back.

"I not only seen his footprints there, I followed him from Marion's camp. I took care to stay way behind him, because he half-killed me once before. He swum the river to spy on you, Cunnel."

"*Major*," snapped Fay, "—and call me *sir*. I ought to hang you along with him."

Had his guards not held him up, the Schofilite would have groveled. Fay was raging.

"Take him away! If you let him escape I'll hang *you!*"

The wretched man was dragged from the scene, crying aloud for mercy. His cringing had infuriated Fay. He could, without conscience, have watched the deserter swing; but the deserter had proved that this tall Partisan was a spy. The only thing to do was to get it over and go back for another half bottle of port. He swung on the young man with Lex's cap.

"Leftenant Saunders, pick your detail and hang this rebel spy!"

The young officer looked even more frightened than Lex felt. He started stammering: "Yes, s-sir. Doesn't he g-get a trial first?"

"Trial?" said Fay between his teeth. "His compatriots hanged the King's officer when they hanged Major André. It will take more than a dozen such as he to pay the debt, but—on my word—I'll collect on it."

45

LEX WAS WONDERING DAZEDLY: IS IT ME THEY'RE GOING TO hang?

His strong young body was icy cold, colder than river water and the night wind could have made it. He knew that he was a spy; but they hadn't stopped to prove it or even given him a trial. Fay—who had burned his home and as a result killed his father—had taken the word of the Schofilite whom he plainly despised.

Lex had heard of "Tarleton's quarter," and he was now experiencing it.

To him it seemed that the stable yard had come alive with soldiers. Their red coats were dark in shadow, but the torches lit them to scarlet. They were bringing forward tar pots and torches and lanterns, and the fire was making the tethered horses nervous. Lex could hear them blowing and pawing the ground. One of them whinnied plaintively, as only a mare can whinny. She was near enough for him to see her red-bay coat and her rolling eyes. He knew that death and pain disturbed animals, and he realized that this one was troubled on his account.

But just then he saw a squad of eight men approaching Leftenant Saunders. They had no muskets, but they walked in strict formation and their leader carried a coiled rope over his shoulder.

As they stopped in front of him the boyish lieutenant looked at them speechlessly. His face was white and sick as his gaze went from the young Partisan to his commanding officer who was now walking away.

But Fay did not turn in response to Saunders' gaze, and Saunders' clear-cut English voice shook as he gave his orders.

Two men moved over to the tree by the nervous horse and went about fixing the rope to a horizontal limb. The other six fell in around the erect figure in the muddy clothes.

"Guards and prisoner, forward march," said Saunders.

It was thirty steps to the tree. Lex found himself counting them. He was now passing the red mare, and she blew nervously and side-stepped. Through his numbness of horror the thought reached him again that her distress was for his distress. As his eyes went over her it registered through his torment that she pulled back on her halter and her bright hide twitched with nervousness.

Then he looked back and met Saunders' eyes, and he wondered if he looked as unhappy as the young Englishman did. He tried to throw back his shoulders, and the move made the bonds cut into his wrists. *If only I wasn't tied,* he thought, *I might make a run for it. That would at least force them to shoot me. But with my hands tied, I couldn't get far.*

Leftenant Saunders was speaking shakily. "I—I asked you, prisoner, if you had a last request."

At first the words meant nothing to Lex. They were only words, and he looked on death. Then the Calvinist creed of the Back Country rolled on him like a wave.

"Yes," he answered Saunders. "I'd like to say my prayers."

"Do so," said Saunders, thankful for any respite. He wiped his brow with a hand, although the wind blew from the river.

Lex went down on one knee, with his back to the trunk

of the big live oak. All he hoped for was to say his prayers; but when he kneeled his bound hands came in contact with one of his spurs and the sharp rowel stabbed his palm. . . .

As he bowed his head and closed his eyes he recalled that his bonds were cloth, and he sawed them back and forth upon the rowel that also ripped his flesh. It was slow work; but as he worked he was praying sincerely. *"God, let me cut my hands free!"* he prayed. *"If You just give me my hands back, God, I won't ask any more of You. I can do the rest, God—if You'll give me back my hands!"*

A horse snorted and a soldier coughed. His guards had stepped back when he kneeled. As he felt the last shred of the cloth give way, he came up from his knees with a long leap. He came down alongside the red mare, and she did not wheel to escape him. He grasped her crest, and his second jump took him astride her bare back. The yard was a tumult of movement and shouts; but he lay flat along the mare's neck and reached in one quick movement to slip the halter which roped her to the tree. Guiding her with his knees, he slapped both spurs into her sides—and her second bound took them clear of the red-lit stable yard.

She was running like a doe, and he could feel her rise in her stride for obstacles that he could not see in the darkness. Behind, he heard yells and commands and musket shots, and he knew that he was far from clear. Judging from what Major Fay had said, there had been a chain of sentries all along the riverbank in order to trap the spy the deserter had reported. Some might not yet have been recalled. Besides, he did not know this horse. If not bred to the swamp country she might refuse to take water and swim.

They were free of the cedar alley now, and the river lay before them. He knew just where to guide his mount and knew she could see in the darkness. He was riding for a small bluff that would give her a clean take-off. Mud might bog her or throw her at the speed she was going. It was pitch-dark around them now, and the shouts and shots were farther behind. Still—if there were sentries ahead—he might not yet have escaped. . . .

Here was the bluff, and the mare did not even slacken speed for its climb. She saw the broad river before her, and his spurs told her what to do. Without a second's pause, she made the leap that he demanded.

46

THE RED MARE SWAM JUST AS WILLINGLY AS SHE HAD RUN
and leapt. In mid-river Lex felt her fighting the powerful
seaward current. He leaned far over her neck and with the
flat of his hand raised her head and turned it toward the
north bank. He knew it was the only way to aid or guide
a swimming horse. The jerk of a bridle rein could pull its
head down and drown it.

By the time that lights appeared in the Lane garden
behind them they were a quarter mile downstream and
nearing the shore. As he felt her stagger and then catch
footing, Lex threw himself off, caught her forelock and
spoke reassuringly to her as he steadied her upbank. She
did not try to pull away. She shook herself like a big wet
dog, blew loudly through her nostrils to clear them of
water, then stood trembling but obedient while he looped
around her nose an improvised hackamore of the buck-
skin strips in his pocket. As he drew her forward by it,
she pawed and snorted again with excitement. But when
he spoke gently to her she lifted her feet high in the marsh
and followed.

It took him the rest of the night to lead her through the
north shore swamp. Even in darkness, her silhouette and
his touch showed she was young and slender enough to be
called a filly still. He did not wish to bog her or strain her
legs. He knew that the swim under his weight and at full
speed had been an exertion. So he took a longer way,
guiding her around cypress pools and morasses. Just be-

fore dawn they crossed the Georgetown road into woods which were just as thick but on dry ground. He had taken care to let her drink from the brown swamp water, and he tied her now to a live oak's low limb. Turning out his pockets and even using his belt, he re-enforced the hackamore with headstall and lines. Then, while daylight was creeping into the forest, he rubbed her down from muzzle to pasterns with pads of gray Spanish moss.

On that wild swim he had had no chance to think; but during the long walk which followed he had told himself he might have the Red Doe. Full daylight assured him that he was right. Never before had he seen such a bright bay, and her teeth told him she was less than four years old. A man of Fay's weight had no right to ride a filly on long marches. But she was sturdily built. Fire had said the Red Doe strain had sturdiness, sufficient speed and great courage.

The big dark eyes rolled trustingly to follow him as he moved around her. She whinnied very softly and swung her head to snatch a bite from the moss in his hand.

He stroked the dark mane, combing it with his fingers. The bay coat gleamed where his crude grooming had cleaned it of dried river water and mud. He ran his hands down the long, well-shaped legs. She allowed him to pick up her feet, and he found her hooves hard and healthy. She was sweet-tempered as well as bravehearted, and she seemed content to accept him as her master. She stretched her neck to smell him now—blew her warm breath against the back of his hand—and then rubbed her hard flat cheek along his arm.

His heart went out to her with all the affection of the true horse lover toward a favorite steed. She was beautiful and gentle and brave. Even when Fire described the strain he had not guessed it could be like this. He had not dreamed—in all his dreams of getting a horse—that he would ever possess one with these qualifications. No wonder the Fays prized the breed. But this officer Evelyn did not deserve to own one. To have shot the filly's brother—the magnificent stallion!

Lex's blood ran cold as, in memory, he again faced Major Fay in the torchlit yard. He had hoped for an encounter with the man who had burned his home—the man who had dared to annoy Fire until he drove her from her home! But he had hoped for an encounter with even chances: for a fight with swords or pistols—or better still to drive a fist into a scornful face. . . .

He looked at the rowel scars on his wrists. His cavalry spurs had served him well. He blessed the unknown captor who had fettered his hands with a dirty neckcloth instead of using leather or metal.

But he still saw Fay's face: narrow and proud and sneering. Could any woman call that face handsome? Fire must not have thought so, since she did what she did. But then, Fire was different from all other girls.

His torn wrists gave him a stab of pain, for his fists had clenched at thought of Fay and Fire. Oh, for only a fair chance—a chance to break with one blow that fine arched nose—to smash it so completely that no girl would ever again consider Evelyn Fay handsome!

But he, Lex, had not done so. He had run away. He had by the skin of his teeth—or rather by the skin of his wrists —escaped being hanged on an oak limb at Fay's orders.

All that day Lex thought, while he petted and tended the young mare. He would not have dared sleep, and he was too excited to. He led the horse to places where grass still grew green—as it does in winter in southern woods when it has dampness and shelter. He picked tender twigs and sprouts and the first leaf buds for her.

"It's the best I can do for you, sweetheart," he told her. "We'll drink at the first branch we cross tonight. You'll have the day to rest; but—remember!—when we start you'll have to carry my twelve stone as fast as you can without hurting yourself to reach Snow Island before daybreak."

She was shivering with eagerness as he untied her in the dusk and put a hand on her crest to vault to her back.

As he did so she plunged and reared—eager to go where he guided.

What shall I name her? he asked himself. She reminds me of wind and fire. . . . Fire . . .

And, thinking of it, they were alike: young and clean and spirited and beautiful and tender.

They were alike in that Major Fay had coveted both of them. The woman had escaped him. He—Lex—had taken the horse.

By all the stars in the Winged Horse above, why couldn't he—Lex—take the woman too?

She was as far above Peggy and Sal as a star was above a candle.

This war in which he was risking his life was for liberty and equality. But Fire had never made him think he was not her equal. It was Peggy who had played with him, and Sal—of his own stock—who had betrayed him.

Could it be there was no question of caste when the right man found the right woman? Had he been a blind fool who couldn't see his luck? Captain Conyers had said, "You're a lucky devil, Mourne."

As they cleared the wood and settled to a gallop for the open road north, he leaned and stroked the neck of the Red Doe.

"I'll call you *Flame*," he told her. "For you run like a flame through broom grass."

47

THE RED DOE TOOK HIM DIRECTLY NORTH ON THE SANDY CART road. It was the same road he had ridden when he escorted Fire to the Sellers farm. He would have given a great deal to detour upriver to see her, but he knew he must reach Snow Island as soon as he could. He had the information for which he had been sent, although his discovery and escape had probably ruined all chance of surprising Major Fay and his allies. For that matter, Major Fay had already had the surprise of his life.

Lex grinned with joy at the thought, as he sat the galloping mare bareback. He was part of her, relaxed to the rhythm of her stride, leaning with her and trailing his legs like an Indian. He felt himself safer with every mile that she took him; for few Tory patrols dared go near Snow Island.

They entered the Peedee swamp before day broke, and as soon as he reached its cover he dismounted and led the mare. She told him—with rolling eyes and soft snorts of apprehension—that she was unaccustomed to such terrain. But she obeyed his every word and touch without hesitation: lifting her feet high and daintily to follow through half-submerged cypress knees, or plunging after him into pools whose depth she could not know.

When he led her into camp it was full morning, and he saw signs of excitement on every side. Scouts were saddling and riding off. Lovely, whom Lex had not seen for many weeks, was the first man with whom he came face to face.

"You're just in time, Mourne. Colonel Watson—"

The bowlegged scout's eyes went wide as they took in the red mare.

"But—where'd you get that horse?"

"From King George's stables," said Lex. "She was His Majesty's favorite. That's why I decided to take her."

The group around him was growing so fast that he could hardly proceed to Marion's tent. These men knew horses, and they saw that he had a treasure. They crowded him and the Red Doe, running a hand on her flat saddleback or stroking her mane, leaning to look at her slender legs, crying out their questions.

Among them Lex saw Edisto, and he handed the hackamore line to his friend.

"Rub her down for me, Ed. Don't let anyone touch her. But she's cool enough for feed and water."

The crowd deserted him for the horse, and he walked alone to the place where his commander's tent was pitched. Francis Marion listened in silence to the story.

"It doesn't seem to have been your fault that they caught you."

"They wouldn't have caught me, sir, except for the deserter. I had no idea he was behind me, tracking me."

"Lovely would have known—or either of the Conways. A scout is supposed to leave the path and hide here and there watching the path in order to see if he is being followed."

The reproof was anticlimax to Lex's narrow escape from death and to his triumph in getting the British commander's charger. It was true that he had heard of a deserter, but he could have had no idea that the man was making for the Lane plantation. Abashed and resentful, he did not tell Marion about the Red Doe.

"I suppose, sir—since they discovered me—all chance of an attack upon South Bank is done for?"

Marion answered truthfully. "I cannot say that; for I am in no position now even to consider it. Since you left camp I have had other news. The enemy has gathered in considerable numbers, and two forces are now marching upon Snow Island."

Lex found Lovely and Edisto and made them tell him all they knew. Colonel Watson with five hundred men was following the Santee River east. Colonel Doyle, at the head of a regiment, had already crossed Lynch's Creek at McCallum's Ferry and was converging upon them by way of Jeffers' Creek and the Peedee Road.

"All we've got to do," said Lex, "is wait here for them. The whole British army couldn't dislodge us from this swamp."

Lovely said frankly: "The only difference between you and the General is that the General's got brains in his head. He isn't waiting for them to make a junction and then surround us and starve us out."

"Marion's going to meet them?"

"Going to meet Watson before he's joined by Doyle. Peter Horry left last night with a small advance guard. By tomorrow you'll get a chance to test that red horse you stole from the king."

They rode next day. Relays of scouts met them with information, and Peter Horry awaited them in a swamp just east of Widboo. It was decided to make the stand there, using Horry's horsemen as its spearhead.

Lex was one of four hundred men in the main force behind this flying wedge. The band was at its maximum of strength; for during his short delay at Snow Island, the Swamp Fox had recalled to it every man or boy he could reach.

Drawn up, they waited in reserve while Peter Horry

took the first onslaught. In spite of the fact that the causeway they held was narrow, the defenders broke at last under superior numbers. Colonel Watson had several pieces of cannon, and with them he was raking the passage.

As Lex went forward with the first company of re-enforcements, he saw his friend Gavin James turn from the retreat and dash back to the disputed causeway. Alone he rode at a gallop toward the red column approaching, reined in his big gray and fired his rifle point-blank into them.

Putting spurs to his mare, Lex dashed out beside young James. A squad of bright-coated dragoons was riding down upon them. They came to grips with a bayonet fight between the two Swamp Foxes and the half-dozen British. Lex's bayonet was torn from his rifle by a dragoon who rode full tilt against him, practically impaling himself upon its point. The dragoon fell from his horse with the knife protruding from his chest, and Lex drew the filed saw which Jeems had made him for sword.

He saw that another dragoon had boldly seized Gavin James' rifle with both hands and that James was riding back toward his companions dragging along with him the soldier who would not let go.

However, that brief delay had given time for Marion's main attack. Lex heard the hoarse old bugle he knew calling for a full cavalry charge. He saw Captain Conyers, larger than life, riding down upon Major Harrison himself. . . .

Through that melee of hand-to-hand fighting, Lex felt a wild elation at the behavior of the red mare. Young and shy and gentle, she never cringed or held back. She responded quickly and perfectly to the slightest touch of heel or bridle rein, and it seemed to him that at times she responded to an unspoken thought. She found the narrowest crevice through which she could carry him into a fight.

Once she reared and swung him away from the slash of a cavalry saber. She appeared to have been trained to brace herself against the shock of collision with a heavier charger. Between shots and sword cuts and orders and screams and bugle calls, he rejoiced in the certainty that he had a steed to which he had never even dared aspire. Until the battle was over she moved under him like a part of his own body.

When it was over, the British camped at the Cantey plantation, while their weary opponents rested on the damp ground of the swamp which they had used for stronghold. Their scouts brought word that British losses were greater than theirs. But they were not great enough to stop Colonel Watson.

Then a red-coated messenger appeared, approaching them with a white flag and a letter for General Marion. While he read it in his tent, they lay around and discussed it. Presently Captain Conyers emerged from council with his commander and said to the courier: "You may go and tell Colonel Watson that General Marion says there's no answer to that message—except that we'll reply by doing just as he's doing."

As the man's red back disappeared into the jungle, Conyers turned to the men who stared eagerly at him.

"The General told me to tell you. You have a right to know. Besides, you'll each take your part in helping answer that letter."

He clenched hamlike fists with rage and glared as he went on speaking.

"In that letter Colonel Watson dared to tell General Marion that the British were justified in burning homes and hanging citizens."

Lovely spoke from the group. "You mean he's going to keep on doing it?"

"Evidently—since he claims he's right to do so. You

heard me tell his messenger there was no answer from General Marion. This is the General's answer. I'm giving you his order from now to shoot on sight all British pickets and sentries."

48

THE ENGLISH FILLY HAD COME A LONG WAY FROM THE GREEN parks of her birthplace to fight against strangers in a strange land, and then to be seized by that enemy and used against Englishmen. Lexington Mourne had taken her from Evelyn Fay just in time for the incessant and terrible warfare of the spring and summer of 1781.

As he washed her down with swamp water after the battle of Widboo, thoughts of her and of Fire washed briefly from his mind the tragedies of that engagement. For he recalled Fire's description of the Red Doe breed. That breed was now his. By getting the mare he had not only got a perfect cavalry mount, he had acquired a new strain for South Carolina horse breeding.

And what a superb saddle horse he had got for himself! She had beauty of color and conformation, three smooth and clean-cut gaits, docility and great courage. Although not so large as some of the chargers in camp, she was tall enough to suit him and she carried his weight with ease. She had been cavalry-trained by the British, and she performed every maneuver he asked. Yet she was neither afraid nor uncertain in a country which must be new to her. She swam willingly, did not panic and struggle in a bog, kept her footing in jungle, and jumped all obstacles in her stride.

Lex had a chance to prove all that, for Marion's band was on the move. Colonel Watson continued his march paralleling the Santee, and his cannon and greater numbers of men cleared the road before him. All that Marion could do was to delay and harry.

The Red Doe carried Lex well in the charge made by Colonel Hugh Horry's troop at Mount Hope, where the British had stopped to build up bridges wrecked by the Partisans. But in accordance with Marion's orders, Horry made his charge and then withdrew when artillery fire was turned on his small band.

The strength of this artillery enabled Colonel Watson to continue toward Murray's Ferry, although worried by the Swamp Fox scouts as a bear is worried by dogs on his flanks. Then, realizing that his foe's objective was the lower bridge, Marion sent Major James on ahead with seventy men to see that the bridge was completely destroyed. Meanwhile the main force continued by wood paths and byways. And with this force Lex crossed the river at a ford just above and arrived in time for the spectacular engagement.

Major James' men had already wrecked the middle arches of the bridge. Upon the eastern side where they had taken their battle station, the broken stringers were burning from shore out into the stream. But the stream was fordable just below, and the enemy knew it.

So upon the east bank of this possible crossing, Major James drew up M'Cottry's riflemen: a band of Back Countrymen who were the pride of Marion's Brigade because of their marksmanship.

From the west shore where he wished to commence fording the river, Colonel Watson covered the attempt by opening fire with his field pieces.

Then an officer waved his sword and led his men toward the bank.

Captain M'Cottry himself stepped out and with one shot killed the officer in his tracks.

At that signal his riflemen began dropping the British gunners with deadly accuracy. They killed every man who had followed the officer into range. Colonel Watson withdrew his guns to a ravine behind the low bluff. But from that angle their balls passed over the Partisans' heads, smashing the tall trunks of the pine trees behind them. And still M'Cottry's riflemen, from across the wide river, continued to drop every Redcoat within sight.

Under that slaughter the British attempt gave way. When night fell they returned to remove their wounded and dead. In the next twenty-four hours Marion's scouts brought word that Colonel Watson was camped at the Witherspoon farm, and that he and his officers said no troops could hold their position under such shooting.

Hatred had lent precision to that marksmanship. Among M'Cottry's riflemen there were few men who had not lost loved ones at British hands under circumstances they considered outrageous. Hatred was causing the whole Brigade to fight more savagely than it had ever fought before. After Widboo their commander had issued orders which he had until then refrained from issuing. There was little quarter given now by either side. Reprisals became more frequent and more cruel.

Marion at this point sent Captain Conyers and Captain M'Cottry across the Santee to harass the British camp at Witherspoon's. He made his own camp below the ford upon a spot of high ground known as "General's Island."

Conyers' Irish sallies and M'Cottry's sharpshooting cut down Watson's pickets and videttes as soon as they were sent out. Either because of that or because provisions at Witherspoon's were exhausted, the British commander withdrew to Blakeley's plantation and there made his camp in a more open place.

But his tormentors followed and gave him no respite. Captain Conyers rode out in full sight, yelling insults and invitations to Colonel Watson to duel with him. His wild riders swooped down upon any party sent out for scouting or forage. M'Cottry's men hit their targets from incredible distances. Sergeant McDonald one day walked calmly into sight and from three hundred yards away sent a rifle bullet through Lieutenant Torriano's knee.

Bold and efficient as was the British commander, he realized that his men were in panic, that supplies were low and his camp really besieged. His losses were so severe that in the countryside around there was speculation as to how he disposed of the corpses. Gruesome stories were brought to General's Island by both civilians and scouts. Men claimed to have seen at night weird burial parties carrying wagonloads of their dead to an abandoned rock quarry nearby. These onlookers vowed that the corpses were weighted and dropped into the deep pool far below— both for burial and to hide the enormity of the losses.

Colonel Watson at this time wrote General Marion, asking safe passage to Charles Town for Lieutenant Torriano, six other wounded men and six guards. Marion sent him a written pass for the thirteen.

But this concession did not prevent the Swamp Fox tightening his lines around the camp at Blakeley's. Still losing soldiers and unable to renew provisions, the British officer broke camp and started on a forced march to Georgetown.

Through swamp and wood the Partisans followed him. They attacked from ambush, they cut off stragglers, they surprised his advance guard with sudden charges at crossroads. Colonel Peter Horry's cavalry, with deadly riflemen among them, were sent around and ahead to bar the Sampit River crossing while the rest of the Brigade attacked from the rear.

But after the first skirmish there, a Partisan courier dashed up with news from Snow Island. This news was of such grave importance as to cause Marion to abandon his plans in regard to following Watson and to turn back to the Peedee Swamp.

49

AS USUAL LOVELY KNEW ALL ABOUT IT, AND HE IMPARTED the knowledge to Lex.

"While we been chasing Watson, Doyle's took Snow Island."

"How'd he get there? Couldn't Erwin defend it?"

"He got a guide through the swamp—a Tory born in this section. How could Erwin defend it with the handful of men we left?"

"I know we only left him a few—and most of them down with fever. But—did Doyle get our supplies?"

"Erwin destroyed them. That was all he could do. Soon as his scout warned him Doyle's regiment was 'most there, he ordered every man who could walk to throw everything into Lynch's Creek."

That was better than allowing it to fall into British hands, but it was a body blow to the lean Partisans. They were cheered to hear that Watson had arrived in Georgetown with a depleted and hungry column and with two wagonloads of wounded men. But they knew that he had strength and supplies upon which to draw; and they knew they must now deal with Doyle's forces—fresh and strong and emboldened by success.

The arrival of a second courier informed General Marion that this new enemy was at Witherspoon's Ferry. To engage superior numbers with men weary from skirmishing and marching, with ammunition low and no longer any reserve at Snow Island, was taking a fearful and apparently hopeless chance. But it was a case of "needs must." The devil driving the Swamp Fox was knowledge that if he slackened and allowed Watson and Doyle to unite, South Carolina would again be in British hands and every man of his Brigade a hunted man.

They all realized it and discussed it through the camp. When their commander made and announced his decision, they got to their feet and cheered.

Captain M'Cottry was to take his riflemen in ahead and do what damage he could by a surprise attack. Then the rest of the band would go in to support him.

M'Cottry's company dismounted near the place and, leaving their horses, crept through the woods. Across the deep, swollen creek they could see the enemy destroying the boat which served as ferry. Making every bullet tell, the Back Woodsmen opened fire.

In spite of the surprise and of the terrible loss, Doyle's men rushed gallantly to arms and returned a shattering fusillade. But they shattered only the trees from behind which M'Cottry's men were shooting. While volley after volley crashed above and around them, the riflemen chose their targets carefully and disposed of a Redcoat with every ball. Before the rest of the Brigade had a chance to get into action, Colonel Doyle withdrew his men from the useless slaughter.

The ferryboat had been destroyed and the creek was high and running fast. Guided by old Conway, the Partisans rode for a spot five miles upstream where they could more easily swim their horses across. There they discovered that Doyle had already passed. He was marching even faster than they and was well ahead of them.

All that night they rode as fast as tired horses could be pushed. Before the next noon they came upon proof that the enemy had destroyed all heavy baggage in order to travel even more swiftly.

There the Swamp Fox gave up the chase. For a short time he devoted himself to licking his wounds and taking stock of his losses.

Then Lex and Edisto, anxious for news of Fire and Samantha, asked leave to ride to the Sellers farm. Marion listened to them, his thin face thinner than ever and his eyes deep-sunken between cheekbones and brows.

"If I could, I would let you go, in spite of the fact that Doyle's pickets are between us and the Santee. I'd let you go, Mourne, because—"

He paused, and Lex asked anxiously: "Because of what, sir?"

"Because a scout from Charles Town has just brought me a message from my old friend Jervey Lane. Two weeks ago his son was killed in action in North Carolina."

"Toff?" asked Lex. "You mean Toff?"

He knew Mr. Lane had no other son, but something made him keep repeating senselessly: "Toff? Toff? Fire's brother?"

General Marion nodded. "I mean Toff Lane."

"Does—does Fire know yet?"

"That I cannot tell you. But you shall go to Miss Fire the first moment I can spare you. Right now Watson is at Catfish Creek and scattered bands of Tories are pouring in to him. I cannot spare a single man."

"You mean we're going to attack Colonel Watson, sir?"

Marion turned his back, his thin hands clasped behind him. He walked a few paces away, then turned to Lex and Edisto.

"We are five hundred men, and you know as well as I do that not one of us has more than two rounds of ammunition. If we attack it will be the end—for us and for the liberty of South Carolina."

He turned and walked away again, and they saw the

muscles twitching in his clenched hands. When he faced them this time his black eyes smoldered.

"Still—hark you, Hawkins and Mourne!—we are not yet beaten. I believe in the justice of our cause, and I know that help will come to us from somewhere. Meanwhile we'll hang on Watson's heels and worry him all we can."

The lack of ammunition was known all through the camp, and it cast a gloom over the usual rough gaiety of comradeship. Peter and Hugh Horry, John Erwin and James Postell, who were Marion's colonels, and his majors, Alexander Swinton, John James and John Baxter, stood shoulder to shoulder with him in his decision.

Meanwhile fiery Gavin Witherspoon was all for attack with naked bayonets and knives. He exhibited his powder horn.

"It's full. What else do we need?"

"Bullets," said Lovely, "—and only a thousand more men to make our chances equal."

"Well, we've got to fight them soon, or else be cornered and starve. Old Baker Johnson just came in so hungry he's eating cold rice."

"What did he come for?" Lex asked. He knew Johnson as a scout and a true Patriot.

"He said something about having news for General Marion, but he refused to say any more until I gave him something to eat."

They walked over to the place where the old Whig sat on the ground, scraping the last of the cold rice cake from the iron pot between his knees. They questioned him, but he still chewed.

"Yes, I got news for the General."

"Why don't you go to him then?" Lex demanded.

"I ain't going nowhere 'til I get my belly full. This is the first thing I had to eat since day before yesterday."

A crowd was gathering, and someone informed General

Marion. They made way for him as he walked through them.

"Well, Baker, have you any news that can help us?"

Johnson wiped his mouth with the back of his hand, took a long pull from his water bottle, and rose to his feet.

"I sure have, Francis. I took a short cut to tell you. I just seen Major Conyers and Captain Irby. I seen them down by way of Long Branch, and I cut through the swamp to bring you word."

Marion prompted him: "Yes? Word of what, Baker?"

"Word about who was with 'em. I knowed you'd be glad to hear."

There was a rustle of movement as more than a hundred men closed in eagerly around the old Patriot. Marion was patient and brief.

"Who was with them, Baker?"

"Lee's Legion," said Johnson. "They ought to be here any minute. All of Lieutenant Colonel Lee's infantry. Conyers and Irby are guiding them here."

He patted his stomach full of rice and added: "I came to tell you. But I was hungry and I had to get my vittles first."

50

RELIEF HAD COME AS IF HEAVEN-SENT—AS IF SENT BY THAT source in which the Huguenot Marion had said he still believed.

But with it had come friction: the bickering and disagreement and rivalry which always comes at the fusion of volunteers and regular troops. Lee and Marion were completely at variance in their ideas and methods of warfare. Only their common need for ammunition led to the agreement that the Swamp Fox should storm Fort Watson.

The Brigade took it against odds, although their old enemy for whom the post was named escaped capture. Shortly afterward General Marion dispatched Colonel Harden for the attack on Pocotaligo. When they received news of that success, they knew they had driven a small wedge into the arc of British defense. Next news to come into camp was of Greene's engagement at Hobkirk. It was then that Marion and Lee moved with all their strength upon Fort Motte.

Sitting the Red Doe, Lex Mourne looked up the long hill called Buckhead. He was in his own country again, far from the deep lowland rivers. He was not far from the Congaree, sister to his own Wateree. He was seized with a great homesickness for their broad stony shallows where a barefoot boy might wade across or a man ride a horse from bank to bank. He knew that it was their meeting which formed the great Santee: the tawny, rushing watercourse which ran by Fire's home. Against the background

of Buckhead Hill she came into his mind's eye. His country
would be strange to her. Could he ever persuade her ...

He heard Nathan Savage's voice. "The General's lookin'
for you, Mourne."

Marion told them: "Mrs. Motte is staying at her overseer's house, where she moved when the plantation house
was occupied by the British. You are to convey to her my
respects and inform her that I regret the necessity of opening fire upon her home."

Savage knew a path through the woods, and by it they
reached the overseer's house on another part of the plantation. Rebecca Motte herself met them at its door. Her
manner was decisive, and her eyes were snapping.

"Tell Francis Marion that if I had his cannon I would
have opened fire before this. I would rather see my home
in ashes than in enemy hands."

For two days they bombarded the house with the small
field pieces which were their artillery; but its location on
a height and its wall protected it. Then Mrs. Motte arrived
in their midst, carrying an Indian bow and arrows.

"Enough of this nonsense," she told the Swamp Fox.
"My husband always said that the house was impregnable
to guns. He said the only way to attack it was by flaming
arrows."

The men about were staring at her, their eyes bright
with astonishment and admiration. Marion spoke.

"Madame, you are a true Patriot—brave and unselfish.
I had hoped to spare you this which you urge upon me.
But my scouts are bringing news that Lord Rawdon is
drawing steadily nearer as he retreats from his meeting
with Greene at Camden."

Her eyes snapped sparks. "I know that too. Were I
younger and stronger, I would myself draw this bow."

"I can at least spare you that. My men are woodsmen.
With your permission—"

She interrupted him there. "Not with my permission, but with my *orders*."

That night the Patriots saw in the north the glow of Lord Rawdon's campfires. His army, even in retreat, could have overwhelmed their band. They waited two days longer, then knew they could wait no more.

Nathan Savage was the man chosen to creep up Buckhead Hill. He carried no bow but a crude sling, such as David used on Goliath. His officers knew that he knew how to use it, and they had prepared and given to him a ball of brimstone and resin.

For an hour they waited. He had been told to get near enough to make his aim sure. When the flaming missile rose and curved its arc against the dark sky, Rebecca Motte cried "Bravo" and the men began to cheer. Almost at once flames flickered and sprang along the wooden roof of the building.

Dismounted, they charged then, uphill and in a run. Lovely was alongside of Lex and keeping pace with his long legs. From behind the wall which encircled the height British musket fire was pouring down upon them. By the time Lex and Lovely were halfway to their objective they could see the defenders above in dark silhouette against the illumination. The two dropped, each on a knee, chose their targets against the light of the blazing roof, fired and rose again.

And as they did Lex heard at his side a horrible thudding sound that he knew: the sound of lead striking and rending a thing more soft than itself. He recognized it because he had heard it before; but he had never heard it quite so close. He recognized it as the sound of a musket ball striking hard and directly into the body of a man.

As he paused and turned he saw Lovely spin completely around. His legs buckled under him and he would have fallen had Lex not dropped his own rifle and caught him in his arms.

In that smoky, leaping red light he cradled his friend's small body.

"I'll get you right to the doctor. Don't you worry, old man.

"I ain't—worryin'—no more," said Lovely.

He sighed very deeply, and when he tried to speak again his voice was only a whisper.

"I ain't—worryin'—no more. You put me—behind a bush —and go on."

His head fell back across Lex's arm, and his face was calmer than Lex had ever seen it. It was far calmer than Lex's face bent close over it, calmer than the faces of the yelling men who jostled them as they ran by in the charge upon Fort Motte.

Lex leaned to secure his rifle, and as he did the short bowed legs dangled helplessly from his grasp.

It broke him as even the old scout's dying words had not. Those bowlegs had taken Lovely from the Wassamas-saw to the Back Country and through the Tidewater. They had taken him on errands for the Swamp Fox all over the battle-torn terrain—and at the end up his last long hill.

Lex laid him down gently behind the nearest clump of sassafras. Then he reloaded his rifle and, with smarting eyes and lips drawn thin, he followed Marion's rearguard up Buckhead toward Fort Motte.

51

BY THE TIME THAT LEX GOT INSIDE THE WALL OF DEFENSE, the fight was over. Leftenant McPherson was surrendering his small command, and Marion's men were swarming over the Motte house to put out the fire which its valiant owner had urged them to set.

Then Lex and Edisto and Jeems and Sonny buried Lovely behind the clump of sassafras bushes. Buckhead Hill was a far cry from the dark morasses of Wassamassaw; but both were the South Carolina for which Lovely had died.

They were cheered by the news that General Sumter had taken a strong British post at Orangeburg, and shortly afterward they heard that he had seized Fort Granby.

Meanwhile Marion's Brigade crossed the Santee River again, made camp, and settled down for rest and reenforcement. Georgetown was their next objective; but they needed recruits and equipment in order to take it.

Upon this encampment and on the march to Georgetown, they were not far from South Bank or from the Sellers place on the north shore. The great rice plantation and the small farm both lay alongside the great river and a short way to the south. Lex's longing to see Fire was increasing with every day. Not only was he constantly worried about the two women alone in a lonely place, he wished to know if Fire yet knew of her brother's death and to give her what comfort he could. And along with these big things he wished to tell her of smaller things, as lovers

wish to tell each other. He was anxious to show her the
Red Doe mare and tell her how he had got it. He was
fretting to know what Major Fay had done or said to make
her run away from her own home. He longed to assure her
that he wanted to care for her, to protect her forever from
all that troubled her.

And then his heart would go cold with the thought that
she might not love him at all. She had been friendly and
comradely because he was Toff's friend. Was he not pre-
suming to dream that a rice planter's daughter would be
willing to go with him to a farmhouse in the High Hills?
He had not even the house now, but he intended to build
it. He was a dirt farmer and not a Tidewater planter. It
never even occurred to him that he might live in her section. His wife would go with him and he would build her
a home on the hill where the tall white oaks threw shade
and the sycamores were pale.

There was no fight at Georgetown. Before the victors'
advance, its garrison evacuated and went aboard their
ships in Winyah Bay. The hunted Swamp Fox band was
drinking a heady wine. Instead of being obliged to hide
and take their foe by surprise, that foe was giving way at
word of their approach. But the greater part of the section
was still in British hands, and Marion realized that he must
not give them time to rally and reorganize. He could not
spare a single able-bodied man. At his orders Colonel Peter
Horry had forced Gainey to sign a treaty which was ad-
vantageous to the Patriots. Sumter was marching down
from the Back Country, striking right and left as he came.
The Swamp Fox took his men back to their late encampment at the Cantey plantation and there waited to effect
a junction with the Game Cock. Between them Colonel
Coates had entrenched himself at Biggin Church, and as
soon as Sumter's forces arrived they joined battle with his
cavalry.

For some time victory wavered between one side and the other. Coates was a valiant and skillful officer, but under Colonel Hampton's attack he finally gave way. Setting fire to Biggin Church in which his baggage was stored, he began a retreat on the Strawberry road, destroying all bridges as soon as he crossed them. Pressed hard in spite of this, he turned aside and took refuge at the Shubrick property.

Sumter and Hampton had borne the brunt of the fight at Biggin. General Sumter, who ranked General Marion, now sent the latter in to lead this attack.

As they massed for the first charge Lex looked across cleared space at the big house and outbuildings. Unlike most Low Country plantations, it offered no shelter of avenues or alleys or groves of oak. Only open and bare ground lay between them and the British riflemen whom they knew to be waiting at blind windows and doors. The Americans would have to cross that terrain in order to reach even the frail shelter of yard and paddock fences. He knew just what they were in for as he looked from his tight-faced comrades to Colonel Taylor's regiment which was starting off in formation. Bad as he knew it must be at best, Lex thanked Francis Marion's training in Indian warfare for the fact that his Brigade was breaking ranks and going in singly.

Running singly, they started toward the houses which crouched in wait for them—in wait like wild beasts which hid until ready to make their kill. To one side, volleys of rifle fire were pouring into Taylor's command. Even though preoccupied with trying to save his own life, Lex felt a pang of horror at that slaughter. Then a bullet went by him with the high whine of twanged wire, and flashes of fire from doors and windows ahead told him that the defenders were numerous enough and had enough ammunition to attend to his troop as well as to Colonel Taylor's regiment.

Just ahead Captain Perry stumbled and fell. To right and left of Lex the bullets now hummed like bees. He threw himself flat for a second, remembering as he did a childhood day when his father and he had captured a hive. Yadkin Mourne had moved with quiet assurance, but at his first sting a small boy had screamed and fought. They had been all about him then—humming and fighting and stabbing—until his father caught him up and threw him in the big horse trough.

At the second's end he leapt to his feet and ran on—zigzagging—praying to his father's God for help in dodging these bees of death. His objective was the main house, and the closer he got to it the more numerous were the men who fell around him. He heard somebody call: "They got Lieutenant June!"

In spite of the fact that they were going in as they did, the Brigade was taking the worst of the punishment. Their approach had been ordered across the most exposed and dangerous ground. It was awful to take such fire and not be able to return it. Lex Mourne set his teeth and ran on, gripping his rifle with hands which were white-knuckled and wet with icy sweat.

He could hardly believe it when he reached the fence unhurt. He threw himself flat behind its low boards, and other men began to throw themselves around him. The house was within range now and he rose to his knees, took a quick sight over the fence and fired at a red jacket just within a door. At once a volley came back, ripping the top rail from the fence.

And just then—from behind them—their bugles ordered *Retreat. . . .*

52

LEX MOURNE THREW HIMSELF FACE DOWN ON THE GROUND in rage and frustration. Around him his forlorn companions wept or swore. They had just crossed the front yard of hell, and had left in it friends they loved. Now, at the very door of assault, they were being denied their revenge.

In the frame of mind which was theirs, they could not realize that to go on would have been total annihilation. But their commanders realized it and were salvaging what they could from disaster.

Return was of course impossible. They would have to wait for night. Those behind them had obeyed the bugles and turned, but those in the advance had gone too far for that. They numbered about a score, angry panting men sprawled in the inadequate shelter of a wooden fence. Looking back the way they had come, they saw the ground thick with their dead and wounded. A hoarse voice said in Lex's ear: "Bet you more'n fifty of the Brigade's out there."

Staring across the open field, Lex agreed with him silently. About a hundred yards to the left was the plantation well house. Hiding behind its brick coping and quaint shingled roof were several Partisans, visible to the men by the fence but not to the enemy in the house. Service Dalzell crawled up to Lex.

"You seen Jeems or Edisto or Sonny?"

"Not since we started across that field. Your cheek's all bloody. You hit?"

"No. I just scraped it on the ground. When I got within

fifty feet of this fence I dived and slid the rest of the way."

Service wiped the blood and sweat from his face with a dirty sleeve.

"Two field pieces would have taken this place."

"Yes," said Lex, "but we didn't have 'em. Doyle took all we had at Snow Island."

They fell silent. All around them men were tending small wounds and cursing the order which had sent many to useless death.

The shadows were growing longer. They gazed with desperate yearning toward the cool mossy bricks of the well.

Suddenly Dalzell whispered: "By gum! That dead man wasn't there just now, Lex."

Lex looked and saw a man flat on his face between them and the well. He recognized the thick black hair, the broad shoulders and lean waist. He whispered back: "Service— it's Jeems. I'm going out to get him."

But at just that second the man supposedly dead turned his head slightly and looked at them from one bright blue eye. With a slow swimming motion he dragged himself half a length toward them—then lay still again. The enemy in the house either did not see him or mercifully did not shoot because they thought him a wounded man.

Slowly he moved his body a few feet at a time. Then a dozen hands reached out and dragged him the last yard. A dozen voices whispered: "You hit, partner?"

"No," said Jeems. "I ain't hit. But Sonny is. He's hit bad."

"How bad?" demanded Lex.

"Whereabouts?" asked Service.

"In the chest. He's bled a lot—and he's spitting blood too. We got a bucket of water there, so we could let him drink and wash the wound. We made a pad of Ed's shirt and tied it on tight to try to stop the bleeding."

He passed a hand across his eyes. "That young one sure

is game. Ed wanted to hoist a white handkerchief and take him to the house. Said he'd rather for them both to be captured than to let Samantha's boy die for need of a surgeon. But Sonny wouldn't hear of it."

Lex spoke as much to himself as to Jeems. "What can we do?"

"Can't do anything until dark. That's why I crawled over here to tell you. Edisto and I figure to lay Sonny on the well cover and get him back that way. But we need you and Service to help. Sonny's bigger than any of us except you."

It was only half-dark when Lex and Jeems and Service began the precarious journey from the fence to the well. One by one they crawled across the danger of the open ground. They found Sonny half-conscious. He moaned and whimpered and muttered his mother's name.

They laid him on the well top, with his head on a pillow of shirts and his long legs hanging helplessly off the crude stretcher from his knees down. They walked slowly and without mishap on that return trip across the field. They knew that a jolt or a stumble might make their errand useless. To their horror Dr. Irvine, beloved by the whole Brigade, was lying under the shed where the wounded were being dressed. He raised his head to look at the pale face and the bloody pad.

"I'm waiting my own turn. Dr. Skinner has a line that'll keep him working all night. But this boy can't wait. Sit me up against the wall, Jeems."

Service opened his medical bag and handed the instruments asked for. Lex steadied the doctor with both arms, and Edisto held Sonny in position. Dr. Irvine extracted the ball and Service, at his instructions, washed and bandaged the wound again.

"Give him a swallow of brandy from that flask," the doctor said, "and leave him lying here by me. When Dr.

Skinner gets to me, I'll have him look at young Sellers."

Edisto rose from his knees. "Doctor, what kind of a chance has he got? I just feel like I couldn't go back to Samantha if—"

"He's got about even chances, so far as the wound is concerned. But he's got youth and cleanness and strength. We'll get him back to his mother."

All that night the three kept returning to look anxiously at Sonny and the doctor. Not until all others of the wounded were tended did Dr. Skinner dress Dr. Irvine's wounds. But Sonny rallied, although he tossed with fever and kept calling for his mother in his delirium.

In despair of taking the Shubrick place and made more hopeless by news that Coates was expecting re-enforcements, the Brigade withdrew to camp near the Santee. Sonny was carried on the same well cover, and at the Peyre plantation his wound began to heal slowly. But a fever had by that time set in, and in midsummer General Marion advised Edisto to take the boy home.

Lex knew that he was going into action again, and at once. Trying to recoup their losses, the British were active at Monck's Corner, Dorchester and Parker's Ferry. He could not go with Edisto, but he could write Fire a letter. He thought of danger or possible death ahead, and he made up his mind to tell her he loved her.

Dear Fire, he started it, *I've loved you ever since I pulled you out of the river. I didn't know it myself, and I know you'll be surprised. Maybe you'll be angry. You have no reason to care for me——*

She had no reason to care! That thought rushed upon him again. He heard Edisto calling his name and knew that he and Sonny were starting.

Lex tore his letter in small pieces and scattered them.

"No," he told Edisto. "I didn't have time to write. You just give my respects to Samantha—and to Fire."

53

ON THE LONG RIDE TO PARKER'S FERRY LEX WAS SO PRE-
occupied that Jeems and Service demanded what was the
matter. If I'd only written it and sent it by Edisto—he was
telling himself again and again—Fire would have it by
now and she'd tell me *yes* or *no*.

But he had let Edisto go without the letter. Fire had
no idea that he cared for her. In fact she knew that he had
made a simpleton of himself about her sister. She was
probably engaged anyhow, to a man from Charles Town
or to some planter's son.

No, he told himself, why should she care for me? I'm
a Back Countryman. If she married me she'd leave her
home and the Low Country. I haven't even got a home for
her yet. All I could give her at first would be a log house
on a hill. And I'd have to build that.

When he did not even reply to Jeems' and Service's
questions, they laid his distraction to grief about Lovely.
All three of them had cared for the bowlegged scout from
Wassamassaw. Lex finally roused himself for news of Captain Cooper, who had been left with a troop of cavalry to
engage the enemy behind them while the Brigade went
hunting bigger game.

Major Fraser was camped at the Edisto crossing, and
as they approached Marion set his trap along the road:
riflemen hidden in the woods covered it, while Colonel
Harden rode on with a small party of the swiftest horses
and best horsemen.

The Red Doe picked her feet from the swamp as lightly as a marsh tacky. She knew that danger was close by, for she did not snort or blow. But from behind her head Lex could see her great brown eyes rolling watchfully, and he felt between his knees her occasional shiver of anxiety.

In that same interchange the horses could sense the nervousness of their riders. Although seasoned scouts to the last man, the small group being used for decoy was by no means tranquil. As they made the hazardous approach they expected at any second a volley from the enemy whom they knew to be ahead. Moreover they knew that when that volley came and they turned they would have to clear their own ambuscade well ahead of the foe, or else risk being shot by their comrades.

When the first shots rang out, they wheeled at Harden's order and dashed back as they had come, pretending surprise and confusion.

Fraser took the bait and dashed after them, leading his corps into the line of Marion's deadly ambush. By the time he discovered his mistake and attempted to withdraw, he merely succeeded in giving the hidden Partisans a second chance to mow his men down in the turning and the retreat. His cavalrymen and his horses fell so thickly that they blocked the narrow swampy road. All that saved his survivors from death or capture was the advance to their rescue of a formidable force of infantry and artillery. At the approach of these re-enforcements Marion's mounted riflemen took their departure.

They had not yet cooled from this success when a letter from General Greene told General Marion of the hanging of Colonel Hayne in Charles Town. It increased their fury, and they marched to Eutaw determined to force to complete victory the advantage of their recent achievements.

Here General Marion met General Greene at Burdell's plantation. Around the ice-green lakes and their deep, mysterious, subterranean streams the Americans were gathering for a concentrated attack upon one of the main British armies. Marylanders and Virginians, North and South Carolinians were massed in the desperate hope of striking a final blow. Their prayer was for terrain and circumstances in which they could use their cavalry to greatest advantage. Only in that did they feel themselves superior. They knew the enemy was better equipped with both infantry and artillery.

On a hot, dusty August day the Brigade rode into battle. Pickens' men rode with them, and they fired as they advanced. Back and forth the outcome swayed, now for one side and then for the other. All around the pale green springs other corps were in action. British artillery held the Charles Town road. The Virginia and Maryland troops were engaging the foe with bayonets. Colonel Wade Hampton made his magnificent charge, and Colonel William Washington went directly in behind him. Tide was turning fast for the Continentals when Major Majoribanks and Major Sheridan saved the British from total defeat. Together they seized and occupied the building known as the "brick house"—a building whose bricks withstood the little and light artillery commanded by Greene and his supporting generals.

Bitter at being deprived of total victory, weary and dirty and wounded men began to fall back. All those unhurt or not badly hurt hurried directly to the nearest fresh-water pond.

Lex was with them, his face smoke-blacked and half of his hair scorched off by the close discharge of a musket which had blown his cap from his head. Flame was dark brown with sweat, and her red-rimmed nostrils blew in and out. But neither he nor she had suffered a scratch in the wild foray.

He dismounted at the edge of the pond, loosened her

girth, then slaked his thirst from cupped hands while he allowed her to drink. Relief at finding himself alive and his beautiful mare unwounded was surging through him, making the swamp water wine. He looked Flame over as he had done on the night he took her from Fay, alert for strained tendons from the battle or greasy heels from long marches in mud. There was no gray moss at hand, so he wiped her down with pine straw.

While he did so, more and more of his comrades were riding in. A few arrived on foot, reporting horses shot under them. Jeems came to tell him that Service Dalzell had suffered a slight saber cut.

"It ain't serious," he assured Lex. "It's just enough to get him leave, like I got for that ball in my leg."

Lex's anxiety for his friend turned into a pang of envy. "Wish I could get me a wound little enough not to cripple me, but big enough to get me leave to go to the Sellers place."

Jeems did not smile, but his blue eyes grew even bluer. "You weren't thinking about going to the High Hills?"

"No," said Lex. His face felt hot, although it was wet with the pond water. He added defensively: "I want to know how Sonny's doing."

Jeems looked hard at him. He had seen Fire at Marion's camp and he knew that Lex had taken her to Samantha.

"I'd like to know, myself," he said. And then he changed the subject. "Look at those fools scuffling in the middle of the pond. Seems like they'd have enough fighting without fighting each other."

The brown wine of relief was affecting men in different ways. Standing knee-deep in water, a group of rowdies were trying to hit each other over the heads with their rifle butts. Lex's eyes went from them to figures sprawled on the margin: weary figures who lay relaxed as death, in gratitude not to be dead. He looked back at the half dozen engaged in the water fight.

"Peter Horry'll cut their ears off if they get their powder wet or drop a gun in the pond."

Then he heard the crack of the explosion and a strange numbness began to spread from his right hand up his right arm. He tried to move his right fingers, but they refused to respond. With his left hand he cupped them to hold the gush of blood which filled the curved palm as he looked in astonishment at it.

54

THE BALL HAD GONE COMPLETELY THROUGH, SO THERE WAS
nothing to remove. But Dr. Irvine's cleansing probe was
red-hot agony.

"Hold still! You're lucky it missed the bones. Your hand
will never be pretty—but it wouldn't have been that anyway—and you'll be able to use it after six weeks or so."

Lex's grimace of pain turned into a grin of joy.

"You mean it'll get me leave for six weeks?"

"Francis Marion has the say about that. I don't see why
he'd want you hanging around camp eating the rations of
a man who can fight."

He finished his bandaging, knotted a strip of homespun
for a sling, looped it around Lex's neck and bent the fore-
arm into it.

"Keep it there. Don't let it hang down. And by the way,
when did you get it? All the wounded who could walk
came in hours ago."

Lex and Jeems looked at each other. They had agreed
not to tell on the men in the pond. The culprits had been
even more frightened by the accidental shot than by the
fight against the British. They had at once surrounded Lex,
expressing their regret, while other men warned them what
Marion and Horry would do to them.

"Let 'em think you got hit in the battle! That way you'll
be a hero—and we'll keep our ears."

"I'm not telling the officers," Lex had assured them

sourly. "But I'm telling you right now, if you'd hit my horse I'd have killed all four of you."

Dr. Irvine looked shrewdly at their embarrassed faces.

"So—that's the way it is? I should think you boys had enough fighting at Eutaw to leave off fighting among your-selves. Well, it's none of my business. I'm sending in my report that Mourne will be of no use to the Brigade for six weeks or two months to come."

It still seemed unreal to Lex, as he rode Flame in a walk toward the Sellers farm. He still feared he was dream-ing and would awake to find his right hand undamaged and himself in camp. He was obliged to ride slowly, for the slightest jarring disturbed the wound. Dr. Irvine had asked before he left if he would have anyone to dress it.

"You can't do it yourself. Somebody must keep it clean and shake this powder into it."

Lex accepted and pocketed the paper of evil-smelling antiseptic.

"She'll dress it for me. She loves to nurse people. She said so when she was bandaging General Marion's ankle."

"Did she?" asked the old doctor with laughter in his kind eyes. "Well then, get along to her, boy."

But if Fire did not love him—he told himself as he rode —if she loved some other man, he would not allow her to dress his wound. That was a pain he would not be able to bear, although even her touch would be comfort. He made up his mind that he must tell her he had not been shot in battle but in a clumsy scuffle between ruffians. That might seem ridiculous to her. If so he would go on to the hills alone. And if neglected, perhaps his wound would prove fatal. . . .

But he had a healthy aversion to death, and a very virile desire to marry Fire and build her a home and live a long life with her. He pictured her on the Red Doe. When he had called the mare Flame he had, in his heart, been naming her for the girl he loved.

On the second day of his ride he began to feel more cheerful, although the untended hand was pulsing with knifelike throbs. He dampened its bandages with drinking water from his bottle. Dr. Irvine had charged him not to use swamp or ditch water. That seemed a little effeminate to him, since he had all his life washed cuts and bruises from swamp pools or woodcock ponds. But in common with all the Brigade he loved Dr. Irvine, and so he carried out the unreasonable order.

It was dusk when he turned into the road leading from the highway, and he rode undetected almost up to the house. Its door was open, and soft yellow light gleamed from that rectangle and from its windows. He dismounted and tied Flame to the hitching post, leaving his rifle slung on the saddle as Jeems had arranged it. Then he walked almost up to the door and called softly: "Samantha! It's Lex!"

Three voices cried out in response, and he heard light feet running on boards. A tortoiseshell cat flew down the steps without even touching them, and a slender figure seemed to fly after it. He tried to hold out his arms to her, but the sling prevented that. In the fall of candlelight from within Fire saw sling and bandages. She stopped short.

"Lex! Oh, Lex—you're wounded!"

"It ain't anything bad—just a ball through my hand."

He had hoped for a welcome warmer than sympathy. Now he stood, as awkward as she, looking at her in the slanted light. It made a gold flame of her hair and he saw the distress on her face. He moved a step nearer and held out his unwounded hand.

She put a slender hand in it, but pulled back as he drew her toward him.

"Lex," she whispered, "here's Samantha."

Samantha, who moved more slowly than Fire and the tortoiseshell cat, came down the steps to them. She put a soft arm around Lex.

"We're all three of us happy you've come. Sonny's calling for you."

Sonny, a skeleton of a boy, was sitting up in bed demanding to hear of his friends. Lex told him of Parker's Ferry and Eutaw Springs.

"It isn't going to take much longer to lick them."

Sonny frowned. "I know. I hope I get back in the Brigade before it ends. I hear the Tories are beginning to desert."

"I saw one of 'em in the swamp yesterday," Samantha said. "He ran when he saw me. I was carryin' Sonny's rifle —but I don't know how to shoot it."

Lex agreed absently: "There's a kind of man will desert when he think he's beat."

But he had not come to the farm to talk of Tories. He had come to tell Fire he loved her—to know whether or not there was any chance for him. His eyes went back to her, and she dropped her eyes before them. He saw her as slender as before and even more exquisite. Her hair was simply arranged: parted and drawn back and rolled low on the back of her head like Samantha's dark hair. But while Samantha's stayed in place, Fire's escaped and rioted in small red-gold curls at her ears and on the back of her neck. She was wearing a gray homespun dress, such as Samantha wore and such as was woven by the women of the High Hills. Its soft color set off the brilliance of her coloring, and its long full skirt made her waist look as if he could have lapped it with his two hands. But he had only one useful hand now, and Fire would not even look at him. . . .

Sonny said: "Are you deaf, Lex? I asked you how was the Red Doe?"

Only Fire could have made him forget Flame. He exclaimed in contrition: "She's out there tied to the post! She hasn't had grain to eat since day before yesterday."

"There's corn on the cob," said Samantha. "You know the barn, Lex. I'll be fixin' supper while you put up your horse."

Her voice was still quite commonplace, although her words made his heart leap high. "You better go along and hold the lantern, Fire, since he can't use but one hand."

55

FIRE HELD THE LANTERN HIGH WITH ONE HAND AND WITH the other lifted her long skirt. It was only thirty feet from door to hitching post and she cried aloud as she saw Flame.

"Oh, Lex, she's lovely! She has the conformation of the stallion I saw at the Fortesque place, but I think she's even more beautiful."

"Edisto told you about her?"

"Yes—and Sonny too. I'm so glad you got her, Lex. You're the only one I know who rides well enough to deserve such a horse."

They were moving toward the barn, he leading Flame with his left hand. He stopped.

"Ever since I got her, I've been picturing *you* up on her."

Fire said politely: "I'd like to ride her sometime."

She moved around to the other side of the horse.

"She must be tired and hungry now. Let's feed her and put her up, then go back to the house and dress your hand."

Fire was doing all she could to avoid him, he told himself. It was as he had feared. She cared nothing for him. She approved him as a horseman but not for a husband. She was anxious now to go back to the house and was making his hand an excuse, while he had hoped with all his heart for a tête-à-tête in the barn.

His heart was aching far more than his hand as he led

266

the red mare on. He was telling himself for the hundredth time that he had been mad to allow himself to hope.

He fed and watered and stabled his horse, while Fire stood by with the lantern. Then they walked back to the house, primly, side by side. Sonny was in a big chair, and Samantha was cooking supper. She came toward Lex.

"We'll clean up that hand, now you're through with a dirty horse. I got a kettle of hot water here. Fire, bring the basin off the piazza."

He had pictured Fire dressing it, but she only helped Samantha. The bandages were stuck to his flesh with blood and pus. When Fire saw it she moaned very softly.

She had not moaned when she dressed Francis Marion's ankle. It made him feel that she was less willing to help him, Lex.

"Don't you stand there," he told her, "if the sight bothers you."

Samantha told him sharply: "Fire ain't the kind that's bothered by sight of a hurt. She ain't selfish."

He knew that she was not selfish. He had seen how she sacrificed herself for her mother and father. He was too modest to imagine that she had been sacrificing herself when she stood aside and lent him her horse to ride with Peggy. His heart hurt so much that he hardly felt Samantha's thorough dressing of the festered wound. Then he and Fire pulled Sonny's chair to the table and they sat down together for supper.

They told him all the news of the farm, and he told them of the Brigade.

Sonny said: "You must of just missed Edisto. He wrote us a letter saying he was at Monck's Corner."

Lex described the ride to Parker's Ferry and the successful ambush of the British there. He told them of Eutaw Springs.

"That was by a long way the biggest battle I've ever

been in. I wasn't wounded; I came out without a scratch. Then those fellows scuffling in the pond did this to me."

As he spoke he looked at Fire, in fear that she might be disgusted with him. She was staring with parted lips and eyes big and dark. She dropped them instead of meeting his look, and he saw her flush.

He had not yet spoken to her of Toff, and his grief for his friend was deep. While he sat with Sonny and the women washed dishes, he made up his mind to do so. When she came back into the room he rose.

"Fire, I want to ask you about Toff. Would you come out on the steps with me?"

She went so white that he saw a few small freckles on the bridge of her nose.

"I wouldn't want to give you more pain. But he was the best friend I had."

"I know it," she said. "I want to tell you all I know. But you can ask me right in here. Samantha and Sonny know about it."

Toff's death had been swift enough to be merciful. Her parents had sent her word by one of Marion's men who was Charles Town born and who went in and out of that city even while it was occupied by the British.

"Are your father and mother still there?"

"Yes—and Peggy's with them." She paused and looked hard at him. "She likes it there. In her last letter she asked what I knew about you."

For some reason his face and neck grew hot, although he no longer cared what messages Peggy sent. Fire's eyes were still on him. "Peggy has more beaux than ever. But she isn't married—or engaged—in case you want to know."

This time it was he who dropped his eyes before hers. He managed to mumble: "It's no concern of mine. I was just thinking Mr. and Mrs. Lane might send for you to come there."

She shook her head so decisively that several curls came loose from their knot.

"General Marion sent them word that I was safe here. Besides, they'd rather I stay hidden after the way Major Fay acted."

Lex rose to his feet with his good hand clenched. He felt a sharp flash of pain as he tried to clench the injured one, and Fire stared with parted lips at the expression on his face.

"What did that blackguard do? I wanted to kill him the night I took his horse! What did he say or do to you? I'll yet kill the scoundrel!"

Fire dropped her eyes to hide their expression from him. Her voice was both demure and teasing.

"It's kind of you to be so concerned about Peggy's sister. But you needn't bother your head."

Demureness and teasing did not suit her. He loved her sweet gravity and her youthful eagerness. He was almost as angry with her as he was with Evelyn Fay.

"You've no call to talk this way! Toff was my best friend, and besides—"

He stuck there. Toff's name had wiped all except sadness from her face.

"I know you were his best friend, Lex. I thank you. But you might as well own up to yourself that I'm the less attractive twin and I can take care of myself—while you and all the other men run after Peggy."

"Less attractive?" he shouted. "Have you gone crazy, Fire? Captain Conyers told me no man would look at Peggy again after he got one glimpse of you."

She rose swiftly—a tall girl but inches shorter than he. Her hands were clenched now and her eyes dark with anger.

"So it took Captain Conyers to tell you?" she asked. "Well, good night. I'm tired—and going to bed."

56

WHILE HE STOOD IN SILENT RAGE, SHE HAD TURNED HER BACK on him and gone into the room she shared with Samantha and closed its door with a slam. Samantha had come to him then and put a hand on his shoulder.

"Help me get Sonny back in bed. Then I want to talk to you, Lex."

They had taken hold of each side of Sonny's chair, and he talked eagerly as they dragged him along.

"I hear tell they got chairs with wheels on 'em, Lex. If I had a couple wagon wheels on mine, it would save Ma and Fire a lot of work."

"You're most well now," Lex reassured him. "You won't be troubling them to haul you much longer."

Samantha pointed to a corn-shuck mattress and cotton quilt in a corner.

"I put that there for you. But before you go to bed, I'm goin' to talk some sense into you."

Out on the dogtrot she opened with heavy artillery.

"Seems to me, Lex Mourne, you've lost all the sense God ever gave you."

"What reason you got to say that?"

"I'm talking about Fire. What makes you treat her this way?"

He was angry already—angry and sensitive from Fire's rebuff. Now his temper flared.

"She's the one who's treating *me* wrong. I came here to tell her I loved her."

"Why didn't you tell her, then?"

"She wouldn't let me. She made fun of me. She pretended to think I was stuck on Peggy."

"Well," said Samantha calmly, "from what I've heard you *were* stuck on Peggy."

"I don't know what you heard—or who made it their business to tell you—but I love Fire and nobody else."

"Hurry up and tell her then. She loves you, but she's got her pride. She knows you were crazy about her sister and engaged to marry Jeems Gaylord's sister."

That set him back on his heels, for it sounded as if he were a ladies' man like Captain Conyers. He scowled.

"I can't help what's past. All I can tell you is I learned better sense."

"If that's the best you can tell Fire, she'll probably refuse you."

"She's practically done that already. I got an idea she's engaged to some rich man in the Low Country."

"Well, you got a fool idea. Fire hasn't got any man but you in the back of her head. She loves you so, she'd die for you."

"If I could just think that," he said. "If I could just believe it!"

"If you had any gumption you'd see it for yourself. You're the hardest-headed man I ever came across. Now, stop wavin' that sick arm 'round and go get a night's rest!"

He did get a night's rest; for the shuck mattress was a feather bed compared to Swamp Fox sleeping quarters. He awaked at first dawn and leaving the silent house started to the sheds to do the feeding and milking. These were tasks for which he needed only one arm.

As he left the cow stall with the wooden bucket in his left hand, Lex came face to face with two mounted men. They must have ridden up quietly for he had not heard their approach. They wore the uniform of British officer and private.

"You rebel horse thief," said Evelyn Fay. And he spoke coldly, confidently, with a note of victory in his voice.

Unarmed, and hampered by the pail, Lex stood looking up at him.

"How did you come to find me?"

Fay's laugh was a sneer.

"Did you think I'd let the Red Doe go as easily as that? Tory scouts have been on her trail ever since you took her. I set one of them to watch this place as soon as I knew you held Miss Lane here, you presumptuous son of treason."

His voice clipped the endings of its words more sharply.

"Miss Lane is here of her own choice. I happen to love her and I'm going to marry her. And what are *you* going to do about it!"

As he spoke Lex, now enraged beyond caution, hurled the milk bucket with all the strength of his left arm. Bucket and contents struck Fay's horse full in the face.

The affronted animal, with milk in its eyes and nose, reared high in the air, bucking madly. Fay was a horseman and kept his seat, but that was all he could do. Unable to draw a weapon, he yelled to his orderly: "Shoot the scoundrel down!"

Lex saw the orderly's hand go to his cavalry pistol, and he leapt back toward the shelter of the door. As he moved he heard the report of a gun and saw the orderly pitch forward across the neck of his standing mount.

Lex was upon him with one long jump. As he jerked the pistol from its holster, he was wondering whether the man had clumsily wounded himself or whether Fay was shooting wild from the back of the plunging horse. But he did not delay to question his luck. He ordered the writhing man on the ground, "Lie flat or I'll kill you!" And he turned the weapon on Fay.

Then, while the fighting horse was being quieted, a girl stepped up beside Lex: a girl with a face white as fear itself and with eyes dark as the smoke which still curled from the muzzle of his long rifle.

She was gripping it with both hands, and she looked at the fallen soldier.

"I don't care if I killed him," she said. "I don't care if I kill them both. I heard Fay tell him to shoot *you*, Lex!"

57

AT LEX'S DIRECTION FIRE PUT THE RIFLE DOWN. BUT HE noticed that her hand was steady as she held the orderly's pistol on a direct line with the middle of Major Fay's scarlet coat.

"My father taught me to shoot a pistol before you ever showed your face at South Bank," she informed the officer. "It was only luck I hit your soldier with the rifle, but I'll not miss you if you don't obey Sergeant Mourne."

Fury and humiliation made Fay's face as white as hers, but he kept both hands on his bridle lines while Lex took his pistol.

"I am your prisoner—thanks to a yokel's trick and to a woman's assistance."

Fire cried out: "Two of you rode up on him! I saw you from the house, and I ran for his rifle then. Two of you— armed—rode up on him—while he was unarmed and had the use of only one hand!"

"He made good use of that one hand," Fay told her sourly. "I am not surprised at anything *he* does; but I am surprised that *you* take his part against an officer and a gentleman."

"An officer and a gentleman would not have done what you did. I have not forgotten the night when you got drunk at South Bank and followed me out in the garden and tried to force me to submit to your attentions."

Lex's voice was a roar of rage.

274

"I'll take him now! Leave him to me—and you watch the orderly!"

Fay was not a coward, but the pistol in Lex's hand was aimed directly at his head from just a few feet away. It was his own pistol, and he knew it was loaded and oiled. He took pride in the fact that subordinates feared him and kept his tack and weapons in exquisite order. He knew, too, that some of these rebels shot with the left hand as easily as with the right.

This one had a finger tensed against the trigger and was commanding: "Get off that horse!"

It flashed into Fay's mind that if he could put the horse between them, perhaps—

But as he freed his left boot from the stirrup the girl spoke scornfully. "Do His Majesty's officers dismount from the off side?"

Crimson now with humiliation as well as anger, Major Evelyn Fay dismounted in perfect order from the near side of his horse. Hands clenched, he stood a few feet from his enemy. He was thinking of his sword. If he had time to draw it—

The tall young man who had once faced him in similar circumstances was saying: "Fire, there's a coil of rope on the door of the cow stall."

This time Fay's face went yellow-white.

"Sir, I remind you that the rules of war—"

"Are not supposed by your command to apply to the Swamp Fox's men," said Lex. "But I happen to want the rope only to tie the horses."

Fire reached out and with her left hand gathered both bridle reins.

"I can hold them this way—and hold the pistol too."

"All right. But keep that man on the ground while I attend to this one."

He stepped farther from Fay.

"Draw your sword and drop it. If you try to lunge I'll kill you."

"This, sir," said Major Fay, "is an uncalled-for indignity."

"Never mind the indignity! I don't trust you in a fight."

"A fight? How can I fight you without either sword or pistol?"

"With your fists. You've got two of them. And while I've only one, I'm finding out a few things I can do with it."

"No gentleman uses his hands upon another," said Fay. "I give you my word that I'll fight you fairly with either pistols or swords."

"I have no sword, and I don't want your word. All I want is to knock you down. If that blade isn't on the ground by the time I've counted three, you have *my* word that you'll get a bullet through your right shoulder where your orderly got his."

Fay dropped it sullenly but refused to remove his coat. He was no boxer, but neither was Lex. Both had the same height and reach. Fay had more weight and both his hands, Lex was stronger and quicker. But he did not anticipate that his foe was going to hit directly for the wounded arm.

His blow knocked the torn hand out of the sling and sent him up against the side of the cow shed, dizzy with agony. But it also brought him back again, more dangerous with fury.

He left the bandaged hand swinging. It had gone numb, and at his side it was less apt to be struck again. Fay pressed his advantage and stepped closer. As Lex gathered himself he tried to recall every move he had seen made by Toff Lane or Jeems Gaylord. He went through Fay's inadequate guard with all his lean weight behind his left fist and landed squarely upon the officer's handsome Roman nose.

Fire's voice brought him back from his satisfied contemplation of this fallen Redcoat who had cost him so much. Her question held interest, not anxiety.

"Is he dead, Lex? He's lying still, and his whole face is covered with blood."

"Nothing's wrong with him—except that I broke his nose and knocked out a few teeth. Fire, tell me—did you shoot in order to save me?"

The quick flush of her white skin brought two spots of carmine into her pointed face.

"I saw them riding in from the road. Samantha said you were at the barn. I ran into Sonny's room to get your rifle. He told me to rest it on something and pull its trigger just like a pistol."

The orderly on the ground clawed at his wounded shoulder and groaned.

"I didn't know you could lift it. It's a miracle you hit him."

"I was less than six feet behind him. I laid the barrel across that board sticking off from the shed corner. I was close enough to you to hear—to hear what you said, Lex."

He knew it was time to risk everything—as she had done when she ran to his help with a weapon she did not know.

He stuck Fay's pistol in his belt, took the orderly's from her and laid it and the sword behind him in the cow shed. As his left arm went around her waist she dropped the bridle reins.

"Are you close enough to me, Fire," he asked her, "to believe what you heard me say to Major Fay?"

"I believe it—now—Lex."

With that first kiss the world and the war and the daybreak spun pinwheels around them.

"And you'll marry me? And go back to the hills with me?"

"I'll marry you, Lex—and go wherever you go."

Only the sound of eight galloping hooves brought them back. They raised their heads to see Fay and his orderly escaping in a full run on the dusty farm road.

Lex's face was so rueful that Fire comforted him.

"I'm glad they got away. How could you have guarded them? You'd have left me in order to take them somewhere."

That was a catastrophe which Lex had not considered.

"Captain Conyers is patrolling the Georgetown road. If Fay tries to bring a party back, Conyers will gobble them up like a duck gobbles a June bug. But that doesn't excuse me for letting two prisoners go. I don't seem able to do anything with just this clumsy left hand."

She took it in both her hands, examined its skinned knuckles and put them against her lips, then replaced the arm around her slim waist.

"What more could you do with two arms," she asked him gravely, "than work on a farm and fight a foe and hold close a girl who will be your wife?"